MIDNIGHT MAGIC

A FANTASY LESBIAN ROMANCE

Cameron Darrow

Not everyone who sees us start will get to see us finish. It's for them that we must ensure we do.

1

Vimika was generally kind to her doors. They served an important purpose and were a pain to replace. But if it was boot hers open as hard as she could or choke to death, she didn't even slow down. Unfortunately, her front door opened inward, and she was forced to expend precious breath on all the swearing. When she managed to throw it open, the plume that roiled out was acrid and greenish-black, streaming into the sky with such speed that one could be forgiven for thinking it was trying to get away from something. Hacking and coughing, waving a frantic hand that was more effective at shooing away the smoke with menace than wind, she burst from the door in a race she had lost the moment it started.

"Boiled piss!" she wheezed, though thankfully in frustration and not in declaration of the source of the haze curling out from her doorway. She stalked up the stairs in shoes not-at-all adequate to the fact there was nearly a foot of snow on the ground and deliberately avoided looking back. If she did, she would quickly have a hammer in her hand again, followed by more bashing and sparks, cursing and someone certainly calling the fire brigade.

The goggles she wore did wonders in keeping the smoke out of her eyes, but did nothing about the sun. She squinted in defense against the sudden brightness almost fast enough to miss seeing passers-by covering the ears of their children or making panicked dives into the street.

Retching and spitting, Vimika fell onto the pavement just short of the brownish hillock of sleet that marked the edge of the road and looked resolutely down at it and not the flow of traffic on the other side. But as she was dressed for sorcerous experimentation and not the freezing cold, it wasn't long before Vimika felt someone staring down at her.

Two someones. So was the horse.

"Are you all right, young lady?" a man said, peering down from atop his mount with something that might have been pity, but could just as easily have been the dawning realization that he may have just made himself responsible for the answer.

Something gritty that tasted remarkably like metal shavings coated Vimika's tongue, a flavor made stronger by all the blood. Gathering as much as she could, she spat into the snow, confirming the presence of both.

"I'm-" --*hork*-- "fine," she said. Raising her goggles, she looked up at him with eyes like shields of hammered bronze, only not terribly effective shields, as they had great vertical slits in them. "And no lady."

"Clearly," the man replied with a face suddenly more sour than it had been before Vimika had taken her goggles off. "Where is your hat?"

"On fire at the moment," Vimika said with a glance over her shoulder.

"See it replaced or I'll report you to the Watch," the man said, and urged his horse forward without another glance. For the horse's part, it did spare her a look of concern, but seemed more enthused about the idea of getting away from whatever was in the haze gathering around it than it was about the state of dress of the young woman at its feet.

Vimika looked down at her thick leather apron, her white shirt spattered with burn marks and unnamable fluids (it had been a long day), the sleeves rolled up to reveal arms blackened with singed hair and pebbled with gooseflesh.

No robes, no hat. In public! Her stomach dropped while the grime coating her forehead suddenly became a lot damper, though unable to freeze from the heat of her shame. The tips of her long, blade-like ears were freezing and burning simultaneously.

"Yes, sir. Thank you, sir," she said with all the grace she could manage, which was more than she'd thought before she learned she still had her eyebrows. Heaving herself back onto her feet, she found herself surrounded by people thankfully content to gawk and little else. A little boy pointed.

The smoke had ceased its advance, but as there was no wind to speak of, it was now fog. Vimika descended into it anyway, blowing it all up the stairs and into the crowd of onlookers with a whispered command and a wave of her hand.

When the door slammed shut, the sign hanging from it jiggled and danced against the faded wood.

V. A. Malakandronon
WIZARD

~

"Thank you *sir*," Vimika muttered to herself with a little sneer and a shake of her head, tossing an afterthought of magic at the hat smoldering on the floor. What had been glowing orange and red faded quickly to a cool, crispy black. She swiped off the worst of the charring, which had been limited to the edge of the wide brim, and mercifully found no holes. The fireproofing had done its job, so she tugged it back on, the point flopping over into its customary position, melting down the left side of her head like a deflated candle.

Every wizard's hat bore the marks of its owner's mistakes, in some ways the most accurate record of their work. A pristine one meant you were lazy, rich, or fresh off wizard school, and Vimika was decidedly none of those things. Though the blue patterning that spiralled up the cone would never tarnish or fade, she very nearly took pride in how beaten up the rest of it was.

But not quite.

Her heart was still hammering at how close she'd come to a citation for being caught outside without it on. A citation didn't sound like much, but word spread quickly among wizards, and the only one Vimika ever wanted said about her was 'Who?'. It was times like these that she wished she had a proper chair in her laboratory so she could fall into it with her feet splayed out and a look of discontent on her face. As it was, she only had a stool, and every time she tried falling onto that, it tipped over. And while she would still end up with her feet splayed out, she would also be flat on her back staring at the ceiling, which wasn't nearly as effective at encapsulating her mood as a good slouch.

The Atvalian Empire was not the most ideal place in the world to find oneself a wizard, let alone actually practice the magic unique to them. The mandatory hat and robes were only part of it, but thinking about all the others only drove her to drink more than she already did. She'd heard it wasn't like this everywhere, but people said that about a lot of things in Atvalia. Besides, she wasn't entirely sure how she was going to afford lunch tomorrow, let alone leave a country that took up half a continent, to say nothing of what could happen to her family if she tried.

But here and now, it was a more pedestrian (and much less hypothetical, but more cowardly, if she was honest) goal that drove her to today's despair.

She set her hands on the edge of her workbench and stared down at the little pile of gears and springs as they stuck out at all kinds of inappropriate angles, looking for all the world like an inside-out cockroach with guts of brass and a carapace of silver.

How such a trifling little thing could prove such a vexing pain in the arse was a mystery that only time and most likely several more explosions was going to solve, if she was lucky. If she was unlucky, it would stay a mystery. If she was *spectacularly* unlucky, she would be further pondering why amidst the charred remains of what was left of her home. Should she find herself in the space that lay beyond bad luck in the realm of 'curse of some description', she would find her head on a spike for trying to shove magic into metal.

People had done it before, which is why a penalty existed for it: death. It was called mechamagery, but as Vimika quite enjoyed her head right where it was, that wasn't what she was doing. Oh, she'd toyed with the idea of magicking a clock so it would run forever, but that came too close to forbidden magic for the average person. Clocks had moving parts, and animating them magically (even if said average person couldn't have said how they *actually* worked beyond 'Little springs, innit?') would just be a rather involved form of suicide.

No, no. Vimika had far more mundane plans than all that.

Rats. Lice. Termites. Relatives you didn't know you had until your name came up in your late uncle's will. All unwanted and difficult to get rid of, normally. Magically, it was relatively straightforward, and if she could find a way to contain a banishment spell in a neat little talisman, normal. And profitable.

But magic wasn't normal, as her incident with the man and the horse had proven. Her ability to drive off rats and mice was the only reason she could afford to live in Durn proper. It was a steady, if unglamorous income, but gold was gold, and the reason she didn't have to spend any of hers on at least one hot meal a day.

Breakfast, usually.

But now it was closing in on supper, and she still hadn't made any progress in her latest attempt to scrape true independence off the floor of a life caked with wasted potential. That she had been trying since she'd graduated from the Academy several years ago didn't salve her feelings in the least, and in fact made them worse.

Her subjects had shown quite a bit more fighting spirit than she had anticipated from watches, but she put up with it because magic encased in something that wouldn't corrode, say gold or silver, was essentially eternal. It would zip around in an endless loop, with no degradation, unheeding of such paltry concerns as 'time' and 'this shouldn't actually be possible'. Permanent solutions commanded premium prices, with the side benefit of only having to do to the work once. She didn't need the watches to actually *work*, they just had to look like they did so as to conceal the *scaaary* magic that was keeping the client's grain from being eaten or shit in. Or eaten and *then* shit in, which was the usual order of such things.

Preservation spells and the like were happily absorbed by objects without even the mildest explosion, why would this be any different? She couldn't even ask for help with it, either. One, she had no one *to* ask. Two, she didn't dare tell anyone for fear of them figuring it out first. Or cutting her head off just in case.

On either side of her workbench, presently bookending the corpse of the watch, were myriad vials and jars filled with myriad-er fluids, all of which bore an alarming lack of labeling or demarcation of any kind.

Grabbing the nearest one, filled with a thin amber liquid,

Vimika brought it to her lips and tossed it all back at once, swallowing with a grimace.

Apple brandy.

The last dregs of her last bottle, she had meant to nurse it well into the evening, but the metal shavings needed to be washed down with something more than blood. Being a practicing wizard, the shredded little abrasions had already healed themselves, but that hadn't made her mouth taste any better.

Neither had the brandy. For once.

She pushed around the cold scraps of the exploded watch with a fingernail, listened to the little clinking noises, carved patterns into the soot.

Ironically, watching her dreams catch fire made her tired.

Tired of being stared at, whispered about, judged. The hat, the robes, the preconceived notions they set in people's heads before she even had a chance to open her mouth, all of it. The fear of having to tangle with the city Watch because she'd run out of a burning(ish) building without putting her hat on first. She just wanted to… go away. *Further* away even than Durn, which, according to most Atvalians, was already the end of the world. It wouldn't matter what country she was in if she never talked to anyone. But that required money, and being a freelance wizard wasn't exactly the bed from which flowers of gold sprouted.

Sighing, she turned away from one failure to check on the ongoing progress of another.

In a little ceramic bowl filled with a mixture of milk and silver-laced mineral water were floating several orange cat hairs, slightly aglow with the magic 'tag' she'd placed on them. Aligned due north, it meant their former owner still hadn't responded to the Beckoning spell, which meant *his* owner had no reason to pay her.

That was enough confidence beating for one day, she

decided.

This time, she treated her front door with considerably more care so she could turn the sign that hung from the knob from 'open' to 'closed'. It was getting dark, and as it did, the noise coming in from outside got louder as the streets filled with excitable talking, laughing, and on Deer's Day, the last workday of the week, singing. Off-key and slurred, but still a melodic arrangement of syllables. To call them 'words' was unfair to the Common tongue of Atvalia.

But as Vimika turned away from the sounds of life, it meant she had to take in her little domicile, and the lack of any within it.

Off to the left was her workbench, with racks of ingredients and tools both above and below. On either side, within easy reach, were her texts. They were mostly there to hold all the things her head couldn't or wouldn't, as she wasn't called on very often to deliver a baby dragon, which would have just taken up space she needed for scrying out lost cats. One helped pay the bills, the other had been thought extinct for half a millenium.

Set in the opposite wall was the hearth. Black iron cauldrons squatted on either side like rotund little gargoyles, crusty with use, but cold from not recently.

Straight ahead was a another door that led to what she had made into a bedroom, also cold from disuse, and still smelling faintly of the ghosts of the ale and brandy casks that had been moved out to make way for her.

All of it was spotlessly clean, as a wizard's place of work and rest should be, though it had taken her a solid week of scrubbing when she'd first arrived to get it that way. In that respect, it could pass as a normal flat, but the low wooden beams in the ceiling and the total lack of windows would make anyone who thought that begin to ask questions.

Probably starting with the bubbling mystery liquids. And

the jars with the brains in them. The sharp, unmistakable odor of air that had been repeatedly tortured by magic would prod the blind, and the deaf had the squeaking.

Vimika told those who asked that it was just the bats, but really it was a few loose floorboards.

When it came to a wizard's belfry, people *expected* bats, not a tavern.

~

The Crowned Cock was only a funny name if you were of a sufficiently puerile mindset to ignore the rather nicely-painted rendition of a rooster wearing a gold circlet looking down proudly from the sign, or if the Common tongue was your native language.

For Vimika, it was the name of the roof over her head and why she hadn't frozen to death (yet), thus it was only a modest titter, hidden behind a voluminous sleeve of the type only wizards and eccentric people wore, that shook her shoulders as she pushed open the door into a riot of heat, color and noise.

The escape from winter never really ended in a tavern, it just sort of rolled over from one day to the next, along with the patrons, as the slightly-less inebriated tried to keep them from choking on their own vomit. That said, the crowds at the Double C, as it was known by those tired of talking to smirking people, were generally well-behaved.

The proprietor, one Wilim Hagshead (something about slaying monstrous snake-women in a past so distant and likely mythical it had snake-women in it), made sure it stayed that way. Bringing to mind the world's most hospitable bear, he merely had to cross his massive arms and shoot a withering look to get across the idea that You Can't Do That Here. Another contributing factor was that he had been blessed with only daughters, four of them, and anyone who got out of hand while they were working would generously be given the flagon they had been drinking from to carry their teeth home in. It was expected to be returned the next day, spotlessly clean.

To find a corner table available at any time was a rare enough sight, and on a Deer's Night all but impossible. But Vimika's luck had turned, at least for as long as it took her to scurry across the room and slip into a chair just ahead of a pair of gentlemen who clearly had had it in their minds that they might be able to get away with acting on the look in their eyes if only they had a secluded corner in which to do it.

"The inn is next door if you need a room," Vimika said with a smile. They looked happy, and she wasn't about to ruin that. But every activity had its proper place, and the corner table was for single people to sulk in. At least, it was as long as *she* was the single one.

The two men glanced at each other before each giving Vimika a sweeping bow. "Who are we to spurn a wizard's advice?" the one on the left said.

"Indeed," Vimika said, and the two stumbled away in each others' arms, giggling and somehow navigating the crowded floor without looking at anything but each other.

Sighing, Vimika set her chin in her hand and took in the merriment going on around her.

A veritable cloud of white candles burned overhead, lending extra movement to the shadows they cast below as people leaned in close to one another to be heard over the din of everyone else trying to be heard over it. On a small stage off to one side, a bard was plucking at his lute in time with a slow song about keeping warm in the night with company and drink. A little on the nose for being sung a tavern, but the gaggle of young women around him was evidence to the fact it was exactly the song he should be singing if he wanted either of of those things for himself when he was done.

It was what a respectable tavern should look like. A roaring fire, laughter. The harvest had been bountiful this year, and the snows both later and less of a smothering blanket than the year previous. Though winters this far south could be harsh, this year's had started off mild, looking to shape into what the locals called a Fruit Winter. A time they got to enjoy what they'd spent the rest of the year breaking their backs preparing for. The larders were full, and the merchant trains had all managed one extra trip through the passes, which meant wine and spices aplenty.

A warm, insistent presence made itself known against the side of Vimika's leg, and she looked down to see Hewer, the Double C's resident rat-catcher sidled up against the hem of her robe.

"Aren't you friendly, considering I put you out of business?" Vimika asked. Though the change in circumstances seemed to be a welcome one, as the black and gray tom was now more pillow than predator, looking up with eyes that were slitted just like her own to mew in what Vimika took to be forgiveness. He Smelled of magic tonight, but that should have been no surprise, given that she'd almost burned down his house with it earlier.

Some recompense was in order. "You keep my legs warm, and I'll see that I'm a little clumsier than usual with the scraps. Deal?"

Hewer mewed again and leapt into her lap. He took his time in settling, sniffing and kneading at the tops of her thighs, but seemed content enough with his final choice when he eventually made it.

Good enough.

"Yer usual, or do ya wan' sumthin' with a li'l more kick tonight?" said Delica, the youngest of Wilim's daughters, as she looked down on the wizard only a year her senior. For being built like a warhorse, she was very good at sneaking up on people.

"I think tonight calls for the strongest you've got," Vimika said.

"Tha' bad?"

"Thinking about it's making it worse," Vimika said as her chin settled into her hand again.

"So tha' stink-cloud earlier was ya, then?" Delica asked, pulling a lock of tousled blond hair down to her nose and giving it a sniff. She grimaced and let it pop back into place with a lip upturned just enough to say she didn't mean it.

Delica had a face and figure that were *exactly* the reason she'd learned how to twist a man's arm in just the right way to snap it if he kept on like that. She shared Vimika's proclivities though, and knew how hard it was for a woman to find another woman in a town that was almost entirely men. Vimika had never admitted that that was nearly the entire reason she'd chosen Durn in the first place. She couldn't be tempted by something that didn't exist.

The rock sparkling on Delica's finger removed any doubt as to the state of *her* relation to Durn's population, however.

"It was. Sorry. That mean what I think it does?" Vimika asked, curling a pinky from under her chin to point at the ring.

"She was gonna ask on Midwinter's Day, but I found the ring 'fore I was s'pose ta. Asked me right there in the toilet."

"Congratulation- wait, she hid it in the toilet?"

Delica smiled. "Pretty goo' place, I though'. 'Til I though' we was outta bog roll and I tore it apar' lookin' fer more. Found this instead." She held up her hand and wiggled her fingers. Though the stone sparkled in the candlelight, it didn't sparkle *right*, and Vimika Looked into it hard enough to do a minor cast she had learned the day she decided to move to a town built on gemstones.

16

The results, however, put her in a dilemma. Her eyes flicked from the stone to Delica's cheerful face and she swallowed hard. A wizard's reputation was built on honesty. At least, an honest wizard's was.

"Delica…"

"'S fake. I know."

Vimika started so hard her hat flopped over the other side of her head. "You do?"

"'Course. No reason to waste all tha' money. Jus' make people think we did. 'Sides, I'm quick, but no' always tha' quick. *Shoomp!*" She mimed the ring being yanked off. "'Da says I shouldn't even wear i', but people usually respec' a ring. I needs ta get back ta work, though, so I'll jus' tell ya the Soft Sea Gold's pretty strong this year," Delica said with a knowing smile

At that, Vimika's heart lifted so much it made her sit up a little straighter. "It's in already?"

"Aye. Don' suppose ya wanna-"

"Don't stop until I have to be carried home."

~

True to her word, Delica hadn't stopped, as Vimika could still find the privy without falling over. When she returned for the third time, she plopped down in her seat to find someone sitting in the one across the table. As that hadn't been the case when she'd gotten up, Vimika blinked several times until her brain caught up with what was coming in through the holes in front of it.

"Seris?" Vimika asked. She was sure, but not *sure*, and it was only polite to confirm the state of things before she said anything personal. Or at all, really. A lot could come out of a drunk wizard's mouth, only a fraction of which counted as conversation.

"Aye," Delica's fiancee said with a tankard raised to Vimika's ability to recall names. "Just got back from my last run of the season. You looked like you needed someone to keep an eye on you."

A trader by... trade... Seris had been swept off her feet (literally) on her first visit to the Double C when Delica had carried her back to her room after one (or five) too many pints. A full head shorter and several stone lighter than her stocky mountain fiancee, Seris was pretty in a hawkish sort of way, her prominent widow's peak beak-like in its attempts to split her eyebrows apart in her constant near-sighted squint.

"I keep my eye on myself... my *third* eye! WooOOoo..." Vimika said, wriggling all ten fingers above her forehead.

"That's bullshit," Seris replied, and took a sip of what smelled like mead, but could have just as easily been vomit. They smelled the same to Vimika, and she was too pissed to tell the difference.

"'S not. I have the Sight," Vimika said.

"Yes. I've been around wizards, you know. *Sober* ones."

"*Psshh*, no such thing. 'Sides, you drink like a... bird... too. So don' say an'thing 'bout soberty," Vimika managed.

She knew how red her face was, but of course it was, it was so hot! All she wanted to do was take off her stupid hat, but then she'd get yelled at, and that would make her remember where she was and why, and who wanted that?

"And I'm going to catch up, don't worry. Why don't we talk before I pass you? Or you pass out," Seris said with a little crook to the corner of her mouth that Vimika had to stare at really hard to confirm was a smile.

"'Bout what? Why you wanna talk to a wzzzrd?"

Seris handed her flagon to Delica, who had once again appeared from nowhere, or maybe had been standing there the whole time. "I don't. Believe it or not, Delica and I care about you. I want to talk to *you*, Vimika."

A concerned hand set atop Vimika's, but Seris being human, it was only a gesture of comfort. There was no magic to feel from the connection. Nothing like when wizards touched. Gods how she missed it! Just *once*, to remember who she was...

But she knew too well who she was. It was why she was drunk.

"'K."

Leaning forward, Seris retracted her hand to take her flagon in both, talon-like fingers nearly long enough to encircle the whole thing. "Every time I come back, I find you in here. Why do you do this to yourself? Even Mrs. Hagshead is worried about you at this point."

Vimika rocked side to side, either in attempt to dodge the question or because she had to pee again already. Since it was more likely the former, she took another swig of golden wine. "Do what? Have a good time? For once?" she added a lot less quietly than she'd imagined it was going to be.

"You're a *wizard*!"

Vimika looked up at the brim of her hat. "Ooohhh noooo, you're right!"

She snapped her fingers, and a ball of light bloomed into an unstable, hesitant kind of light that seemed to wonder what it was doing here. Settling it into the palm of her hand, she held it up to Seris. "I made this. With *magic*. Something you can't do, but *I* have to wear the hat."

"Yes, you did. And you can do a lot more. Yet you're down here in a tavern in the ass-end of nowhere drinking yourself to death. You want to tell me why?"

Vimika yanked the brim of her hat down over her long wizard ears, flattening them painfully against the side of her head. "'Cause I'm in the ass-end of nowhere living under a tavern."

"You don't have to, you know."

"I know," Vimika said to the table. "I'm moving soo... some day. My own house. Away from here. Away from evr'buddy. In the woods somewhere."

"That sounds lonely," Seris said.

Vimika nodded, the point of her hat flopping forward. She glared up at it, but it was as much a part of her as her hair, only with more freedom of movement. "Ran from Maris aaaallllll the way down here, but wasn't far enough. Still hurts, still 'member. Still... everyth-" --hic-- "why're you so nice to me?"

"Why wouldn't I be?" Seris asked.

Vimika brandished her light again. "'M a wzzzrd. People don' like wzzzrds. 'S why I wear this." The benefits of magelights being heatless became apparent when her robe failed to burst into flame upon thumping her chest.

"I like you just fine. So does Delica. That's why it's so hard to see you like this. I drink because I'm tired of talking to people trying to cheat me and from being stuck on horseback for weeks on end. I suck Wilim's casks dry because I have so few chances. I make them count. You can do magic... yes, just like that. No, I don't want to try to hold it. Vimika, you have a genuine talent. You've made so many people happy by finding their pets, taming their horses, driving out vermin. I've seen you call songbirds, and had to resist the urge to write a terrible poem about it."

"You write poetry?"

Seris shrugged, flicking an eye at Delica. "Not often, hence it being bad. And beside the point. I heard you blew up another watch this afternoon."

The smile that split Vimika's lips wasn't out of pride or pleasure. Or a smile really. More of a grimace, but the alcohol was making it harder to tell the difference. Another glass or two and she would get to the point she could admit they were the same thing nowadays. "Yep. Real good. Almost choked a horse."

Seris *tsk*ed and took a good long draught from her flagon. When she set it back down, the face it revealed was less than impressed. "Why are you wasting your time with that shit?"

"You swear a lot."

"I work with horses and assholes, you would, too," Seris said.

"Not complainin'. Wish I could."

"Why don't you?"

"'Cause I'mm wzzzrd! A *girl* wzzzrd... a slit-eyed witch. I have t'be good. No cursing around humans. Keep my hat on, wear the robes." Vimika held out her enormous sleeves, waving them around, brushing over her wine glass. She watched it wobble with panicked intensity. "They only see the wzzzrd. Always the wzzzrd. Get pointed at, whispered 'bout... don't say anythin'... pretend I don' see. Don' hear. Who sees Vimika? Nobody. Jus... magic. Don' need *me*..."

She snatched up the glass and threw everything in it back in one gulp before the floor had a chance to drink it first. "Magic... objects... worth a lot o' money. Then I can go away. Can't get hurt there."

Seris looked across the table over her flagon. Held it out and brought it back full somehow. "Who hurt you? You never talk about it."

"Sure don't. Now, I gotta go bedtime. I live downstairs! If I fall down them fast enough I end up in my bed," Vimika said, jabbing herself in the temple. "'Cuz I'm smart."

"Vimika, I'm sorry to pry, I just-"

"I know." Vimika swayed to her feet, swatting at Seris several times before managing to thump her hand onto to the trader's shoulder. "I know. You worry. I 'preciate it. But y'won' have to much longer. Now go play kissy face with Delica. I'll be fine."

"I don't think you will," Seris said.

21

Vimika shrugged. Or tried, instead her entire upper body swayed like a top-heavy tree. "That's okay, too."

2

It was a pulsing white morning Vimika woke up to, full of blurry things and wishing to be dead. The blurry things eventually coalesced into the rugs hung on the wall around her bed, there to both muffle noise and at least pretend to try to keep the chill at bay.

Right now they were acting in their tertiary capacity as lodestars, and Vimika was slightly more confident in which side of the bed was less likely to result in injury if she rolled that way. The lack of certainty came from the fact it took her longer than she would care to admit to realize her head was where her feet should be, which was appropriate since it felt like someone was walking on her skull.

That didn't explain the scratching.

With a few more blinks to orient herself, Vimika oozed out from under her covers and into some semblance of dressed. Whatever was doing the scratching, she doubted she needed to look impressive for. Things that needed impressing were usually louder.

From the lab, it became clear the sound was coming from her door, for which she was relieved. From the walls or ceiling would have meant rats, and rats would have meant questions about her magic proficiency and little squeaking sounds.

Though the noise was quiet, it was insistent, and couldn't talk. Or read, since the sign clearly said she wasn't home.

Scritchscritchscritch.

"Just a moment," she felt compelled to say as she went to undo the set of ensorcelled locks. They both looked, and were in fact, impressive. Anyone who wasn't Vimika, or didn't have the equally ensorcelled keys, would be surprised at just how creative a magicker could be when it came to dissuading would-be thieves.

Scritchscritchscritch.

Meow.

The door opened and the snow drift that had built up against it during the night collapsed. The bulbous orange cat that had been perched atop it surfed the mini avalanche straight into Vimika's laboratory, alighting on the floor like it was intentional.

The cat wasn't terribly remarkable, as cats went, so much so Vimika had no idea why it was now in her house, looking about the place and finding it wanting. Only when she looked at it in pure wizard Sight did anything make sense for the first time that morning.

"I scryed for you three days ago!" Vimika said, peering down at the little animal the way only wizards could See things.

Apricot, her hangover-addled memory supplied, was aglow with magical energy, the 'tag' she had sent after him glowing the same color as the hairs in the bowl. Sure enough, they were pointing right at him. Everywhere he'd been since she'd sent the tag, he'd left a little trail of magic behind, and Vimika followed it back, tracing his journey.

It was a knot of overlapping, re-tracing steps, meandering down alleyways and over rooftops, peering into windows and chasing birds.

"I see you took the long way. Three days to go a half mile?" Vimika asked. Beckoning spells usually only took a few hours to work, even on animals as stubborn as cats. She'd had all but given up on the little cretin.

The deeper she looked, however, the more apparent the possible reason became. There was a trace of magic in him that wasn't Vimika's. It was faint, like a rat fart in a fog bank, but obvious once she'd noticed it. Who else would want to do anything magically to an ordinary house cat, and why? She hadn't noticed anything when she'd placed the tag, had someone been checking her work? If someone had Borrowed him, it would explain the magic and his meandering course over the last few days, but any wizard skilled enough to do it would have plenty else to do with their talents than sniff around back alleys and peer in windo-

"Ew," Vimika said through a grimace. Apricot cocked his head. "I'm sorry little friend. If you'd come when I first called, you might have been spared."

It was no matter, however, he was here now, and she tossed Apricot a dried fish from her jar of thinking-time snacks so he would stay long enough for her to get dressed enough to be seen. She took another fish for herself. Salty and tough, it was all she had time for if she was to make it across town before her bribe wore off.

~

Though somewhat put out by the timing, Apricot's family was grateful to have him back, and in time for Midwinter. Apricot, for his part, had treated his return with the same sniffy indifference he treated everything else. Vimika had left with thanks, pockets jingling with silver and a reminder of why she didn't particularly care for cats very much.

They weren't popular among wizards at large, either. If

you could banish vermin with magic, why would you put up with such haughty little things? Maybe it was because cats reminded wizards of themselves: intelligent, doing as they were told only with great reluctance and a fair bit of bribing, seen by everyone else as arrogant and entitled; slitted eyes, pointed ears.

The last two were the primary arguments wizards had against being forced to mark themselves with robes and ridiculous hats. They were all *born* looking different, but then someone had gone and invented sunglasses and long hair.

The reasons why wizards had slitted eyes were lost to history, now solely the domain of myth and what they told people after a few glasses of wine. That they were descended from cat-people was a favorite, but as Vimika didn't have a tail and the only wizard she knew with fuzzy ears was her grandfather, it remained only as one of the more entertaining for her. After enough Soft Sea Gold, however, she would happily help to elaborate on how it had come to pass, with lots of scratching and tail-pulling.

The theory favored by Vimika and others however (when they took such things seriously), was that they were the remaining descendants of the long-lost race of elves, and the eyes were what let them See with what used to be called magesight. Now, it had lots of rather less impressive names, like wizardvision or magiceye, but was most often just shortened to simply Sight. Just the way Vimika had Seen Apricot and followed his travels, it was a way of perceiving magic without having to do any spells or look into crystal balls. The ears were much the same way, although being able to Hear magic took considerably more practice. Not all magic was glowing wisps and fireballs, and magic that had been imbued deeply into inanimate objects, old ones especially, put out more sound than light.

The magic accessible to wizards came in three flavors.

Mana was the most common, the raw magic that flowed in and about the world the way water does, appearing green to Sight. In different forms and concentrations but omnipresent, it was the type that smart wizards drew on. Well, smart in that it was virtually inexhaustible. It still had to be absorbed, channelled and filtered into anything usable, which took technique and concentration.

Animata, the animating force of every living thing that had a brain (by wizard reckoning), was white. Beginner wizards had to learn to filter it out or go blind from the fact their own eyeballs were full of it. After a while, however, one's own *animata* became simple enough to ignore naturally, the way one does the smell of their own house.

Then there were high-energy magics, the *alumita*, the very creative (and destructive) energies of the universe itself. They were intensely blue, and what stupid wizards drew on. Or tried to, anyway. The *alumita* were very powerful, but the world was dotted with craters that attested to how wrong trying to harness them could go. It was quick energy, and so would your death be if you made a mistake.

No ability to See or channel magic, however, prepared Vimika for the sight that awaited her at the top of her stairs when she got home.

The coach was lacquered black and completely spotless, which was saying something in a place where it snowed half the year, and pulled by a team of animals so fine they now epitomized the word 'horse' in Vimika's mind. Equally black, they stood in perfect tranquility, their bobbed tails barely swishing as they regarded Durn the same way Apricot had regarded Vimika's cellar.

The kind of money they represented was the kind that Vimika had long ago decided couldn't be earned honestly, or by pleasant people. She knew the allure of it well, the same way an alcoholic knows the allure of ale or brandy. In this case it was ostentatious and public at least, which made it moderately more honest than being behind closed doors and feeling of silk, smelling of incense and perfume...

She almost turned around.

No, this is Durn, not Maris, she reminded herself.

And in Durn, the Southern nobility had hoarded their wealth behind barricades made from the corpses of all the miners necessary to make them wealthy, not just rich. Rich people had second houses and butlers, *wealthy* people had titles and a presence at Court to go along with them.

The eight Houses in Durn had been minor ones relative to those up north, left to freeze-dry in the southern mountains. But when rich deposits of gold, silver and jewels had been discovered, the resulting feeding frenzy shat out four survivors, rulers of the southernmost, and most remote, part of the Atvalian Empire.

Vimika, however, was a wizard. And that meant that even if she did hail from Atvalia's capital, she was still forced to approach her own front door with eyes downcast, leading with the brim of her hat.

Waiting for her was a woman dressed much like the horses. Her ponytail didn't swish, however.

"You Milkdragon?" the driver asked, her beady eyes flicking between Vimika's sleeves and her hat. Or might have been, the shadows were long this time of year.

"My name is Malakandronon, yes," Vimika said tightly, trying to keep the suspicion from her voice. Each of the Four already had a house wizard, they didn't need to come into town for a freelancer. Nothing good could come from this conversation, but it wasn't as though she could hide. Did they know about her watch experiments, or did they have rats?

Of a height with Vimika, the woman looked straight through her before crossing arms clad in perfectly-tailored fabrics, ending in gloves made of leather so soft as to be sybaritic. Her reflection was flawless in the polished black side of the carriage she had driven here with horses that had stepped out of a painting.

"Good. My mistress has a job offer for you, and if you can keep quiet and manage to not break your neck getting into a carriage, you may find it lucrative." She glanced down at the sign on the door. "For a witch."

"Wi…" Vimika swallowed. "When do we leave?"

~

The house of Lady Malivia Tarsebaum, when Vimika arrived, wasn't a house at all. Or a mansion. Or a yacht that had gotten terribly lost.

Surrounded by a high wall whitewashed to within an inch of its life (solely to blind passersby, as near as Vimika could guess) the black iron gate swung open to reveal an entire compound. No less than four buildings of approximate size orbited a massive one in the center, which was all windows, spires and showy bits with gargoyles on the ends.

The carriage pulled up to discharge Vimika (or vomit, really, given how underdressed she felt in relation to even the servants), clattering away the moment she was under the supervision of someone else. Namely, a white-haired gentleman dressed equally monotone to the carriage driver, only with more frills and other extraneous accoutrements that could only be practical on someone who stood around and looked snide for a living.

"This way, Miss," he said, turning so perfectly on his axis it looked like his hair subsumed his face and absconded with it through the front door.

Inside, the sound of his heels snapping on the polished marble floor echoed in the cavernous main hall, while the scuttle of Vimika's soft leather shoes whispered among the paintings and tried not to be noticed. Or laugh at how overtly ostentatious every single thing in the house was. Who was it supposed to impress? Anyone who knew the true value of any of these things likely had them too, and anyone who didn't probably had taste.

"Miss Vimikathritas Malakandronon," the butler announced as he admitted her into what looked to be a kind of study.

Vimika's eyebrows raised at him in appreciation for being the only person in Durn to pronounce her name correctly on the first go. Then again in alarm that he knew what Vimika was short for. She never used her full name, except on official paperwork.

"Thank you, Billsly, you may go," said a rather disinterested voice from a chair near the window. A woman's voice, one that had more years behind it than ahead, most of them full of cigarettes. "Come over here, girl, I won't shout at you."

Doing so revealed exactly who Vimika had imagined the voice belonged to: a woman so near the sunset of her life she was squinting into it. Her round, wizened face was perched atop a pile of brightly-colored scarves capping a cone-shaped mound of fine furs. Her silver hair was done up tightly, bundled within the peel of a former rabbit. All of the above were necessary because the window she sat before was open for some reason.

"How may I be of service, madam?" Vimika asked.

Many students at the Academy openly complained about wizards having to learn a proper vocabulary, with accent and diction to match, but not only did it help in enunciating spells well enough to keep them from backfiring in some ironic way, it also prepared them for the day a rich person might have money to throw at them in exchange for a bit of magic.

"I understand you have a way with animals," Malivia

Tarsebaum said without bothering to introduce herself, peering up at Vimika from behind spectacles that had more glass in them than the window did.

"It is indeed one of my specialties, yes," Vimika replied, acutely aware that being able to use words like 'perchance' and 'heretofore' in a sentence didn't account for much when you were standing in a mansion with a hangover, dressed like a freelance wizard and covered in cat hair.

"Very good. Normally, I would enlist my house mage for this, you understand."

"I understand," Vimika said flatly.

It's only because he already failed that you're standing here grubbing up my rugs, and I am too old and indifferent to your feelings to care about using the word 'mage' in front of you, said Malivia's expression.

"Good. Now, I expect utmost confidentiality from you on this matter, Miss…"

"Malakandronon."

"Yes. Why magickers insist on such ostentatious names, I will never understand."

Though Vimika very much got the impression the old woman had said that to herself, she was very old, and now, Vimika knew, hard of hearing.

"It's my birth name," she said. She tried to make it sound like a simple explanation, but was unable to completely hide the sliver of pride that glinted from every word. There were many things that made life difficult being a wizard, but shame was not one of them. However far she might find herself from her family, blood was blood, no matter how many hats she was forced to obscure it with.

"I'm sure. As I said, I expect you to keep a secret. Mages are good at that, aren't you?"

"Wizard. And that is another of my specialties, I'm happy to say." Vimika did so tightly, to the point her lips hurt.

The old woman considered Vimika another moment, though she had no idea what part of her was undergoing the most scrutiny.

"Very well. I need you to find a gilded fennec," Malivia said.

Vimika had to snap her eyes shut in order to keep them in her head.

"Those are... exceedingly rare, madam. I can't guarantee..."

"He escaped two days ago. I fear what might become of him out in the untamed wilderness."

Escaped? Gilded fennecs weren't *pets*, they were wild animals! He was *from* the untamed wilderness! They weren't even *legal*...

The scarves. The coach. The house...s.

Of course.

'Legal' was just a word, like 'haberdasher', or 'obsequious': it didn't mean anything unless you needed it to.

"I will be happy to try, madam. I will need more information to increase the odds of a successful scrying, you understand."

"Yes, of course. Anything. Just find my beautiful Oliver and bring him back to me," Malivia said, her voice cracking. Reaching into her sleeve, she dabbed at her eye with a handkerchief a shade of red that looked like it belonged on the other side of the rabbit skin. "He's been my closest companion for nearly fifty years. I shan't imagine what life would be like without him."

As Vimika swallowed her reaction at such a mundane name for such an extraordinary animal, she felt the first shots of a war within herself go off. The fennec was where it needed to be, free from cages and ridiculous names, but an old woman missing a companion was a sight sad enough to move statues. But fennecs only lived, at most, twenty years. Either it was the most bloody-minded, well-looked-after example of its species in history, or…

The woman was quite old. Were the staff just indulging her, ready to laugh at the stupid wizard as they sent her off into the woods on some impossible task? Testing whether she would bring back one she found at random since there *were* no fifty-year old fennecs? A wizard's reputation may be built on honesty, but wasting their time for sport was just mean-spirited.

On one hand, she needed the money. On the other, she could just lie and say it was impossible, preserve her dignity. On a mysterious, disembodied third hand, she could ask for an advance and then figure out the rest later.

That one. She did that one.

~

Her broken brass cockroach swept away and forgotten, Vimika stared down at the new, much better, much shinier metal on her workbench and counted it all again for the fourth time, unable to trust that she still knew how. She had never seen this much money in one place before, and it didn't look right.

The work she did earned her silvers and coppers, because that's what it was worth. Gold? Actual gold coins, with a man's face on one side and a dragon on the other? She'd set out from home with two, and that was supposed to last well over a year, enough so she could at least put a roof over her head until she got steady work and still have some left over for things like not starving to death.

In front of her were six.

The first thing she'd done was a casting to make sure they were real. After that she'd had a hyperventilation and a lie down.

Spending any of it hadn't even occurred to her yet, she was

just emerging from disbelief and had marched straight into paranoia about being robbed. No one who saw that coach parked at the top of her steps would think it had been there so its occupant could get a tankard of mead, and Wilim didn't rent rooms by the hour.

And this was only half!

It was too much. She would have to use most of it just to buy something secure enough to keep the rest in. Preferably something that would bite whoever tried to open it. Something magic and *weird,* so anybody who managed to break in would just turn around and leave.

Granted, anybody who broke into a wizard's laboratory had to be prepared to spend the rest of their life as a toad or a brain in a jar (the two Vimika had were just for show), but there were some out there desperate enough to take that risk.

Durn was nice enough, a sleepy mountain town with rich people on the outskirts, and so free of crime the members of the city Watch all shared the general roundness of the gold in front of her. But until now, she'd never had enough worth stealing to worry about it.

No freelance wizard did. If you were a house wizard, like her newest client had, or if you ran a school, you lived fat and happy; if you were of the sorcerous persuasion willing to explode people with lightning, you could become a mercenary and grow rich avoiding all the people who would kill you on sight because of what you did for a living. But they were few and far between. Most wizards valued, above all else, stability. Ambitious, power-hungry ones were booted out of the reputable magic schools, ensuring that it stayed that way. House wizards were just lazy toffs with 'good breeding' and 'connections', they weren't any better at magic. Most were worse, since they'd spent their time at school with their noses in more posteriors than books; even if their reputation was that they were retained for 'security' reasons, it was really all backstabbing skullduggery. Magic was opaque to the common folk, and if a wizard was being paid by the most powerful families in Atvalia and being dressed in the finest robes money could buy, it had to be for a real reason.

Wizards knew better.

And because of it, Vimika had all but impoverished herself by choice. But now she had a minor fortune and a fistful of fennec hair with which to double it. More than enough for what she had planned: she could give up the whole talisman enterprise altogether and live as she truly wanted to, away from people, away from expectations. No one to point, no one to stare. No suspicious glances, no one to cross the street rather than brush up against her on the sidewalk. No one to break their promises, no one to lie to her, no one to hurt her.

Except herself.

But money seemed to solve everyone else's problems, why not hers?

~

A scrying for something as rare as a gilded fennec should have been no problem. Vimika had his name, hair samples, had seen where he slept, the genuine desire of his 'owner' to see him returned. More than enough to figure out where he had gotten off to.

She'd just found a lot more than she was looking for.

Following Oliver's trail hadn't been difficult at all, since it was a blazing white trail of magic the likes of which Vimika had never seen in something so small. It would have been difficult for her *not* to be able to follow it, since it would have required her to be not a wizard.

The question, as it always seemed to come down to, was *why*. Magic would explain the little critter's long life span, certainly, but that only raised more questions. Did he spend every night in suspension, time locked every minute the old woman showed no interest in him? He was just far enough away that Vimika couldn't work out any answers, but she knew he had to be a lot more than the product of the most perfect pedigree in history to have survived almost triple the lifespan typical of his species.

But thinking about it only made it worse, because the more Vimika thought about it, the more she began to suspect that he was even older than Tarsebaum knew. Or admit to, at any rate. For an animal to be suffused with as much magic as Vimika could deduce from Oliver' trail, he should have a lot more eyes, be partially inside-out and sport a tentacle or two. And be made of shadows. And make a sound like a pig being juiced by a horde of rusty hinges. Underwater.

As such a thing would have been noticed by the staff at least, if not an old woman who had a vested interest in making sure her only trusted companion wasn't a nightmare from a place no one could give name to without going insane, Vimika concluded that Oliver was one of two things, both of them impossible.

One, he was an illusion.

Two, a relic of a time when all the great magickers of Atvalia had collectively decided to jump off the planet by being stupid.

For One to be true, then Two would have to be as well, since there were no wizards strong enough to make an illusion stand up to fifty years of scrutiny the level of which Oliver had been receiving.

Not anymore.

Vimika would be the first to admit she wasn't a great wizard. She was good, she would give herself that much credit, but the fact she had only been able to draw two conclusions, both of which were impossible, was leading her to reassess her own self image.

The intelligent thing to do, when faced with a dilemma like this, would be to consult someone smarter than herself. There was no shame in that among wizards. If there was, there would be no wizards, because they would have all melted, exploded or dissolved from both the trial *and* error of avoiding it.

But.

If Two was true, then that could only mean Bad Things, and wizards kept Bad Things to themselves so there would continue to *be* wizards.

Sheer probability said that a few mechamagical creatures had to still exist. In addition to the immortality was the fact that so many had been made, regardless of the number that had been destroyed along with their creators. The survivors would be so highly prized by their owners that it stood to reason a few would have been 'lost', 'escaped', or 'get off my property or I'll have my private army take that crown off your head the long way'.

Every wizard knew it. Their continued survival depended on them ignoring that fact, however.

The race of magic practitioners had barely survived the culling brought on by the hubris of their forbearers. A lot of bowing, scraping, regulation and acting invisible were the only reasons there were any wizards left at all some 200 years later. The meek had inherited a messy, ugly legacy, not the world someone had mentioned somewhere. Anything that reminded those in power of a time where they almost weren't anymore, or at the very least humbled them with a reminder of what *true* power looked like, which was worse, risked a renewed scrutiny that wizardkind couldn't survive. Magic was *useful*; it wasn't *necessary*. Having grain stocks that were never lost to weevils, or being able to tell fake jewels from real ones were both, in a word, neat.

Being able to tear the lifeforce out of a living creature and put it into a metal shell regardless of the wishes of said lifeforce's owner, was, in a word, not.

The former could be done the hard way if it meant expunging the ability to do the latter from existence. And that had been the reaction before anyone could ever manage it with people. Doing it to animals had been enough to spur a minor genocide, doing it to people would most likely have meant total extermination.

The very idea of true, *animata*-stealing mechamagery was horrifying, and Vimika sat back from her scrying implements slightly light-headed. Little tingles pricked at the backs of her eyes as she looked about her laboratory as if it was someone else's. What had it been like to be a mechamage? To be in a place not unlike this (actually, considerably not like this, as the entire reason one got into mechamaging was the money), a place of discovery and experimentation, and have the idea that 'I'm going to rip the life out of this puppy and stick it in a body that looks exactly the same except all the bones are made of gold'?

Perhaps the origins were as benign and altruistic as the apologists made them out to be. That it had only been done on the sick and dying in a last-ditch attempt to save the animals' lives, or some version of it, but more blood had been spilled than ink in the name of good intentions.

It was sick. A complete perversion of the magickers' gift. Though it was easy for Vimika to say with as much time as had passed since, there was a part of her that was glad someone had stood up to her people and said no. Much easier to do when backed up with a forest of swords and being able to fill every shadow with the world's best assassins than as a lowly apprentice seeing what their master was getting up to, raising a finger and getting out 'Um...' before being liquified and poured into a ditch.

But what was she to do now? She had every reason to track Oliver down, and just as many not to. Yes, she was being paid handsomely to do it, which was a handsome reason indeed, and how many had the chance to see a genuine mechamagical creature? As repugnant as the idea was, they were relics of a bygone age, little fuzzy miracles that shouldn't exist at all.

And had led to Vimika's people being nearly wiped out altogether.

Then there was the law, which, nicely in line with Vimika's cynicism on the subject, didn't seem to apply to Malivia Tarsebaum, since she was still (mostly) alive. She had to know what Oliver was. He would have been passed down through the family for over two centuries, since you couldn't acquire a new mechamagical creature once all their creators had been killed in gratuitous but symbolic ways. The market for them was so far past black it didn't even have a name. It was more like anti-light. A void.

Nearly impossible to get rid of without scrutiny, in a number that would only ever get smaller, they were literally priceless.

The gold sitting under Vimika's bed made a lot more sense now. The silence required on her part was such it hadn't even been spoken. Tarsebaum knew what Oliver was, and knew that if her house wizard was caught with him…

"Shit," Vimika said, hurling a *wakasha* nut across the room to plink off of a beaker. The clear fluid inside suddenly glowed bright pink in response to being awoken, but soon settled back to sleep.

She was expendable. A freelance nobody with a name that didn't mean anything in this part of the country. It would in the capital though, which meant she could, at the very least, disgrace her entire family if she was caught transporting Oliver, or even keeping the knowledge of his existence secret.

She could shut up or ruin her family. Or worse.

The gold was just to keep it from blowing back on Malivia and her family. If Oliver had been living in that house for hundreds of years, it would be impossible to hide from the most cursory magical probing, so a return to the status quo behooved (or beclawed) all of them.

It was the chance of a lifetime for a wizard, even if she would have to take the story of it with her to the grave. With the money she would make from taking that chance, however, she wouldn't have to talk to anyone again if she didn't want to. She could take her story and her shame, and disappear with both forever.

Odd how it was the last part that won out.

3

There was a strain of magickers far to the north and east of Maris that held with riding brooms as the preferred mode of transport, since they were widely available, simple, cheap, and were both portable and inconspicuous once you landed. If you didn't want to carry it, you just set down and propped it up against a wall with no worries anyone would look at it twice. No stables, no grooming, no oats, no poop, none of it.

But Vimika was quite aware of her own anatomy and the very idea of straddling a stick barely wider than her thumb and trusting her entire weight to it started a little noise in the back of her throat that she had to consciously stop by thinking of soft pillows and hot baths while crossing her legs several times.

Masochists, the lot.

It was the skill of the wizard, not the shape of the object that let wizards zip around through the sky unimpeded, and Vimika was of the school of thought that since the latter could be whatever the level of the former allowed, it should be practical and not at all painful.

Thus it was that Vimika was hurtling through the icy winter air perched atop the upper half of an old door. Faded blue, she had never actually seen the lower half, but knew it had been severed violently, with lots of jagged edges splintering the bottom that made it look faster. A broken door was practical, as far as flying refuse went. She could keep small items in the recesses without fear of them rolling off, sit in virtually any position she wanted, even lie down for small stretches if she was brave and not near any mountains, and the knob was perfect for hanging her worn, well-traveled satchel from. Today it contained a few magical implements and the gold coins she couldn't leave behind without at least a tiger guarding them.

Tightly cinched into her flying trousers below her flapping robe, her legs dangled over the side, fuzzy insulated boots kicking empty air as she sped along several hundred feet above the quiltwork patches of farms that stretched away in every direction from Durn. The further south Vimika sped, however, the sparser the farms grew, as south meant cold, and soon, mountains. Big ones.

She sat up.

Looming ahead, stretching the breadth of the horizon were the foreboding Dragonback Mountains. Strikingly beautiful in the clear, sharp air of a dry winter's afternoon, they rose up from the surrounding plains to scrape the clouds from the sky, weaving them into blankets of snow in which to drape themselves all year round.

There were nothing like them where Vimika grew up. Like many of the old (surviving) wizard families, the Malakandronons had lived within sight of the capital city of Maris. Sight being relative as well, since the great spires of the palace were so tall that the curve of the world was less of a hindrance to concealing them than one would imagine.

Maris had what the locals called mountains, but having lived in Durn for a while now, Vimika could join the Southerners in laughing at how naive she'd been to label them as such. The brownish lumps that ringed Maris were hills. Here, if it didn't have snow on it year-round or hadn't exploded at some point, it wasn't a mountain. Locked into their winter finest, the Dragonbacks were simply *more* white than in the summer. Just like people, they wore fewer layers when it got warmer, but they still wore something.

At their feet lay the true end to Atvalian civilization, the Shadowbridge Forest. Tightly packed with speartip pines, which in most light appeared blacker than greener, Vimika had always found herself giving it a wider berth than the mountains, which were like a great, unknowable wall. Vast and old, they radiated indifference to lengths of time shorter than those she had to put a great deal of thought and humility into imagining properly.

Shadowbridge was different.

It *wanted* you to come closer.

The section Vimika was slowing down to avoid entering did, anyway.

She set down in daylight amidst a field of unblemished white and immediately blemished it by heaping snow atop her door before casting a spell of Weight on it. The winds blowing down from the mountains could be as strong as they were finicky (and so would any people be who were mad enough to live here), and she wanted to make sure she had a ready ride home should she need to flee in a hurry.

Satisfied her door wouldn't go anywhere, Vimika slung her satchel over her shoulder and Looked into the woods.

Blazing straight into the heart of the dark was Oliver's magical trail, vanishing less than a dozen yards into the shadows of the immense trees that seemed to somehow take a keen interest in the little creature staring up at them and trying not to use her imagination very much.

It was tough to get going, however. Everything about the place felt wrong. The woods could be scary, of course, it's why scary stories were set in them. But as Vimika stood in the snow, for the first time taking comfort in being near blinded by it, there was a sort of extra darkness to the trees that couldn't be accounted for by simple lack of light. Shadows had color, the darkness amidst the boughs above was just *black*. Little detail was visible to her naked eye, but through Sight, it was intensely green with *mana*, which wasn't surprising given its likely age and the fact it had achieved said age completely unmolested by people.

It was alive and thriving, just dark and ominous, not unlike what she imagined the inside of a snake looked like to an unwary mouse before its eyes were digested. Almost as if the Shadowbridge Forest had been named appropriately.

It had to be her imagination though, didn't it? A trick of light that happened so often when you were alone on the border of a dark place filled with unknowns but had no real choice but to enter.

That described the privy half the time, so with a spasm of sudden decision, she stepped forward. Her boots sank into snow softer than she'd thought it would be, a discouraging representation of her confidence as she left the warm embrace of the sun for the shadowy chill of the forest.

What made her stop short wasn't a sudden noise, it was the sudden lack of any. Utter silence, a sucking vacuum of noise that made her lean forward so she could listen harder to find some.

Jerking back ramrod straight, the feeling of 'nothing' ahead of her continued, as though she were standing on the edge of a cliff. She didn't want to look over. She knew she should back away, but was drawn by some inner compulsion to creep closer. To grab the watchman's truncheon, to stick her hand in the yawning dog's mouth, to say 'surely the soft wooshing sound coming from the depths of this cave is just a draft.'

People say cemeteries are eerie because they're so quiet.

That fact only made them good neighbors, in Vimika's mind. But this, the complete anti-presence of noise, wasn't eerie either— it was terrifying, like she'd been entombed inside her own head.

The forest had stripped away every single sound save one: her own heartbeat. In a way, it was reassuring. She hadn't gone deaf and she was still alive. She tried shouting, but the only proof was the vibrations in her throat. She tried again, louder, but only succeeded in adding pain. Still her heart thudded in her ears, all the more noticeable for the lack of any meaningful competition.

That's what made her turn around.

Stumbling back into the light, sound returned in an overwhelming rush, the wind and the crash of her feet through the snow near deafening after total silence. She threw her hands over her ears, breath coming in frantic, sucking wheezes until her hearing adjusted to the real world again.

She shot a withering gaze into the forest, which returned it somehow.

Vimika looked away first.

"BAAAAAAAAA!"

Anything to drown out the memory of the sound of her own heart.

No one ever understood when she told them. They called her strange and backwards, one of her old girlfriends had even been hurt by the fact that Vimika couldn't stand the sound of her heartbeat. That Vimika was cold. Weird. Wizard-y. But it had nothing to do with being a wizard, and everything to do with being alive.

Everyone else found the sound comforting, like a reminder of the womb, they said. To her it sounded like proof of mortality. Every beat, she feared the next one wouldn't come, that the rhythm would stop and that would be that. Every lover she'd lain with, Vimika'd put her head on their shoulder, not their chest. She didn't need a reminder of her final moments during her most contented.

The worst part was, she couldn't even explain why. If someone had died under her ear, or she'd seen some horrible variation of a heart outside its former owner's body beating its last, that might explain it, but no, it was just the simple fact of death. She didn't need anything more than that. Brains were silent and invisible when they were working, so were spleens and livers, they didn't *mark every second on the march to oblivion out loud.*

"*Baablghghrmnphgrblgappbpbpbpbp!*" She spat out more nonsense noises. There was enough nonsense in the forest, she needed some in her mind to distract her from that fact.

Once she had herself back under control, she took a deep breath, a thick plume of white roiling from her nostrils like a dragon who'd just discovered cigarettes.

Something had stolen her hearing and she had no idea what. Peering back into the forest, her eyes had nothing to tell her, light or magic, and neither did her ears, or her nose. There was nothing to indicate… whatever it was. She didn't even know what she was looking for. It had to be magical, didn't it?

She was a wizard, which meant she had extra senses, one of which should have told her what was lurking in that wood. But there was nothing. As a wizard, she couldn't abide the unknown if magic was afoot. *Hidden* magic? That was new.

And scary.

Yet all that was out of place was Oliver's trail. He was in there, a few hundred yards away, unmoving. And, something told her, waiting.

Vimika stared down at the edge of the snowfield in resentment. Whatever her misgivings, whatever else she may find on the other side, she had to keep telling herself that the only thing that mattered was the gold she would get for crossing into it.

Or, if she chose to downplay her own avarice, she could say that she found herself genuinely curious about just what kind of place a mechamagical fennec would choose to retreat to. Wild fennecs lived in dens, a fennec with gold bones animated by magic that had been holed up in a mansion for possibly ten times its natural lifespan lived in... what? A hole he'd found? The stomach of a bear who was in for quite the surprise when it came time to visit the little bears' room? As far as anyone knew there wasn't anything else in these woods beyond trees and the beginnings of the mountains. What drew him here and why did he stay? Why now?

All questions that should have consumed her before she'd left. Or taken the money. Or gotten her hopes up with what to do with said money.

Had she thought about just keeping Oliver for herself? Of course she had. But where would she fence something like a mechamagical animal anyway? She wouldn't even know who to ask other than the police, which was a bizarrely comforting thought. The reason she couldn't be a criminal was because she didn't know how. Her mother would be proud.

No, she would return him and he would be fine. If he had been up to this point, there was no reason to believe he would be anything other than *more* coddled than he already had been when she returned him. If she didn't, then he would be free forever, both of which suited her better than a slow execution.

All that mattered was getting paid.

Yes. That was it. Nothing more. No more moral quandaries to sort out.

In. Out. Done.

House. Solitude.

Go.

She didn't even brace herself this time, she just barreled into abject silence.

Raging, terrifying silence. Aggressive silence that felt like it was jamming itself into her ears in a bid to reach the bit responsible for balance so it could throw her down and laugh at her. She had to fight for each step she took, keeping her eyes straight down to make sure that her feet were still going in the right direction.

Without another sound to mask it, it felt like her heart was trying to break into her head, pounding away at her brain to force it out through her eyeballs in order to make room.

Boom-doom. Boom-doom. Boom-doom.

How many more of these do you have in you?

Boom-doom. Boom-doom. Boom-doom.

Louder and louder it grew, the rhythmic march of the shadow she was born with, the one she couldn't shake, the one that looked exactly like her except it had no eyes and no mouth. And no mercy.

Waiting. Watching. Stalking.

Boom-doom. Boom-doom. Boom-doom.

But it was always behind, and could only catch her once.

Use it.

Eyes forward, she matched every other beat of her heart with an answering step.

Boom-doom.

Thud.

Or, there would have been, if she could have heard it. She was a wizard, she had a good imagination.

Boom-doom.

Imaginary thud.

Boom-doom.

Imaginary thud.

She braved a look behind her, but all there was to see was

the progress she'd made. Two dozen footsteps, (mostly) forward, only one back. No shadow. No sign of impending mortality.

Wait, no shadow?

The world turned.

Upside-down or inside out, or both or neither, the trees began to spin and swirl like the forest was being rung out by some unseen giant. The ground rose up to meet the sky, white with snow, white with cloud, rushing like the foam of a river over rocks made of trees. With the silent thunder of a world come loose from its moorings, the ground reared up to meet her, smacking into her knees first, then the shock of her hands breaking the fall before her face could.

Her eyes were full of snow, her mouth with bile. She swallowed hard against the urge to throw up when all at once, her hearing returned, but all the sounds were wrong.

And it was too warm.

She forced herself upright to sit back on her heels. Scraping the snow from her eyes, her vision cleared enough to see where she was.

Maris.

All around her were the spires of the capital, pointing accusatory fingers at the stars for daring to lie beyond their power. The cobblestones, the bridges, the flats, all hunched and bent from bearing the weight of the eyes looking down from the spires. The laughter of the river slithering through the city, in no hurry to find the sea.

It was dark, where was she? *Why?*

Laughter.

Her ears twitched at the sound. It wasn't the water anymore.

All around her was laughter. Girls' laughter.

Tearful, side-splitting laugher. Pointing, tears streaming down faces.

From the walls past the door, through the open window.

No.

It didn't matter how or why anymore, she couldn't be here again.

A breeze blew in with the laughter, over her bare skin. Her arms, her back, her legs.

"You thought I meant it?"

This isn't real. This isn't happening.

"The look on her face! She had no idea!"

Wake up, Vimika!

Cold, hard impacts pelted her, the soft thump of coins raining on the bed. The sound of her clothes being passed around, more laugher. Fabric fluttering out the window and a soft splash into moving water.

"Good thing you don't have much to cover up!"

With a scream of rage as much as at herself as anyone, Vimika shot to her feet and spun to face her tormenters, her robes billowing out around her. But when she forced her eyes open she was in the forest again.

"You stupid dupe," Vimika said. Another Vimika, standing a few yards away. Stark naked, the way she had been that night, her entire body mottled red with shame. "You didn't even question it. Like a dumb puppy, you just did what she said. How good did that reward taste, dummy?"

"Shut up," Vimika said.

"You haven't been able to make me in three years, why should I start now?" Not-Vimika said.

"You won't let me!" Vimika shouted.

"Of course not. You'll just get hurt again if you forget."

"You're not real," Vimika said.

"Aren't I?"

Power surged through Vimika, a bolt of arcane fire snapping at her fingertips. But as she raised her hand to loose it, Not-Vimika evaporated in a cloud of knowing, satisfied laughter.

~

The only way Vimika knew which way to go next was by where she hadn't yet. Her footprints were everywhere (whether she'd made them or not), along with kneeprints and handprints, the little snow that had reached the ground mashed into a brownish slurry. Thankfully there was no sign of Not-Vimika, but since Vimika had no idea where she'd come from, it couldn't be said for certain that that was a permanent state of affairs.

At least she could hear again.

Granted, all there was to hear was panicked breathing, but she was, for the moment, alone. All that did, however, was give her mind the opportunity to rampantly speculate about what has just happened.

Illusion magic was hard under the best circumstances. If there was one thing that people were universally good at, it was picking out imperfections in other people. But Not-Vimika had been like looking into a mirror. Every line of her face had been replicated perfectly, the cascade of pink that spotted her chest when she flushed, every freckle, the scar on her side she never spoke of, even the little curl her lip took on when she was feeling particularly pleased with herself.

Her memories.

That was a level of magic unseen in centuries. People might be good at seeing imperfections in others, but no deception was more effective than self-deception. Tapping straight into someone's thoughts resulted in the most convincing illusions known to magic. But it was a skill thought lost forever, one of many that had been snuffed out in the Purges.

So why was it here in the woods in the middle of nowhere?

More importantly, *who* was here in the woods in the middle

of nowhere?

Vimika looked ahead, deeper into the forest. Ahead was Oliver. She could still See him there, but only, she was coming to suspect, because she had scryed for him and knew what she was looking for. The illusions had taken her completely by surprise, which was most likely the point of them.

Hidden from her naked eye and her magic Eye, the entire forest was one giant trap, and she was standing in the middle of it. What else was in here? And *why*?

Had Oliver known about it? If he was indeed mechamagical, maybe it would give him some sort of magical sympathy that led him this way.

Or maybe he was made here, Vimika thought, shaking loose a shiver that rattled her from the top of her hat to her toes. Any wizard capable of illusions as strong as the ones she'd just endured would easily have been capable of mechamagery, if they weren't otherwise occupied being dead.

But if a few mechamagical animals had survived, then perhaps one or two of their creators might have, as well. There were stories of mages escaping justice, but always in fanciful (and impossible) ways like teleporting or on a pillar of fire, usually involving some amount of taunting and assurances about forthcoming revenge. The current state of wizard society was ample proof that those promises had gone unfulfilled.

Leontofen Stovkovr, Azrabaleth Kalinostrafal, Ikaliza Fantokiribas, they were notorious among wizards. Heroes to some, villains to the rest, the outstanding bits of unfinished business that made it impossible for people like Vimika to go outside without donning the hat and robes first. Two hundred years later, they had to all be dead, of course, but it was a lingering aftertaste that no amount of gargling with the freedom of living wizards could quite rinse out.

A mystery was already a dangerous proposition for a

wizard, but multiple mysteries layered on top of one another could get them to do all manner of stupid things, like take another step forward into a place that had already made clear it didn't really get on with visitors very much.

Vimika was freezing, she hadn't eaten since her fish with Apricot, and she'd just been forced to remember something she'd spent quite a lot of money on alcohol trying to forget. All she had to do was turn around and go back to her cellar.

There were other ways to make all the money she needed in a single afternoon. She wouldn't at all dwell on just what was happening in this forest, what secrets it was hiding or why Oliver had run here in the first place. None of those were thoughts that would occupy the mind of a young, lonely wizard trying to find any excuse at all to think about something other than where she was.

No, drinking herself into an early grave was a much better use of her time.

So.

Onward into the unknown, or back into the very well known? The well-trod, the featureless blank plain of the future she'd settled on largely for lack of a better idea.

"Yes, hide. Like you always do," said Not-Vimika from behind.

"No thanks to you," Vimika replied. She turned to see herself standing amidst the the swirling cyclone of footprints she'd made when she'd first been disoriented. Not-Vimika was clothed this time, exactly the same way Vimika was, a perfect mirror image.

"I *am* you. So..."

"Shut up. So shut up. That's what comes next. Shut. Up."

"You don't even know who I am," Not-Vimika said with a little pout. "Not *really*."

"I know only too well who you are, which is why I told you to shut your mouth," Vimika snarled.

"Or what?"

"I'll ignore you. What you like best, isn't it?"

Not-Vimika laughed into her sleeve, then looked down it in puzzlement, as if she'd never seen it before. "If only you could. Your tab at Wilim's is proof enough."

"I don't run a tab. It's why he tolerates me."

"That was more a figure of speech. A little more elegant than saying 'the amount of money you've thrown down your gullet in that bar you live under.' Or maybe that would have gotten the point across better after all. Your mind is a confusing place," Not-Vimika said.

"Well aware of that, thank you. Why are you here, and who are you? Really?"

"I'm not telling and there's nothing you can do to make me," Not-Vimika said.

"You sound like a child."

"And since I'm a figment of *your* imagination, who's fault is that?"

Vimika narrowed her eyes and tried to Look *through* the maddening phantom wearing her face, but it was perfect. Almost. It was too weak in *animata*, but that kind of energy was difficult to fake. Magic had its own truth, you could only bend a lie so far. But in every other respect, Not-Vimika looked as solid as Vimika's own reflection, and almost as sad. "You're an illusion. A powerful one, but just an illusion."

"Am I? Maybe this is all in your head. Maybe this is a dream. Ground's a little soft, isn't it?"

In an eye blink, Vimika's footing collapsed beneath her and she spiralled down into the freezing mud. The world around spun and swam, twisting into shapes and patterns she had no words for. The trees soared into the sky at the same time they bent low over her like a cage, pine needles becoming like daggers and teeth, snow like haze, the sun too bright to stand at the same time she was plunged into darkness.

"Go home," said a voice from the shadows.

But not shadows of light. Of time.

"I have no use for you anymore, *witch*."

Screwing her eyes shut so tightly it hurt, Vimika shook her head violently. "No. No! Shut up! Leave me alone!"

"I will, if you'd get out of my house."

The air was warm again, heavy with perfume and incense. The ground was no longer mud and snow, but a plush rug, one that Vimika had fallen to her knees upon before. Stars exploded in her vision as she doubled over on herself, her forehead smacking through the thick pile onto the hard wooden floor beneath. Her chest swelled against her arms as she held herself and sucked back the sobs she would *not* let come again.

"Get up Vimika, you're embarrassing yourself. And me, frankly."

A voice like honey. Sticky and sweet. Enticing, and inescapable if you got sucked in by it.

"You said you loved me," Vimika whimpered.

"I said a lot of things to get you to do as you were bid. A wizard *should* do as they're told, but you never would. Well, you won't be the last one I bed, and I doubt the next one will take nearly as much work for so little reward."

"You don't mean that," Vimika said.

Honey exploded into spun sugar, a full-throated laugh that left Vimika tangled in a web of tacky threads that only got stronger the more she flailed against them.

"Of course I do. I can afford someone better trained, you know. A good girl who doesn't ask questions. She'll work her magics and hurt the people who need hurting without talking back. She'll be seen and not heard. Warm my sheets at night, go back on her shelf during the day, and thank me for the privilege. Unlike you, you ungrateful, slit-eyed harlot. Now get out before I summon the Watch."

The world spun again, sucking the breath from Vimika's lungs and she found herself back in the forest on her side, her right cheek half-buried in slush. White clouds geysered from her lips, limning the scattered pine needles in white hairs of frost.

"I hate you," she whispered.

"I know," Not-Vimika replied. "So why don't you go back home and prove it? All that yummy brandy, the Soft Sea Gold you spared the other night just waiting. Then you can curl up and wish you were dead again. Or pretend you already are."

Vimika looked up at herself. "Is that what you want?"

"You're the one who fell for the 'I love you' trick twice, you tell me."

Sodden and freezing, Vimika forced herself back to her knees. Her right side was numb, her robe splattered with clots of sodden filth. The brim of her hat was crumpled and heavier on one side, covering an eye. "What are you hiding?" she asked.

"Nothing. Which is why I can be so honest with you," Not-Vimika replied with a maddening little rictus that might have been a grin.

With a grunt, Vimika managed to get one foot underneath her, sloshing freezing mud into her other leg. "Liar. You're saying those things for a reason. Making me re-live... that... for a reason. You want me to listen to you..."

"To yourself, you mean?"

"Shut up," Vimika seethed.

"So you've said."

Swaying and unsteady, Vimika managed to get to both feet. She looked again towards the unblemished ground, the path untaken. With a wrenching effort, she heaved herself forward without looking back.

"You aren't worthy of her!" Not-Vimika shouted.

Vimika didn't reply. Instead, not for the first time, she fled from herself.

Headlong into the unknown she ran, in the only direction she hadn't been. She didn't care what she would find anymore, because what was behind was worse. All thoughts of mechamagery and the danger presented by anyone who might still practice it went ignored. She could no longer feel her toes, but she counted it a blessing, since it might be a precursor to not being able to feel anything else.

It was a long, stumbling rush before she could bring herself to look up.

Ahead, the densely-packed trunks began to thin, standing aside to allow her a glimpse of a way out. Clear, unobstructed daylight beckoned, and some animal part of her instinctively pushed her harder, towards the safety of the sun.

She quickened her pace, but the clearer the goal became the brighter it got, to both her eyes and her magic senses. In moments the light between the trees went from potential sanctuary to the gaping maw of the very worst hell. Water fountained from her eyes and she threw her hand over her face, until even that wasn't enough to block the light. It went *through* her hand to stab directly into her brain, and she burst blindly from the trees into open air. Staggering forward a few steps, her toe caught the back of her heel and she pitched straight into the ground, her momentum rolling her into a sprawling heap.

Flat on her back, the entire world was painful, from outside and in. Every nerve was afire, and if her head split open it would come as a relief from the pressure building behind her eyes. She flailed against the assault, but there was no relief to be found.

Unwilling to risk any more surprises, Vimika's mind did the prudent thing and stopped accepting any input from the outside world.

Just for good measure, the inside followed swiftly behind.

4

The world didn't return so much as congeal. A thick, stifling thing that sat astride Vimika's senses like the corpse of a corpulent horse. Every ounce of pain in her body was restricted entirely to her head, which felt like it was about to burst as she coughed and wheezed against the remembered cold. But a few deep breaths told her she needn't have bothered; the only thing nipping at her nose now was the feeling rushing back into it. The air was warm and tasted of spring, which was pleasant, but completely wrong and therefore alarming.

None of that made any sense, but given the thunderstorm wracking the backs of her eyeballs, she was in no hurry for it to start. Yes, the ground she lay on was decidedly hard and flat, and yes the blanket was warm and oh-so soft, but those things made even *less* sense. Maybe if she passed out again it would all go away and she would wake up in a sodden, frozen heap like she'd expected to.

It wasn't the spicy, biting incense that kept her conscious. Nor was it the sensation of a breeze across the top of her hatless head.

No, it was the shadow that passed over her, and the humming that went with it.

Groaning, Vimika girded for another fight with herself. She had been a fool to think she could get away as easily as losing consciousness. Some refuge daylight had turned out to be.

"Oh! Ah, how do *you* do?" asked a woman's voice that was decidedly not Vimika's.

It was a voice she'd never heard before, one of dusk shaded in twilight velvet, with diction so crisp it could snap if used on a cold enough day.

"Ahem. *How* do you do?"

Such insistent politeness made Vimika brave cracking an eye open.

Standing over her less than an arm's length away was absolutely *not* Vimika.

Long, pointed ears protruded from hair as black as midnight, of such length to vanish out of Vimika's peripheral vision. The woman peered down with eyes nearly as dark, almost enough to hide the slits, but more than dark enough to reflect Vimika'a own gawping, fish-like face back at her.

"Vimika, isn't it? Oh, this is awkward. I'd rather hoped you would be sensible when you awoke. Perhaps the question wasn't quite in keeping with your current state. I'm not terribly good at improvising, you see, but I wanted to make sure to mind proper manners in any case. Judging by your expression, your experience may have affected your hearing as well. Oh... my, I hadn't planned for that eventuality. Hmm..."

The wizard had a moment's rumination before she bent over perfectly at the waist, putting her face only an inch or two away from Vimika's.

"*HOW DO* YOU *DO? MY NAME IS AURELAI!*"

A sound that loud from that close needed to be blinked away, and made Vimika afraid to breathe for fear of her lungs being collapsed if it happened again. Holding her breath however, left her light-headed and susceptible to stray thoughts such as 'this is the most beautiful woman I've ever seen.' More sober ones like 'she knows my name' went unheeded. 'This is all very strange' was deemed appropriate. Something about a bizarre flavor of charming was in there too somewhere, but Vimika needed to respond before any windows were blown out.

"Hello," she croaked, half in wonder and half in not knowing what else to do when confronted with something like this so soon after regaining a consciousness she wasn't entirely sure how she'd lost.

The wizard started in surprise before clapping her hands together. "Ah! You can hear! And still speak! Splendid."

Tendrils of black hair reached for Vimika as the wizard swept into a comically deep bow, hooking one ankle behind the other under a dress finer than any Vimika had ever seen on a wizard. A satin red the color of blood, trimmed with icy silver, it was of a style she'd never seen on a living person. Museums tended to frown on exhibits that could talk back.

"How *do* you do?" the wizard asked for the third time.

Vimika blinked, but nothing became any clearer. "I don't know. Where am I? Who are you?"

This seemed to catch the stranger off guard, and she straightened in a remarkable show of balance and poise that Vimika would have been hard-pressed to replicate without hurting herself.

Black eyes cast about as if for rescue, but none came. "I... am Aurelai. And this is my home. Which I should probably explain. Ah... that is, do you remember running towards a clearing when you were in the forest?"

"Sort of. I was aiming for the sun more than anything."

Aurelai nodded. "Thank you ever so much for coming. Your hat and robe were filthy and had little bits of ice in them. I hope you don't mind my removing them before bringing you inside. I do like to keep things clean."

Vimika shot a panicked look downward to see that beneath the blanket she was thankfully still in her tunic and flying trousers, even if they weren't much better off than her robe had been.

"I wasn't about to undress an unconscious person," Aurelai said. "Unless that's acceptable now?"

Now?

"It is not."

Vimika should have been alarmed to the point of some kind of cardiac episode to find herself in the wizard's laboratory. Much like Vimika's own only three times bigger, stocked the way hers was too when she closed her eyes and imagined it really hard. Fortunately, the weight of her envy was enough to tamp down the terror.

Aurelai had *cabinets*! With locks on them! Stone countertops that wouldn't hiss or spit when unfortunate things were spilled on them, with rolls of leather ready to be spread out for fine mechanical work. Shelves and shelves of ingredients, perfectly preserved and meticulously labeled. Beakers, vials, jars, every empty round thing made of glass that had a name, there was at least one Vimika could see. All of it spotless.

Tools were hung on the wall above the workbench in perfect alignment, from smallest to biggest with outlines drawn on the pegboard. Many of them she recognized, some she had never seen before and couldn't begin to guess the purpose of. Saws, hammers, oversized calipers, a sort of wand with metal filament trailing from one end. What was that for? She would need weeks to identify everything, if she ever could.

There was nothing amateurish or freelance about it. Vimika had wound up in the windowless domain of a professional, and with wizards, that was a word that went hand-in-hand with powerful.

And Vimika was laid out on a slab in the middle of it.

"Aurelai..." she said absently. Pieces of her encounter in the forest suddenly cracked across her mind like thunderbolts, the impossibility of what had happened, the skill necessary, the deadness of anyone who could feasibly be responsible. "That's a very old name."

From before the Purges old. It was a *mage's* name, not a wizard's. No wizard in their right mind would give their daughter a name like that any more than they would name her Syphilis. Sounds nice, but when you know what it meant...

"Do you like it? I chose it myself," Aurelai added seemingly without thought, as her eyes immediately took on a cast of regret for having done it. "That is to say... ah... I took it on... But... Vimikathritas! A good, strong name. Traditional too, is it not?"

"It is," Vimika admitted as she pushed herself up on her elbows with middling success.

"Did you choose it?" Aurelai asked.

"What? No, my parents gave it to me... how do you know who I am?" Vimika had never been so well and truly gobsmacked before, but now that her gob was functioning once more, she wasn't entirely sure she would care to repeat the experience.

"I wouldn't have risked trying to bring you here if I didn't know who you were, would I? Would I have? Would I've? Would've... I?" Aurelai shook her head, the curtain of night framing the glowing moon of her face rippling with the movement. "Doesn't matter. You made it here, albeit only mostly alive, but I should think that it counts just as much in favor of my judgment."

Ambivalent to the point of splitting in two, Vimika cast about for an elegant way to change the subject, but nothing was biting, leaving her to set the whole lake on fire instead.

"Are you another illusion? I'm pretty sure you have to tell me if you are. Look, just… dissipate, or turn into something else. If I'm still in the forest, just let me get on with things. If not, then this is a dream, so kindly let me wake up and I'll be on my way. No reward money is worth any of this."

Aurelai looked about long enough for Vimika to notice how slowly the stranger blinked, as though everything that came to her was a surprise. "You're not in the forest anymore, and I'm... *mostly* confident this isn't a dream."

"Oh, good. Then I'm dead. That explains quite a bit. A bit overdone, if I'm honest," Vimika said, casting a look around the meticulously-kept laboratory.

"Did I say something wrong? I'm sorry. I practiced, too," the wizard standing in the middle of it said, crossing one arm over her chest and holding herself tightly, closing her grip one finger at a time.

She *had* to be an illusion, Vimika thought. Surely someone like this couldn't be *real*, could she? You could cut diamonds on her cheekbones! Her ears were perfect grassblades, eyes nearly black, inviting Vimika to get lost within them. She was breathtaking, and Vimika didn't have that kind of luck. Or patience. Or breath to spare.

She needed it to blow sharply out her nose. "Tell me then... angel. Demon. Figment, whatever you are... All of that, out there-" she tossed a hand in a direction that probably answered to that description, "did you do that? Did you put me through that nightmare? Which hell is this?"

Such dark eyes were remarkably expressive when set in such pale skin, making them look even more enormous when they expanded in genuine horror and no little offense. "What? No! Of course not. I didn't know what the forest would do to you, and I'm sorry to have made you face it, but I need the help of a strong mage, and-"

"Wizard."

"What?"

"I'm a wizard."

"I thought your name was Malakandronon."

"It is! And I'm a wizard. Like you."

"I'm not a Wissrd. Could you please just call me Aurelai? There's only two of us, there's no reason to get hung up on such semantics. Yes, I wanted you to come here, Vimika. No, I'm not responsible for the illusions that I should have inquired about first because they've clearly had a profound effect on you and I've done nothing about it as of yet and am now beginning to feel a tremendous amount of guilt concerning..." Aurelai's eyes flicked sideways as a thought seemed to occur to her. "That is to say... I don't know what you saw. I can't. But I imagine whatever it was was most unkind, and you have my apologies. I didn't mean for you to get hurt. I just need your help. Oh, and no, this isn't any hell I am aware of, just to be clear."

"But it was so powerful! If not you, then who? Is there someone else here?" Vimika asked, her voice rising in panic as it settled in how stupid she'd been to trust that the Aurelai was alone. Distracted by a pretty face so she wouldn't see the knife in the back coming!

She whipped around, spinning off the slab and backing into the closest wall that didn't have any mystery fluids on it, firing her entire attention at the only door, which remained open and empty.

Picking up the blanket, she ran the thick wool between her fingers in agitation. It was warm from her body heat and smelled of closet, just like it should. She shook her head in maddened confusion at such normalcy. What if *this* was an illusion, too? All of it. Where *was* she?

But when Aurelai spoke, she was conciliatory. "No. Vimika, I'm all alone, and that's why I need your help. The illusions aren't just for keeping people *out*."

"Then how did I get here? If I am here. Wherever this is."

"I don't know. You're the first and only person to ever make it through. But I give you my word that you're safe. For now."

Vimika's eyes tried to consume the top half of her face.

"That... was a lot more ominous than it was when I thought it. Apologies. I meant that I mean you no harm, Vimika. Truly. I need you, hurting you would be... counterproductive. It's just that getting out might be tricky, so I can't guarantee that you will come to *no* harm while you're here, but *I* have no reason nor intention to hurt you. In fact, I'd like to feed you and make you comfortable, but now you look even more suspicious and I don't know how to fix this so I'll stop talking."

Vimika felt her brain trying to crawl out of her ears so she could deal with this on pure instinct rather than have to think, but her instincts weren't entirely opposed to being fed and made comfortable by someone who looked like Aurelai, which meant Vimika had to force it to stay put.

"Now you're playing on my sympathy, I see. Angry, sad, intrigued, now this? Why? I don't even know what you want!"

Aurelai's dark eyes shifted. "I... just told you."

"My help?"

"Yes. To escape."

"Escape," Vimika repeated flatly.

"The illusions have trapped me here," Aurelai said, nodding out the door. "I can't get past them by myself. But you did! All alone!"

Vimika threw her hands up and pressed her cheeks into her jaw, gnawing on the insides as she thought. Maybe going with the flow would wash her out the other side. What choice did she have? "All right, let's say I believe you. If they trapped you in here, why wouldn't they trap me, as well?"

"Because they were *designed* for me," Aurelai said with

rising impatience. "I've never gotten past them!"

Vimika felt an entirely new kind of suspicion oil itself through her, coating her in mistrust and alarm. Illusions that strong and complex had to be both by and for someone equally strong, which meant Aurelai *had* to be lying. But there was something about her expression, her body language. She was terrified and bordering on desperation in her need to be believed.

"If you're here all alone, as you say, but you didn't cast them, who did?" Vimika with the slow cadence of calm that wasn't so much felt as practiced.

At such speed, each syllable was a hammer blow, and cracks show easier on dark surfaces than light. Aurelai's eyes were no different, the perfect onyx wavering under the strain. Her lips quavered as she nibbled on the inside of her cheek, slender eyebrows dancing atop the grave of her composure. "My father. His death triggered all of this, and I can't undo it."

"Ha! Any wizard that strong would have been killed in the Purges or dead from old age by now! So just how long have you been here, then?" Vimika asked with a mocking lilt.

Aurelai gathered herself before answering. "The simple answer is: I don't know."

Heartbreak, sadness, betrayal, it was all wrapped up in three words that managed to also sound somehow akin to a confession. An admission that couldn't hope to hide the corroded, jagged edge that made it sound like her own fault.

Unless she was lying, Vimika thought as the forest came roaring back, assaulting her once more with her own memories. Of the last time she'd been lured in by a beautiful face that had precious need of her magic...

One thought too many, she couldn't keep it bottled in.

"Why should I believe you?" she blurted, vehemence sharpening every word to lethality.

Aurelai started. "I'm sorry?"

"You could be a criminal, for all I know. A mage who escaped the Purges, set up her own little exile down here in the middle of nowhere, found some way to extend her life to unnatural lengths... There hasn't been an Aurelai born in hundreds of years!"

"My *father* was the criminal, and trapping me here was his last crime. He used his Last Breath to do it, you vexing creature!" Aurelai snapped.

That would explain a few things, Vimika had to admit. A person's Last Breath was powerful magic, especially a wizard's, but Aurelai was a wizard herself and would know that, too. But it made more sense than anything else Vimika had heard since waking up that morning.

"Who was your father, then?" she asked indulgently.

"Azrabaleth Kalinostrafal."

Words tried and failed to come to Vimika's tongue. Instead they just sat in the back of her throat unsaid, too shocked to risk coming out. Her nose and ears were suddenly cold, all the blood having fled her face to hide in her stomach, given how heavy and squishy it suddenly felt. Breath was a struggle. All she could do was blink, so she did quite a bit of that.

"You know him?" Aurelai asked, confusion working at every feature in her flawless face.

"Of course, he perfected mechamagery. But he disappeared during the height of the Purges, conveniently enough... He was hiding down here all along? When did he die?" Vimika added without thinking.

"A long time ago. If I knew precisely, I would have some better sense of how long I've been here, would I not?"

Vimika conceded the point with a half-aware nod, her mind racing off in other directions entirely. Azrabaleth Kalinostrafal was a hero to some, and the catalyst for the Purges to others. Vimika was among the latter. If Aurelai was his daughter, she would be very powerful, and very dangerous. But the young(?) woman standing across from Vimika was neither of those things. In fact, she seemed just the opposite of both.

There was something to her eyes, beyond how beautifully alien they were. Maybe it was the color that lent them an extra layer of depth, but the more they peered at Vimika, the harder she found it to meet them. As much as Aurelai's eyes were windows, they were also mirrors.

Vimika glanced out the doorway again, to the sunlight drifting in through the windows beyond.

Escape.

That's all Vimika wanted, wasn't it? Only she'd never worked up the courage to ask for help in getting it. Wherever she was exactly, it was in the middle of nowhere, cut off from everything (including time, to look at Aurelai), and Vimika had stumbled into it on accident. Or had she? The house wizards, if they all worked together, *might* have been able to construct something a fraction as convincing as all this, but even then, why? Why send her out here? Risk exposing their knowledge of mechamagical animals being sheltered under their noses? Vimika was a miserable drunk living under a tavern, she wasn't worth the level of effort this would have taken. If they were that worried about her, they could have had her *killed* with a lot less effort and risk of blowback. And if that was true, what did that make Aurelai? A victim of a previous game of theirs, trapping her here in a web of illusions? Then why the cover story?

Vimika stared at her hands as they trembled, her fingernails ten grimy crescents wavering on the ends of stick-like fingers, every crease and fold in her knuckles caked with forest floor.

If any of it was an illusion, it was so good she had no hope of uncovering it in her current state. Which meant that, real or not, she was trapped here, just as Aurelai said she was. And Aurelai... was asking for help. She wasn't demanding it or seducing her way into it, she had asked. Whatever Vimika's shortcomings, to refuse someone who seemed genuine in their need for help was not something she could do in good conscience.

Especially a pretty face, because you're a sucker who never learns...

Vimika cast her face upward, not, she told herself, as an appeal to the gods to give her the strength to face whatever was about to happen. "You'll have to forgive me. The illusions were... stressful."

The tension that had been squaring Aurelai's shoulders ebbed, and they rounded off a bit. "It's not your fault. I should have been better prepared for such questions, I suppose. It's not like I've had anything better to do," she said, whether she'd meant to or not.

"If you'll indulge a few more--" Vimika said to a responding nod. "Why me? I'm just a freelancing nobody. You could have called one of the house wizards around here, or gotten them to send to the capital for a proper professional. You're dealing with extremely potent magic here."

Aurelai made a face. "Why would I have done that? You made it, didn't you?"

"I'm still not sure I did. You never did answer when I asked if you're an illusion."

"If I am, I'm such a good one that I don't know it, so I may not be of much help in such a circumstance," Aurelai said.

"Fair enough," Vimika conceded.

"So if we agree that this conversation is actually happening, will you help me? To escape from this prison?"

Vimika searched Aurelai's black, bottomless eyes for some hint, some tiny spark of deceit or mischief born from the bored offspring of the immensely powerful, but found only the light of kindled hope. And once again, her own reflection.

"I'll do what I can. But you should know I've never felt magic that strong before, I wouldn't even know how to begin trying to pull it apart. Just," she said quickly to ward off Aurelai's face falling any farther, "let me get a sense of things first."

But when Vimika tried to use her Sight, her headache snapped back into place with savage intensity, ricocheting around her head and trying to find escape entirely through her eyeballs. Blinking madly, she cast her gaze about with regular eyesight, but there was nothing to see beyond fading white starbursts. "Ow."

"As I suspected. You're in magic shock," Aurelai said with almost callous nonchalance. "I'm sorry."

"What?" Vimika said. Gingerly, she tried to access her magic once more, and was again rebuffed so strongly she fell against the wall, only barely keeping her feet under her as the floor seemed to switch places with the ceiling. "Mother's tits, that hurts! Are you sure magic can be used here?" she asked through her teeth.

"Yes," Aurelai replied. With a few whispered syllables, a breeze blew up from nowhere, swirling about them and snatching at Vimika's hair playfully before dissipating as quickly as it had come.

Unable to think clearly, filthy and exhausted, Vimika found herself pawing the top of her head where her hat wasn't. Her unruly brown hair had wasted no time in taking advantage of its freedom, having burst free from its braids to tumble over her shoulders and down her back.

"Magic shock," Vimika said absently. She'd never experienced it before, but being able to put a name to it made her heart lessen its efforts in trying to tunnel out of her chest. It also hurt a lot more than had ever been mentioned by any of her teachers. Then again, none of her them had ever dealt with magic as strong as Vimika just had.

"It hasn't happened to you? Even when you tried to escape?"

It was absurd to assume Aurelai had never tried, and Vimika wasn't about to insult someone she was even more at the mercy of than she'd already been.

"Thankfully, no." Aurelai said. "But the illusions were made for me. Maybe that included sparing me such difficulty. I'm sorry. Again. Is it serious?"

Shaking her head, Vimika watched her hair sway freely for the first time in years. "I don't know."

"Then may I?" Aurelai asked, indicating the side of Vimika's head.

"Please."

Nodding, Aurelai pressed three chilly fingertips to Vimika's temple as the slits in her eyes widened, expanding over them completely, sclera and all, as she accessed her Sight.

Vimika braced for the incoming sensation of Aurelai's magic connecting to her own, but when it came, it was muffled and distant, like it was on the other side of several feet of wool.

It should have been much stronger, and Vimika's body cried out at the lack of reaction from physical contact with another wizard. From the simple reassurance of 'I'm a wizard, too' between the newly-acquainted to the most intense, soul-cleansing intimacy between lovers, the strength of the interaction of two wizards' magic varied depending on the emotions involved. Even having known Aurelai for all of five minutes, there should have been more than just a dull awareness, and Vimika had to fight back tears at having been robbed of even so small a gift.

From the moment they were conceived, wizards were awash in the magic of their mothers, and the comfort of that feeling never went away. Even blind, Vimika could tell her parents from her siblings, and them from her nieces and nephews just by the feel and 'taste' of their magic. The friends she'd left in Maris, even many of her classmates at the Academy, wizards knew each other better by touch than humans ever could by sight.

Her thoughts went back to when Seris had touched her, the emptiness of it. No matter what happened here or why, when Aurelai put her fingers to Vimika's skin, she should have at least been allowed the reward that was the magic of another wizard's touch. But what she'd gotten was akin to being allowed to smell that a bottle of wine had been opened somewhere in the building when what she wanted was to pour the whole thing straight down her throat.

That Aurelai didn't react with anything but calm spoke volumes about the truth of her isolation. The only way to not miss it was to never have known it.

"Your magic is present, but dormant. Or extremely sluggish, I've never done this before, *but*," Aurelai added quickly, "it's still within your channels. They're just... frozen."

"So, magic shock," Vimika said, her eyes staring ahead as she mourned the loss of something she hadn't even been expecting at the beginning of the day.

The only cure for her condition was rest. The magic channels within a wizard needing to unstick themselves in their own time was something they drilled into every student at the Academy over and over again. Magical senses could be overwhelmed, just like any other, and just like snow-blindness or a ringing in the ear brought on by a loud noise, there was nothing to be done but to wait for it to clear up on its own. Attempting to tinker with one's internal magical workings was a good way to make them external, conveniently mapped out across the nearest wall. And the ceiling.

When Aurelai removed her fingers, Vimika choked down a whimper. Even that barest trickle...

"Was the forest so intense?" Aurelai asked.

"You have no id-" Vimika felt the wizard looking at her. "Yes, it was."

She shook her head with a sobriety that made her wish she was drunk. "I'm sorry. I've never been in magic shock before, and I wasn't that well off before it happened. I feel like someone stuffed my head in a pillow and hit me with a sack of potatoes."

"That's really specific. Sorry! That was a mind thought, not a mouth thought. Oh, I should have practiced more. They don't tell me when I get it wrong," Aurelai said.

"You're not wrong, just really honest. The world could use more of that, to be... honest."

Some light returned to Aurelai's smoke-black eyes as they flicked over Vimika again. "I have more: you look terrible. Could I still offer you a place to rest? Are you hungry?"

Vimika looked from the doorway and back to Aurelai. Wherever here was, she wasn't going anywhere else soon, and certainly not alone. "Yes to both of those things, please."

"Splendid. I expect you'll want to meet my other guest."

5

Vimika's hands found her temples and began to rub at them as Aurelai stared down at her with a look that was part puzzlement and part curiosity, like she was trying to work something out but didn't know what to do with her face in the meantime.

She was remarkably bird-like in her mannerisms, her head cocking in little jerks, even as her blinks remained slow and deliberate. At her sides, her fingers moved one at a time, a rippling wave of motion that was not at all what Vimika's headache needed to see at the moment.

"What guest?" she asked.

"Oh, thank the Mother you said something! Ah! That is... the ostensible reason you actually came here. Our fennec friend arrived days ago, and has been eating his way through my garden since. He's currently sunning himself in the back, if you'd like to see him. Or, he was when you arrived, but then you were unconscious, and I had to carry you all the way here to get you out of the sun, but you wouldn't have any memory of that. Oh. Well. He's... a bit mercurial, that one, isn't he? When he's not being unsociably lazy, at any rate."

Vimika didn't bother to hide a longing glance at the door. "Are there others?"

"Other fennecs? No. All in due time, though. There is much you would like to know about this place, I imagine," Aurelai said, and swept towards the door.

"Aurelai?"

A cyclone of black and red unfurled as she turned at the sound of her name to see the one who'd spoken it still on the floor in an unfortunate heap.

"Could you help me up?"

"Oh! Sorry." Aurelai reached down to haul Vimika to her feet.

"You're a lot stronger than you look," Vimika said, flexing her fingers experimentally. "And have really cold hands. Are you all right?"

Aurelai looked down at their clasped hands with that same bird-like curiosity, only now with an extra dash of satisfaction and more than a little pleasure. Her eyes were remarkably expressive and very difficult to tear away from. Every single thought was written plain on her face, and Vimika found herself caught up in enjoying what she was reading.

"I am now," Aurelai said absently.

Her ears even twitched!

Though Vimika wanted to let the moment continue in the vain hope a proper magical connection would spontaneously happen, the truth was her hands were still filthy, and having dirty hands in a laboratory made her training and instincts join forces to separate them.

"I'm going to need that back," Vimika said not unkindly.

"Oh. Yes, of course. Pardon," Aurelai said, looking down at the streaks of dirt across her palm and marveling.

"Sorry about the mess," Vimika said, wiping her hands down the sides of her legs.

"What? Oh, no, no," Aurelai said without looking up. "It's just... this is the first thing I've ever touched from outside. I thought it would be more different. But it's just... dirt."

Tracing pale white patterns into gritty brown, Aurelai peered down in wonder, rubbing the dirt between her fingers and bringing it halfway to her lips before a look broke out over her features that was so sheepish she could have spun blankets out of it.

Such earnestness was making it harder and harder to believe her plight was anything but genuine. Who would even *think* to marvel over dirt as a means to fake it?

"If you've been trapped here alone, does that make me the first person you've met from outside?" Vimika asked.

Aurelai nodded, unable or unwilling to stop herself from staring.

Vimika was no stranger to being stared at, and the word 'escape' flashed across her mind in giant letters made of experience, but something deeper than that was quite a bit more self-conscious than it was frightened.

"Ah. Well, I could have made a better first impression on behalf of... the world," she said.

"I so looked forward to *any* impression that I am happy to accept it without reservation, dirt included. It confirms that you're real, at least."

Vimika's eyebrows sought her hair. "You doubted *I* was real?"

"Only for a moment, but Father's illusions have a familiar feel, which you lack. As long as I stay within the clearing, they leave me alone. However, I don't think even Father was powerful enough to convince me taking your hand was anything but genuine. I've never felt anything like it."

"Yes, well," Vimika said, trying to tuck her hands together into sleeves that weren't there. "Oliver is here then? Safe and sound?"

"Such a ridiculous name for such an astonishing creature. He's older than I am, and bears Father's marque. I didn't know that until he arrived, however. So, as much as I malign this place, he belongs here. Let me see if he will deign to appear. Just a moment," Aurelai said before her eyes went completely black.

Vimika hadn't watched someone do an incantation from this close since school, and it was easy to see why humans were unnerved by it. Aurelai's lips were moving, but only half-whispered non-words were coming out. Spells were more thought than spoken, the vocalization only serving to focus the thoughts and prevent them from straying halfway through. Vimika recognized the patterns as a Beckoning, which was confirmed moments later when the entire reason for the day's insanity came trotting through the door.

For being a gilded fennec, Oliver was mostly white. It was the smattering of golden hairs throughout their dense coats that gave them their name, making them sparkle in the right light. His pointed ears were enormous, more triangular than blade-like, and his rich brown eyes burned with intelligence.

It was hard to fault the old woman for wanting him back so badly, and without access to Sight, impossible for Vimika to believe he was anything other than what he appeared to be. Vimika *knew* what he was and still couldn't accept it. She *should* hate him. She *should* want to melt him down and erase every memory of his existence. But the little creature looking up at her was a living, breathing animal, not a monstrosity. He wasn't a nightmare from the realms between hells, he was... normal.

All of the death, the pain and suffering, persecutions, restrictions, the entire history of wizardkind for the last few centuries was all because of *this*? Vimika's inability to See him as he really was made the diagnosis of magic shock that much harder to bear. To have such a long-lost masterwork of magic standing only a few feet away but being utterly unable to confirm it was maddening. No wonder they were so hard to track down! Unless you were a wizard, you would have no idea what he was.

He was literally incredible.

"Come say hello, Oliver," Aurelai said.

Oliver did not come say hello.

"He's beautiful," Vimika said absently. The idea of such a perfect little thing bearing a maker's marque was repugnant to the point it made her want to retch. Having your lifeforce stolen was bad enough without needing to be autographed afterwards, but Oliver gave no indication that anything whatsoever was untoward. If anything, he seemed to be enjoying his involuntary immortality just fine. "But... if you didn't know who made him, why did you bring him here?"

"Lady Tarsebaum often told her cats that she would do anything if he ever escaped, but that didn't extend to risking her house mage's life or reputation, apparently. Your skill for finding lost animals was known to her, however, so I Beckoned him here in the hope you would follow," Aurelai said as if it were all perfectly sensible.

"You Beckoned a mechamagical animal? And it *worked*?" Vimika asked, her face unable to hold the amount of surprise being fed into it, and her ears flattened by themselves for the first time since she was a child.

"I wasn't about to Borrow him for my own selfish purposes, was I? He had to come willingly. Turns out I couldn't, anyway, but luckily, he seems content with his choice for now."

Vimika' hands found her temples again.

"Are you all right? I understand magic shock is often accompanied by headaches, but I haven't much in the way of medicines. There might be something in here of use," Aurelai said, and made for the nearest cabinet, stopping short when the sound of Vimika bouncing her head off the wall in weary frustration thumped across the room.

"Do you have any idea how dangerous that was? Our

people were almost wiped out because of your father's mechamagery obsession! How could you risk that again for your own sake? You can't just turn one loose in the world and hope no one notices! What if one of the *other* three house wizards in Durn had seen him first? Or followed him?"

"They said they wouldn't." Aurelai's face was open and completely reasonable for how insane such a thing was to say.

"And how do you know that?"

Aurelai's brow furrowed without actually appearing to move, in a sort of instantaneous consternation. "They said so. They're all harboring mechamagical creations. Didn't you know that?"

Vimika wasn't left speechless very often, her library of swears was too deep for that. But in most other cases, there was a good, universal word that could be applied regardless of company that got the point across just as well.

"What!?"

"It's... what's the word? Blackmail. No. Leverage? Insurance. Help me, please. Father left me a dictionary, but not much context."

For the third time since arriving, Vimika lost her balance and slumped sideways, catching herself on the slab. "I can't believe what I'm hearing," she said to it in hopes its sharp stone corners would straighten a world gone alarmingly curved all of a sudden.

Finding no such rescue, she dipped into her swear box. "*That's* why they're all such pricks. If anyone ever found out..."

"They would be killed, perhaps along with their masters. I am aware of *why* Father sealed me away, Vimika. It's why I didn't try one of them first."

"So you involved *me*, did you? Now I *know* what Oliver actually is. I would have when I found him. Seen the marque. Malivia knew. And knew I would find out..." Vimika smashed her fist into the slab, but as it was made out of solid granite it didn't notice. "Dammit!"

Aurelai blinked.

"She'll probably demand I return the advance, too. Wonderful. Just... *wonderful*. Not only will I not be paid, I'm going to be at her beck and call for the rest of my life. *And* I found the daughter of the worst person in history, with a side of magic shock for my trouble. Thank you for your hospitality, Aurelai, but I really must be getting on with digging the rest of my grave, if you don't mind."

Pushing herself off the slab, Vimika made for the door.

"You can't... you can't go! You said you would help me!"

Vimika spun on her heel without slowing down, marching straight at Aurelai at the same pace she'd marched away. "You *tricked* me! I bought the story about your father, but you know what? I don't care what the truth is anymore. You've just ruined my life, it won't make a shred of difference."

"Vimika, *please!*"

"No. Wizards suffered enough because of your father's obsessions, and I won't let it happen again for the sake of his daughter. He was a greedy, selfish monster, and *that* apple didn't appear to fall very far at all before it started to rot. I won't put my family's lives at risk because you're *lonely*. Quite frankly, if you actually are a Kalinostrafal you *deserve* to stay in here."

With that, Vimika advanced on the doorway once more, every footstep a booming report that echoed through the room and into the hollow cavity where she'd kept her hopes locked away.

She'd been so *stupid*! How dense and starved for anything resembling excitement in her life had she been to walk into that forest? She should have listened to her gut, been content with her lot and sucked down more wine like a good little wizard. She'd poked her head out of the hole she'd dug for herself *once* and now there was light getting in to show her how deep it actually went.

"No!" Aurelai shouted as the air screamed with magic, filling the doorway with arcane power. Spiderwebs of pale blue light laced across it from one side to the other, sewing the air itself solid. "You *can't* leave!"

Silhouetted before a wall of light, Vimika felt just as featureless and lacking in color. "Using magic against those helpless to defend themselves against it is in your blood. Do what you will."

"I'm not him! I'm *not!*" Aurelai cried.

"The wall's still here."

Her face twisted in anguish, Aurelai yanked on the spell, unraveling it all at once. Daylight streamed through, only to be blocked out by Vimika walking through it, leaving Aurelai all alone.

~

Vimika stalked out to find herself at the end of a short hallway. On either side was a single door, but whatever lay behind them would stay there as she tramped across the polished wood. At the far end was a single large room that served as a den, dining room and kitchen, and she had to fight the urge to kick the dining room table on the way out. With how the day had gone thus far, she would probably just shatter a toe in the process, so she let the furniture be.

Outside was unseasonably warm, but she no longer cared if it was real or not. It *felt* real, and that's all she could count on anymore. She also *felt* betrayed. She *felt* furious. She *felt* like drinking herself to death before she could make things worse for herself.

But between Vimika and the sweet release to be found at the bottom of a cask of Soft Sea Gold was a forest full of nightmares, and her pace across a lawn of meticulously-maintained grass slowed. Ahead and all around was a solid ring of trees, with nothing to indicate which direction was which except the position of the sun, if she could even trust that anymore. Looking for which side of the trees the moss was growing on would require her to be near them, and she swallowed hard against that idea, pausing several yards short of the shadows they cast.

How could this have happened? All she'd had to do was tell Malivia no. Or turn around. The forest had warned her, but her own idiocy had made her run the wrong way. She could blame her cursed wizard curiosity, or find some fault in her education or upbringing, but it was all her own fault. The first inkling she'd had something was amiss, she should have washed her hands of the whole thing, not rolled around in it. Now she was covered head to toe, and it was beyond cleaning off.

Malivia owned her. Held her by the same leash she held her house wizard by, and Vimika had handed it to her with a greedy smile on her face. If knowledge was power, then that fragile old woman was a god to two different wizards now and hadn't needed a drop of magic to achieve it with.

Vimika should have run, just like always. Before it had been to spare her heart. At least this time, it would have been to spare her soul.

A breeze suddenly blew in from the shadows, bringing a voice along with it.

I told you, it said.

"Shut *up!*" Vimika shouted so loud it hurt.

Even living underground, she had never felt so trapped. A monster ahead, a monster behind, and she didn't even have her magic to help. She was just a pointy-eared, slit-eyed human, cut off from her means of figuring out just how large a threat either presented. The illusions had fooled even her magic senses though, so maybe it didn't matter after all.

As quickly as it had come, the breeze died away, allowing her to hear footsteps approaching from behind.

"I'm sorry," said Aurelai.

Vimika grit her teeth to the point of pain, fighting the urge to turn around. "It's too late for that."

"Then I'm sorry for that, too." The footfalls stopped. "Please don't make me beg. I can't bear the idea of being left alone again. I didn't know what bringing you here would do to you, or our people. I... only know what Father told me. That we couldn't leave because the world hated mages. When I saw the treatment of the house mages, I had no reason to suspect he was lying. Until I saw you. You were free, you had a home of your own, friends who cared about you. You got drunk in public without worrying about anything happening to you. I thought you were different. That you were stronger than them... that you would understand."

Vimika chose to ignore the last part. "The world did hate us, for a long time."

"He didn't tell me it was because of him. He said the world was jealous of our power."

"Did those house wizards you spied on seem powerful?"

"No. But you did. It's why I thought to try you first. You were already free," Aurelai said.

Vimika's head fell back in a mirthless laugh. "Then maybe I owe you an apology."

"You had everything I wanted, and I thought you could help me get it. Is that not power?"

At that, Vimika turned and saw for the first time just where she'd found herself. The house was a bit rustic perhaps, but well looked after, surrounded by flowers that bloomed in the dead of winter, an idyllic island floating in a sea of luscious green. Isolated from anything resembling civilization and miles from the nearest soul, it was everything *Vimika* had wanted. And she'd been so close. She'd been right to want to get away, and now she had, ironically. But she didn't feel powerful. Just the opposite.

"Do you know *why* people turned on us? What your father did?" Whatever the objective truth, Vimika was willing to play along with Aurelai's for this much.

"Mechamagery," Aurelai said, her voice tiny, her eyes unable to hold Vimika's. For a fraction of a heartbeat, Vimika lamented it.

"Mechamagery. Ripping the lifeforce out of a living thing and shoving it into a metal body so it could live forever."

Aurelai winced, but nodded at Vimika's assessment.

"It was seen as... unnatural. As much as people said they didn't like mechamagical animals, they bought them at astronomical prices. Mages started taking shortcuts making new ones, not waiting for the donors to be on the brink of natural death. Then came all the failures, the monstrosities that killed their makers and then themselves... the common folk wouldn't stand for it, rebellions fomented, so the king put a stop to them before they could start." Vimika paused to take a breath and regretted the split second it gave her to see the impact her story had on Aurelai's features, but it was her duty to continue. "Mages had gone too far, too close to the domain reserved for gods, and they... *we*, were punished. Our people were decimated, leaving barely enough to continue. Even then under strict conditions. Like having to wear the hat and robe at all times, or be arrested. We can't practice magic without a formal education from an accredited wizard school, we have to account for every single public use of it and pay taxes on each. No human woman will risk bearing the child of a wizard and subjecting them to the harassment, the taunts, the *rules*. I've been called a 'slit-eyed witch' more times than I can count. Do you know what 'witch' means? It's a corruption of 'wizard' and 'bitch'. My ears pulled, my hat stolen, I have to ensorcel my locks to keep people from breaking into my home in spite of the fact I own nothing worth stealing. *That's* your legacy. The world your father birthed and fled."

The longer Vimika spoke, the more time it gave her blood to cool. Getting it all out was cathartic, but it was Aurelai's lack of denial, her complete and total supplication to what she was being bombarded with that made Vimika stop.

In the house, Vimika had been defenseless against magic. Out here, Aurelai was against the truth, and now she stood diminished, curling in on herself, her arms wrapped around her waist. But more sure than Vimika had been of anything lately, she knew the look on Aurelai's face was genuine as it turned inward, her ears drooping into limp crescents.

Aurelai hadn't known. As a full-blooded wizard living in the Atvalian Empire, there was no way for her to have not known the truth about the Purges. They *all* did, since no one was about to let them forget. The only explanation for how that could be was that Aurelai had been telling the truth.

In broad daylight, there was nothing at all malicious about her. Nothing illusory or deceptive. Outside of the lab, with none of the trappings of her heritage beyond the eyes and ears, and without being able to See it, there was no sign of the power that lurked within them all. She was a woman like any other.

But if Aurelai was telling the truth, then there was another, much larger truth hanging over her, and she didn't even know it. Vimika hadn't enjoyed *any* of the truths the day had revealed so far, but if her hunch was right, then it was one that also had to be dragged kicking and screaming into the light.

In a moment, Vimika's righteous anger collapsed. Her shoulders sagged, and she no longer knew what to do with her hands without sleeves to hide them in.

"Aurelai... I think you've been here a lot longer than you think you have."

As surely as if Vimika had taken a hammer to them, Aurelai fell to her knees so hard they kicked up clods of dirt, and she sat on her heels in slack-faced dejection.

She looked up with wide, beseeching eyes. "Why?" she whispered.

"Greed. Power. Hubris. There are a lot of reasons."

"Against their will? But he said..." Aurelai choked back a sob, her hand flying to cover her mouth.

"I'm sure he said a lot of things," Vimika said tightly. "I didn't know him personally of course, but history does. And what it has to say is... well, I can imagine what he told you."

Aurelai looked up, twin wells absorbing every bit of sunlight that fell into them. "When? When did all this happen?"

"Over 200 years ago."

"How? How could I have lost track of so much time?"

"How is this all still here, including you? Everything should be dust by now, or at least taken back by the forest," Vimika said.

Aurelai tossed a hand at the very idea. "The slab has suspension spells weaved into it. Every cabinet and drawer is laced with null time; the house is draped in preservation spells. Father was prepared to *wait* for things to... improve. The methods aren't the problem."

"You just waved away two things that are still incredibly difficult, if not outright impossible anymore. That you don't see them as problems *is* a problem."

Dark eyes scanned the tree line, as though it looked somehow different than it had before. "I've always been apart from the world, but to know that I've been apart from *time* as well?"

What could Vimika possibly say to that? The idea was

ludicrous, but every fiber in her being, every drop of intuition she'd ever had, magic or no, told her that Aurelai believed what she was saying. That her reality was even stranger than she had let on, and it was only now occurring to her.

Aurelai's features shifted, and she hooked a sable curtain behind an ear that had regained more of its normal shape. Still on her knees, she held out her hands. "I beg of you, Vimika. Whatever evils my father committed, please don't judge me for them. What he did to me was the last. Help me untangle this... place. Please. Whatever happens when we escape, I will take full responsibility for. I won't ask you to be a minder or- or a chaperone for the modern world, just... please don't leave me trapped here all alone for another two centuries."

It was impossible to look down on a woman on her knees and not be moved, but equally impossible to truly comprehend the scale of what Aurelai was asking. Or set aside the fact that every choice that had been made leading to Vimika standing over her was a sword stroke that had torn Vimika's life to ribbons.

As they floated all about her, she had no idea how to go about stitching them back together, or what shape they would be when she was done.

Or how to even begin.

Where could she go?

Without her magic, she couldn't even open her front door, let alone fly the other one. Could she make it out of the forest? In all the humiliations she'd suffered, she'd never felt so exposed and vulnerable. To be stripped of her self-respect along with her clothes and laughed at was mortifying, but being stripped of a *sense*, a core part of her very identity was something else entirely. The Vimika who had been taunted that night, had her heart ripped out twice, was still Vimika. Without her magic, who was she now? *What* was she?

Aurelai may have been the one on her knees, but it was Vimika who was at her mercy.

But those black eyes didn't know that, and if they did, they didn't agree. They were open and pleading, and the least Vimika could do was grant Aurelai the dignity of not having to vocalize it any more than she already had.

Vimika looked to the house, to the flowers Aurelai had clearly been so carefully tending, finally to the clear blue sky. "If I choose to leave, you won't stop me?" she asked.

"I will not. You won't be made another prisoner to him."

"And if my magic doesn't return..." Vimika snatched one of the ribbons. All that was written on it was doubt, in the colors of fear. "You won't kick me out?"

Aurelai blinked. Already slower than Vimika's, this one shadowed already dark eyes long enough to give Vimika's spirits time to realize just how much further they had to fall.

Then they opened again. "Why would I do that?"

Vimika was standing on ground too unsettled to trust her weight to an implication. "Would you kick me out if my magic doesn't return?"

"I- no. No, of course not."

The fact that Aurelai almost sounded offended by the idea made Vimika return her earnest need for eye contact. But there was more bewilderment on Aurelai's face than offense, and Vimika let go the breath she'd been holding.

"All right."

Aurelai shot to her feet. "Truly?"

"Yes. I will probably regret it, but I need time to think, anyway. There's nothing out there for me right now but trouble. Here, at least, I have a mystery or five to solve."

"Thank you!" Aurelai exclaimed, clapping her hands together hard enough the sound reverberated around the clearing several times, making it sound like there was an audience for her good news. To that ghostly applause, she all but snapped herself in half as she swept into a bow deep enough for her hair to pool on top of her feet.

"I am forever in your debt, Vimikathritas Malakandronon. I receive your acquiescence with praise most highest, of-"

"Ah... what are you doing?"

"Thanking you properly, owner of my most egregious debt," Aurelai said without raising her head.

After everything that had happened, on the edge of both exhaustion and an identity crisis, Vimika barely caught an unfortunate noise not unlike laughter that tried to burst from her nose. She managed to slap a hand over her mouth, but a sound made it out that was something like a sneeze being half-smashed back in with a hammer.

"Have I done something wrong?" Aurelai asked the ground.

"No! No... just... I've only seen that kind of formality in plays. It's a bit... surreal," Vimika said, waggling her foot to signal that Aurelai's bow had gone on long enough.

She snapped right back up again so fast Vimika's back twinged in sympathy. "Do people not read *Manners and Protocol for Polite Magical Society* anymore?"

"I think there might be a copy moldering in the basement of the Academy library somewhere. Ahem. No. No, they don't," Vimika managed with the sliver of composure she'd regained. "Something to eat and maybe a wash would more than suffice for now."

"For now?"

"Well, if I'm going to be here awhile, it might take more than one," Vimika said.

Wizards were, by and large, a people who believed in things like good hygiene, thus keeping magic uncontaminated so it didn't do things like animate mold into seeking revenge for the invention of penicillin. Long hot baths were preceded by a good scrubbing so as to not stew in their own filth, and for that reason alone they were happy to bathe separately from humans for the rest of time.

"Whatever you'd like," Aurelai said. "My home is now yours, for as long as you want it to be."

"Thank you."

Aurelai's sense of time was obviously broken, as she stood staring for a length that careened into uncomfortable with a smile that was admittedly on the endearing side of idiotic.

Vimika cleared her throat. "So, ah... could you... show me around?"

Aurelai snapped back from wherever her thoughts had wandered off to. "Oh, of course! Where are my manners?"

"In a book. Which you may want to forget about if you're to blend in when you rejoin the world," Vimika said as she gestured for Aurelai to lead on.

6

"So this, er, is my house," Aurelai said from inside its shadow, at the foot of the stairs.

"Looks pretty good for being a couple centuries old."

Vimika thumbed the railing that hemmed in the front porch. The white paint was peeling, and she could spot the occasional spot of rust that had once been a nail, but it seemed structurally sound, at least by the noise it made when she knocked on a post.

"The entire clearing is saturated in magic. Spells criss-crossing and interweaving in patterns I could never hope to untangle. Father's illusions are bound to the trees and feed off their *mana,* while the climate protection I made feeds off the *mana* of the things growing in here. The grass and my garden, for the most part. The more I grow, the stronger it is, which gives me some incentive to keep my thumb green," Aurelai said.

"That explains the temperature. It seems like winter never ends in Durn, but *this* far south? Well, there's a reason no one lives out here."

"A reason Father chose this place, you mean."

Vimika shook her head. "Actually I didn't, but you're probably right. It does make me wonder, though. Not to make your situation feel worse, but there is *nothing* around here. I could have walked for days in this forest *without* the illusions and never found my way out again. Why show me the clearing at all? Why not just stay hidden completely?"

"A good question. To see if you'd still come?" Aurelai asked as she led Vimika along a line of white *jamalok* blossoms, the most mature festooned with vibrant indigo stamens. "It took me a long time be able to Borrow as far as Durn."

Vimika stopped to smell the *jamalok*. They were known for their uniquely divergent smell, which to humans smelled like death, but heavenly to wizards. Including the green stems, their coloration was a combination of all three magic types, making them a particular favorite going well back into antiquity. Being able to touch and smell the confirmation of such continuity would have been reassuring if she hadn't known who they originally belonged to.

"You certainly chose the right bait. I couldn't have lost Oliver if I tried, no matter where he led me."

"Is 'bait' really a fair word?" Aurelai asked.

"I mean… lure? Is that better?"

"He was just 'hope' to me. Nothing more. You must believe me."

Vimika cradled one of the flowers between two fingers, the petals soft as silk but slightly waxy. "I'm sorry. It's still hard to believe all of this is actually happening. Certainly not what I was expecting when I set out this morning."

"Then I will do my best to be convincing." Aurelai led them out of the shadow of the house and back into the sun.

Even though Vimika could see trees sheathed in snow all around, the breeze that was waiting for them was warm. Being able to feel it on top of her head was strange at first, since she had been twelve the last time she was outside without a hat on. She had to fight against the urge to throw her hands over her head just to have something covering it, but not a single watchman burst from the trees to arrest her. Without the hat, the world was much brighter (and breezier), even as the sun was beginning the descent into late afternoon. The crisp, brilliant light of a cloudless winter's(?) day was more than a match for the clinging residue of their argument, burning it off of them like cobwebs before an open flame as they walked together.

Aurelai did so with her head higher and her back straighter than Vimika had yet seen, seeming to have settled comfortably into their detente already. She was poised and articulate as she explained the grooming of *jamalok* flowers, but Vimika, simple creature that she so often found herself sharing a body with, was more interested in the one doing the talking than the subject.

In daylight, Aurelai's hair was liquid ink, her skin preternaturally pale, almost glowing. The darkness of her eyes was leavened somewhat, the vertical slits common to all wizards more visible against irises that were now more like thick smoke than solid stone, alive as they hadn't been until now. The deep wine red of her dress was less like blood, the brocade more silver than ice. It was old-fashioned but not unbecoming, even if it was strange to see a wizard in anything but proper robes and hat.

Aurelai glanced back to see Vimika taking in her attire. "I must look odd to you. Like something out of a history book."

"You look very nice," Vimika replied, earning a ghost of a smile.

"Thank you. Do you always deflect with flattery?"

"No," Vimika answered honestly.

Color rose to Aurelai's cheeks, but her smile remained. "Shall we carry on?"

What are you doing? Vimika thought. *The last thing this woman needs is someone trying to flirt with her on accident.*

But that was when she did her best work, unfortunately. If

they'd met at a party, Vimika would have already fallen flat on her face by tripping over her own tongue. In these circumstances however, there was nothing Vimika wanted less than another complication in a life that seemed to be made up of nothing but.

"Are you coming?" Aurelai said from several yards away.

"What? Oh, yes. Just had to... let my eyes adjust. It's very bright without the hat." Vimika squished her face into an exaggerated squint before following. The moment Aurelai turned around, Vimika's face curdled in shame.

Idiot. She clearly likes living things, why don't you show a modicum of interest in your host's obvious talents? Maybe show that you're not going to be a complete clod of a houseguest?

Looking straight down, her charm and creativity slid to the front of her mind, smashing together in a spectacular collision that left no survivors. "So, this grass is nice."

Aurelai knelt down, her dress piling about her ankles. With precise, delicate movements, she plucked a single grass blade and beckoned for Vimika to join her.

"It is," she said, and brought it closer to Vimika's face, waving it in little circles. "What do you smell?"

"Grass."

Nodding, Aurelai made faster circles, brushing Vimika's nose. There was little warning for either of them when Vimika's head snapped forward in a sudden sneeze.

"Oh! I'm sorry!" she said to the Aurelai wavering and swimming in her tear-filled eyes. When she managed to blink them away, the black-haired wizard's smile had gotten bigger.

"What do you feel?"

"That tickled!"

"Good," Aurelai said.

Sniffling and rubbing her nose, Vimika looked down at the lawn she was crouched on like it could swallow her up at any moment. "Why?"

The grass blade spun between Aurelai's fingers as she thought. "I didn't know if this is what it was supposed to smell like. And I'm not ticklish. I've never seen a reaction to it before."

"Are you sure? You can't tickle yourself, you know."

Aurelai looked up suddenly, eyes narrowed. "You can't?"

"Nope," Vimika said.

"So perhaps I'm *not* broken," Aurelai said with a distant expression Vimika was quickly learning to interpret as the one that meant she was talking to herself.

Dropping the grass blade, Aurelai didn't so much stand as unfold, straightening her back before her legs in an astonishing display of balance and no little strength. She hadn't even needed her arms! How was that possible? Her figure belied none of what it would take to move that way. She was just as willowy and waif-like as every other female wizard Vimika knew.

She must be hiding legs like a deer under there to be able to stand like that, Vimika thought.

But why? Maybe it was living in isolation for so long that made her movements so alien. Without anyone to remind her how people actually moved, she'd developed her own tics and habits. More arresting than graceful, everything she did was in a sequence. In addition to being beautiful, she was fascinating to watch, and for the second time, Vimika got caught doing just that.

"You're really going to have to learn to keep up," Aurelai said. She was already at the edge of the house. "Are you all right?" she asked when Vimika joined her.

Swallowing her sheepishness, Vimika answered honestly. "I don't think so. Between the magic shock, the illusions and not having eaten since I woke up, I feel like I've been here for ten years already. Oh. I'm sorry, I didn't mean-"

"It's all right. You do look a bit… drawn. I can't do much

about the first two ailments, but perhaps something to eat before we continue?"

~

"This is amazing!" Vimika said through a mouthful of the juiciest, sweetest tomato she had ever tasted. It was barely even a tomato, quite thoroughly settling the question of fruit versus vegetable in favor of the former. "How did you do it?"

"Just as Father taught me. Is it really so good?" Aurelai asked.

"Yes! Tomatoes are always bitter or bland, like they come off the vine boiled already. Do you really not mind if I have another?" Vimika managed to say before her hand reached out of its own accord.

"As many as you want. There's a lot more." Aurelai indicated the back of the house, but kept looking across the dining table at Vimika with a look of curious satisfaction. "I had no idea."

Her mouth full, Vimika nodded vigorously, her hair falling in front of one eye. Unused to it being free, she tried jerking it away with head movements, then shoving it with her wrist, but it was obstinate in trying to sample tomato juice for itself.

She stopped mid-chew like a startled squirrel when Aurelai reached across and brushed the errant strand away, securing it behind Vimika's ear.

"There," Aurelai said, setting her chin in her hand and considering the woman sitting across from her. "I suppose the hat usually keeps it tame."

Vimika nodded. She didn't care one whit that Aurelai's fingers were cold or that she curled them closed one at a time, it only added to the bewitching otherness that was increasingly hard to look away from.

"So if you get me out of here, I'll be expected to wear one, too? And the robes? Pity."

It was, Vimika agreed. That long, beautiful hair trapped under a wizard hat? *That* was the real crime. She didn't say any of that, of course.

Aurelai pointed to the rack near the front door.

Alone, discolored with char and mud, and hanging from a peg, Vimika's hat looked a lot sadder when seen from a distance. As much as she resented having to wear it, it was still hers, and she felt a little pang at seeing it in so sorry a state.

"May I ask you something about your hat?" Aurelai asked.

"There's not much to tell."

"It looks like someone shot it. Is it supposed to be flopped over like that?"

Vimika turned back to her tomato. "A working wizard's is, yes. They don't keep their shape long, and we can't be bothered to put them back."

Aurelai drummed her fingers on the table as she considered. "Hmm. Wizard… such a strange word. Where are you from, Vimika? That's a traditional Atvalian name. Or, *acceptably* traditional, I suppose."

"Maris."

"So it's not regional? What happened to mage? Why such a bizarre word?"

"The same reason we have to wear the hat and robes. Since the Purges, you don't say 'mage' anymore unless you want to start a fight."

Unless you had money and nothing to fear, then you could say a lot worse, Vimika thought.

"Ah. That would explain your reaction, then. For what it's worth, I'm sorry," Aurelai said.

"It's all right, you didn't know."

"Not just for the slander. If my father was one of the reasons for all of your… our troubles… I imagine the

Malakandronons weren't spared."

"Mm. There was a reason I was so upset with you about Oliver." Vimika sucked the last of the meat off the stem of her tomato. "But, in truth, we came out better than most. The Purges were a long time ago though, they're just as much names in history books as anyone else who died in them."

She couldn't be truly upset about the reminder, as no wizard family was innocent of the practice. It had been too lucrative, too prevalent. Though the Purges that had decimated the wizard race had taken place nearly two centuries before Vimika was born, she had always been thankful that the Malakandronon mechamages were never very good at it. Magically, they had never been a particularly strong bloodline, and that was what had saved them. They had survived by being good enough at mundane magic to be useful but crap enough at dangerous magic to not pose a threat. They'd paid the reparations, watched their own lose their heads over the practice, then kept their (still attached) heads down and had lots of children.

However, the very idea of it all happening again made little worms of anxiety wriggle under her skin, burrowing into her brain so they could shit out nightmares when she went to sleep. It was in the back of every wizard's mind, very often making their way to the front, which is why they endured the discrimination without much resistance. Even if they wanted to do something, the Purges had done just what the name implied, wiping out the most powerful of them all at once. That power never cropping up again had kept the peace, and Vimika would rather not give any further thought to the idea that that might no longer be true.

"You think me a monster for loosing Oliver that way," Aurelai said to her fingers.

Vimika hid her moment of consideration with a chew of tomato that was already liquid. "You didn't know. There's nothing wrong with ignorance as long as you try to fill it in with knowledge. It's a tender subject, one that we'd thought behind us. To know for a fact that beings like Oliver are still with us is troubling, to say the least. It feels like unfinished business. If any of this gets out..." Vimika took Aurelai's measure, but she had to know more to truly understand. "I worry about my family."

"That wasn't my intention," Aurelai said in a voice so small she would have needed a magnifying glass to find it again.

Vimika wiped her chin clean of tomato juice. "I know. I believe you."

Aurelai brightened a little. "Thank you. Tell me about them."

"My family?"

"I don't... have one. You said Malakandronons had lots of children?"

Vimika nodded. "I'm the fourth of five. Two older brothers, sandwiched between two sisters. I have... twelve? nieces and nephews last time I counted."

"That must have been wonderful!" Aurelai said with a sudden glitter in her dark eyes.

"It... was. Mostly. It was also crowded, and we fought a lot. My younger sister Langorifa was a biter, while Kalinostra, as the oldest girl, always acted the princess, including sicking her toadies on me at school. But we grew out of it. Mostly I felt invisible."

Aurelai's brow pinched in incomprehension.

"I'm the middle one, easiest to get lost in the shuffle. I've always... made my own way, I suppose."

"You still talk to them, don't you?" Aurelai asked in rising horror.

"I send letters when I remember to. They accept my choice to leave, but still don't really understand it," Vimika said.

Being a Malakandronon, she had never been of any special

power or station, with no connections, no access. At least, not any more. She wasn't particularly talented or pretty by wizard standards (her ears were too short, for one). Even among her clan, the fact she would never have children was a mark against her, even if it was never said aloud. No one cared that she fancied women; her aunt had married her wife before Vimika was born... but they were also filthy rich.

Historically, the one thing Malakandronons were good at was making more Malakandronons, which meant she'd had two options when she'd come of age: get busy making babies or, failing that, money.

The latter could have been simple, since everyone of power needed at least one sneaky wizard behind them, if for no other reason than everyone else of their ilk already did. But all those powerful women, the ones with gold in their vaults and silver on their tongues, the silk sheets...

Vimika snapped free from the trap of her memories to find Aurelai looking at her intently, thoughts forming behind her eyes that looked dangerously close to becoming questions.

"I think I've had enough of a rest," Vimika said with a brightness she hoped Aurelai wouldn't pick up on the artifice of. "Could you show me where these wonderful tomatoes came from?"

Clear relief washed over Aurelai and she quickly stood, gathering up Vimika's plate before she had a chance to even ask what to do with it. "I would be happy to."

The moment Vimika came around the back corner of the house however, there wasn't a garden waiting for her.

"It's a bloody farm!" she exclaimed.

Row after row of fruits and vegetables stretched all the way to the tree line, from shiny red gooseberries to fat, bright green cask melons the size of Vimika's head. Potato plants crawled along the ground while stalks of corn soared overhead, taller than any she had ever seen.

She gawked at it, unable to believe that one person could maintain such a thing by themselves, let alone so meticulously. It was lush and verdant, not a sign of insects or rot. Then several thoughts got into a big fight over who could leap out of her mouth first.

"Who eats this winter? Ah! That is… who is this for? You can't possibly eat all of this by yourself."

"I don't. It's mostly to feed the climate spells. And a bit of a hobby, I suppose."

"You throw it out!?" Vimika blurted in horror.

"What? No. I give it to the animals. The forest can be unpleasant, but the mountains worse, and the hunters more so. I try to make this place a refuge, if only so I can be around living things. Makes it easier to Borrow them, as well."

Though Vimika was closing in on finally accepting that this wasn't an illusion, she was still entertaining the idea it might be a dream. She knelt down and found one of the spines on a gooseberry bush. Running her thumb over the point, it caught on the fine ridges of her thumbprint and caused pain when she pressed on it, just the way it should.

When she popped a berry in her mouth, her face contorted the way it should, too, pinching into a singularity of tartness.

"Did I do it wrong?" Aurelai asked.

Her face still scrunched up shut, Vimika turned to where she was most confident Aurelai would be. "No, they're actually pretty good," she managed.

"Then why is your face imploding?"

"They usually make me cry, too."

"I see. So this is a… normal reaction?"

Vimika pried one eye open. "It's not for you?"

"I don't usually eat them." Aurelai picked a handful and whipped them towards the trees. Before they even got halfway, a squadron of meteor birds burst from the boughs and snatched them out of the air before vanishing back into the canopy in a cacophony of rustling branches and pleased squawking.

"How did they know you were going to do that?"

"Because I spoil them. They're how I knew about you. Excellent eyesight, fast, common enough no one really notices them, they make very good psychic telescopes."

Vimika's face asked the question for her.

"I don't know what to call them properly. I don't really inhabit their minds as in a full Borrowing, just... look through their eyes. Suggest they go left rather than right. Others animals have better hearing, or can get into smaller places, depending on what I want that day, but flying is true freedom. They see so much. Go anywhere they wish."

"Like... spies," Vimika said with more suspicion than she'd really intended as several incidents that she'd thought isolated suddenly took on a new, more coherent shape.

Like cats that resist Beckoning to go looking in windows or curl up on the lap of the only wizard in the tavern when there were thirty other people to choose from. Come to think of it, the horses had seemed a bit keen as of late, too.

Aurelai shot her a measuring look that saw none of that. "Yes. I've read enough books to know how that word sounds. But do you have any idea what true loneliness is? That's not even strong enough a word. Isolation? Father hadn't been lying when he said there was nothing but wasteland out there, had he? You said yourself there's nothing within miles. Now imagine it before Durn existed, when there was *nothing* within Borrowing range of here. I was completely alone, with no one to talk to, no faces to see, no... interaction. When the first buildings were erected, when they started cutting roads... I cried, Vimika. Ugly sobs of overwhelming relief that I was going to be able to see *people.* Talking, working, going to the shops; just watching people walk from here to there was joyous. And when I learned that a ma-... *wizard* I thought could be of help had finally moved in, I cried again. You were more than a pretty face, you were *hope...*" Aurelai shook her head, hair flowing over her shoulders and into her eyes. "Yes, Vimika, I watched. You. The house wizards. Everyone! The same way someone stranded on an island watches the ships go past. The way someone dying of thirst keeps their eyes locked on an oasis, makes it their goal, helps them power through the last few miles before they can drink. If that offends you, I'm sorry. But I had to know who I thought I could trust before I could risk trying to bring anyone here."

Pain and the need to be believed shook Aurelai's voice, her odd body language now completely familiar in how guarded she'd suddenly become. Closed and awaiting judgment by a stranger. One slow blink. Another.

"I believe you," Vimika decided.

The black curtain parted as it was secured behind a long, pale ear. "You do?"

Vimika looked about the clearing, to the aged house, the fading paint, the moss, the weathering from untold years, and then to Aurelai.

All together, it laid obvious the inner fortitude Vimika had suspected lay at Aurelai's core.

Two centuries, all alone. Even if she'd spent a good part of it in suspension, she must be *unfathomably* strong to have lived her life. That she could speak at all was a miracle of perseverance, let alone so well. She hadn't had to admit anything, sparing herself this moment easily, but she had shared it anyway. Maybe she'd needed to get it off her chest, or maybe it was just more of the honesty that seemed to be her nature, but it made Vimika want to know more. To understand this woman and what she'd been through, to help her recover.

More than a savior, Aurelai needed a friend.

"I can't imagine what you've experienced, and I don't blame you for any opportunity you may have taken to feel even the least bit normal again. I'm surprised, but... I understand. In your shoes, I can't say that I would have done any differently."

"You're very understanding."

"Good trait in a wizard," Vimika said.

"Would I seem ungrateful if I asked for a little more?"

"Not at all."

Aurelai held out her hand. "Please."

To feel that dull, alien connection again was as tempting as it was repellent. Yes, it was better than nothing, but not far enough away to be completely pleasant. It was a long, measuring look before Vimika took the proffered hand.

Aurelai's skin was cold, her grip slightly stiff, but Vimika paid their physical touch little attention. She couldn't actively seek after the missing magic without pain, forcing her to stand passively and be grateful for what little she got.

She'd been taught magic shock could be stressful and disorienting, but no one had ever mentioned this secondary tortuous aspect of it. To look down and see her hand in that of another wizard's and not *feel* it properly? It really was like she'd lost one of her senses, or at least had it numbed to the point of uselessness, as though she'd slept on her hand wrong.

There was *something* there, Vimika had to tell herself, but it was that same tiny trickle that was almost worse than if there'd been nothing at all. An active reminder of what was missing.

But for all the torment of what *wasn't* there, Aurelai would be quite starved for what little there was, and Vimika had to take the whip to her demons to keep herself from denying it.

It was said the most strongly compatible could *taste* the connection, bringing the least-used sense in magic level with all the others, but all Vimika could taste at the moment was gooseberry juice. The slightly metallic tang creeping along the very back of her tongue now must have been from the fact everything she'd put in her mouth since arriving had been grown in a climate that was magically-induced.

Cold as Aurelai's skin was, it was soft as she turned over Vimika's hands, felt them, dragged her thumbs over the backs and down her palms. For as strong a grip as Aurelai had had earlier, now she was gentle to the point of reverent. Could she feel Vimika's magic? Had she spoiled Aurelai forever by allowing this to go on for so long? But Vimika simply couldn't bring herself to let go. In her state, she had to take 'barely anything' over 'sucking vacuum' as long as she was able.

Aurelai's eyes, when they looked up to meet Vimika's, shone, their dark depths filled with things unspoken but clearly felt.

"I've never held a woman's hand before. I wanted to make sure I wasn't dreaming. If I were, I don't think my mind would know how to make it feel, to be honest. Warmer than I'd thought." Her tongue darted over her lips ever so briefly. "I was not expecting to feel your magic, as well. It is... pleasant. Thank you."

Vimika's face grew warmer than her hands, and a little shiver tickled the back of her neck before skittering down her spine and into her arm.

Aurelai looked up to the sun slipping behind the trees. "I suppose it is getting chilly. You could do with a bath, I think. Luckily, there's plenty of hot water. I will go and draw it for you."

A quirk tugged at the corner of Vimika's mouth. "I could, yes. Thank you."

"Not at all. I've been waiting a long time for you." Aurelai's eyes flew open and she dropped Vimika's hand like she'd been caught stealing it. "*Like* you! Someone *like* you. Someone. Like. You. Yes. There, got it."

Whatever urgency there may have been when the day started dissipated in one of Aurelai's languid blinks. Truthfully, Vimika was in little shape to do anything but pass out, but even though she was all but trapped in a strange place with a stranger wizard, she found herself willing to be led inside the house as dark closed in. Granted, she didn't have much choice, but it was *a* choice, and one she made without a glance behind her.

~

One of the problems with living close to the mountains is that the weather can change quickly, so much so that it sometimes feels like it's out of spite. Outside, the wind was howling like a scolded wolf, inside it banged around like a drunken poltergeist, shaking things at random and making sure to point out where all the drafts were coming from in a haughty 'OOOoooOOOooo' sort of way.

Aurelai had said the climate spells would make sure it didn't get cold enough to snow, but that they couldn't do much to blunt wind as bloody-minded as the one set upon them now. Regardless of how fast or cold the air might be, it was certainly dry. Vimika had already been zapped by the same doorknob twice, leaving her to keep her hands hidden inside her freshly-laundered robe as she sat perched atop a pile of threadbare cushions while Aurelai built up the fire. It was slow going, however, as the chimney was funneling the wind into a solid column that kept snuffing out the nascent flames. Were she able, Vimika would have put up a weather shield and a warming spell, but trying in her state would risk blowing the house (or more likely, her head) apart or suffocating them.

Somehow, telling Aurelai didn't make her feel any better.

"I guess you have a lot more to teach me," Aurelai said as she sat back on her heels in front of the hearth, watching her third attempt gutter and spit against the frigid onslaught. "That sounds terribly useful."

"It is. Or... will be. I don't know how you made it so long without knowing how. Don't these kinds of storms happen a lot?" Vimika said, drawing her legs inside her robe as well. She'd even put her hat back on. The residual heat from her bath was leaking out far too fast for how good it had felt, making her extra resentful of the weather. At least Aurelai's magelight kept her from doing so in the dark. That would only encourage the poltergeists.

"They do, yes. I usually just sleep through them. I never wanted to risk burning the house down by using an open flame."

"Weren't you cold?"

"Sorry, not sleep sleep. Deep sleep. On the slab. Especially before I mastered the climate spells, I would just... ignore winter."

Vimika's teeth started chattering. "L-like a- a bear?"

"That's a good way of looking at it. Yes. Like a a bear," Aurelai said, swiping at the hearth with a little roar.

The wind wasn't intimidated, and the flame vanished into a curl of smoke, which itself vanished into the house, making Vimika cough.

"H-have you ev-ver B-Borrowed a b-bear?"

"Once or twice. They smell awful though, and I much prefer the appearance of deer from the outside. It's fun during spawning season, though! The fish jump straight into their mouths." Aurelai clacked her teeth together into an ursine grin, but it quickly faded when she turned completely away from the cold, barely-charred pile of kindling and wood. "You look like you're freezing!"

"I am," Vimika said miserably.

With her fascinating unfolding motion, Aurelai got to her feet and made towards the laboratory. "Just a moment."

When she returned, it was with an armload of blankets.

"Th-thank you," Vimika said, even as she looked down at the first one Aurelai draped over her dubiously. "Lab blankets?" She sniffed, but they smelled as clean as the one she'd used earlier and seemed free of any sign of experimentation or mites.

"They were in null time cabinets. How else do you think they've lasted for so long? However 'so long' is?"

"Maybe you're good with a sewing needle," Vimika said, pleased with the level of cooperation she got from her teeth.

Aurelai smiled and hiked up part of her dress, the former widening when she saw what Vimika's eyes did in response to the latter.

"I *am* good with a sewing needle," Aurelai said, and stretched a section of fabric out flat, revealing a short line of tight, barely-visible stitching. "I'm not quite used to so much... volume. I caught it on a nail not long after putting it on."

All alone in a house in the middle of the woods, she was lucky that was all she caught, Vimika thought. She stopped thinking altogether when Aurelai joined her under the blankets, stiffening more than she would have if she'd been allowed to freeze.

"If I can't get the fire lit, I can do this much," Aurelai said.

Once the shock wore off, however, it was something else that kept Vimika shut up tight. "You're freezing yourself! Why didn't you say anything?"

Aurelai huddled closer, pulling the blankets up to their chins. "I guess I'm used to it. I never really thought about how I feel to someone else. I'm sorry."

"Don't apologize! We'll help each other, then."

As they settled their weight against one another, it was

immediately apparent Aurelai was heavier than she looked. Vimika's thoughts went to strong, powerful legs again, but as they sank deeper into the cushions, their hips pressed together and she quickly needed to think of something else.

"Thank you," she said when she couldn't.

"You're welcome."

As their body temperatures rose, Vimika's shivering subsided, only then letting her notice how preternaturally still Aurelai was. It wasn't just from afar, it was like she wasn't even breathing. Maybe it was the calm she would have had to teach herself to keep from going crazy, Vimika thought. Or the kind of self-discipline they only taught you in monasteries way up in the mountains where they don't allow booze or sex.

But I can't imagine either have been in any great supply for poor Aurelai. Maybe those monks are on to something.

Vimika shuddered. "Have you ever Borrowed a lizard? Or a turtle?"

"I've only ever seen them in books. This is poor climate for them, isn't it?"

"True, but you're so... calm. Your poise and balance, I guess it makes me think of the way they sun themselves on rocks or in trees. They don't move at all, just... bask," Vimika said with the best imitation she could manage using only her face.

"Not exactly basking weather," Aurelai said as another gust shook the house. "Are there lizards in Maris?"

Vimika nodded. "All over. You'll see little black ones even in the city. They like the cobblestones, and it's harder for the birds to get at them with people around. The further from the city you get, though, the bigger they are."

"Like dragons?" Aurelai asked, her question rising with all the hopefulness buoying it.

"Not on this continent. Not anymore. Don't your books say that?"

"They're very old..."

"So are dragons," Vimika said. "Not much has changed then, I'm afraid. If there are any left, they keep to themselves. Can't blame them."

"So you've never seen one?" Aurelai asked, unable (or unwilling) to hide how disappointed the idea made her.

"No. I'd like to, though. Would you?"

"Yes. There is a lot I'd like to see. What about you? What would you like to see?"

Vimika put aside the selfish answer of 'nothing' for the moment, in favor of the honest one she'd been harboring since she was little. "The ocean. All that water, a completely flat horizon. I've read that waves sound like roaring when they crash into the shore, which would make it hard to sleep, I imagine. But a dragon would be something, though."

"What?"

"What?"

The diffuse magelight on Aurelai's hair shifted. "A dragon is a dragon. Why would it be 'something?'"

"Oh... uh... 'that would be something' means it would be a sight to see. Special. Impressive. That kind of thing. I didn't know the expression was so new."

Aurelai was quiet as she stared into the fire that wasn't there. "It seems I have quite a bit of catching up to do."

"Would you like a guide?" Vimika asked.

She hadn't even known the words were in her mouth until they'd already gotten out. It was an innocent enough question normally, there were whole professions around it. But if everyone who asked got the answer Vimika did, they wouldn't be professions, they'd be religions.

Without a word, Aurelai settled her head on Vimika's shoulder.

It should have been surprising, it should have sent Vimika's blood racing, made her forget her own name, or jerk away and storm off in anger at such presumptuousness, or more likely, crying.

Instead she seized up as still as Aurelai. But the longer it went on, the more Vimika relaxed. Magic didn't transmit through clothing very well, leaving just the warmth and weight of another's head on her shoulder to remind her, in this sudden and unexpected connection to a woman she'd known less than a day, just how much else Vimika been missing in her self-imposed exile.

Aurelai had been alone her entire life, the only other living person she'd ever known her own monstrous father. Of course she would seek the reassurance of physical connection as well. Nestled together in the dark, speaking of future plans, it was almost... normal.

"I can't ask that of you," Aurelai said after some thought, "I've asked too much of you already."

"What if I volunteered?" Vimika heard herself say. She knew what Not-Vimika would respond with, but she was apparently confined to the woods, allowing Vimika this reminder of how things were supposed to be, even if it was under circumstances she could have never predicted. After the last few days, the last few *years*, Vimika could sit still for a moment or two, and perhaps make someone else happy.

The wind battered at the house, the wind went 'OOOoooOOOooo,' the wind was nothing compared to the sudden pounding of Vimika's heart or the warm stillness on her shoulder.

A stillness broken by the movement of lips, the fury of the storm silenced by whispers.

Aurelai stirred, her hair brushing against Vimika's neck. "I would like that very much."

7

When Vimika awoke, it was groggily, cold and stiff.

And alone.

The fire was a sad little spark of a thing, just there to show Vimika what a good little trooper it had been since the wind died down, winking out the moment she looked at it. Actually, a wink would have been reassuring just then, because now there was nothing to distract from the fact she was in an unfamiliar old house surrounded by magical traps and her only guide to how or why had disappeared sometime in the night. The wool stuffed between Vimiks's ears was enough to tell her her magic was still just as absent as Aurelai.

When had they fallen asleep, though? Not that Vimika could ever remember falling asleep, she just couldn't quite piece together the awakeness that had led up to it. But as the haze wore off, she found that though she was sprawled out across the cushions, she had been tucked into the blankets, and yet another had been rolled up to serve as a makeshift pillow.

Aurelai.

Where had she gone?

Heaving herself vertical, Vimika folded the blankets as

neatly as she could (though they were rectangles, Vimika wasn't one for doing much with her bedding other than keeping it off the floor, and it took several attempts to get the corners to line up), placing them in a pile atop the cushions.

She gave a quick look into the laboratory, but the stasis slab was empty.

Stepping outside, it was just as warm as the day before. Vimika had expected carnage after the storm, but everything looked largely the same. There were no broken branches, no snow drifts built up against the side of the house (or snow at all), no evidence whatsoever of the violence that had tried to bash its way into the house the night before.

When Vimika came around the corner to the garden, she stopped so quickly she had to throw a hand against the wall to keep from pitching onto her face.

There, in the center of untouched growing things in the heart of winter, was Aurelai.

Still in her red dress, she stood with one hand lifted to the sky, a pair of tiny yellow birds perched on it, one on her pinky and the other on her thumb, as they pecked at whatever treats Aurelai had in her palm. Were her dress white, she would have looked like a statue against the wan light of morning as she stood preternaturally still, presumably for the benefit of the birds. But so much about Aurelai was unique and so invitingly different, it could be for a reason Vimika didn't have the imagination to come up with.

Sheets of sable hair broke over a milky-white shoulder that flowed into an arm held high with effortless poise, eyes the brightest, most polished obsidian. The contrasts of her coloring plucked at strings within Vimika that she had only ever heard the music of in dreams and fantasy.

And feeding birds from her hand at the break of dawn? It was too perfect. This was another damned illusion. Or a dream, but Vimika didn't have ones this nice anymore.

"Good morning, Vimika," Aurelai said.

The only one surprised was Vimika. If anything, the birds pecked faster.

"Good morning."

"I'm sorry for leaving you alone. You needed to sleep and the birds needed to eat." All that moved were Aureali's lips, and even then only just.

But it was enough to break Vimika out of her trance, and she stepped into the garden proper. "What are you feeding them?"

The birds eyeballed the newcomer warily, but seemed content to take their cue from their perch.

"Seeds and dried berries. These two have quite the sweet tooth. Or... beak. Sweet beak." Aurelai smiled. "I think I like that."

"Are they Familiars?" Vimika asked.

"They could be, potentially. Building trust is the first step."

Aurelai's balance was astonishing, and Vimika found herself looking at Aurelai as much as she did the birds. More so. Much more so. What color were the birds again?

"There, you greedy things, I think you've had enough," Aurelai said with a little pout.

The birds disagreed, continuing to feast.

"All right, go on." Aurelai curled her fingers inward, giving the birds fair warning that it was fly off or be crushed. With a few last stabs, they chose the former and burst from their perches in a tornado of flapping wings and feather dust, sparkling like snow in the sun before being swallowed by the long shadows.

The tableau broken, Aurelai moved, turning to face her guest, eyes thoughtful, blinks slow. "Vimika, about last night... I was too forward. I apologize. I hope you'll forgive me."

So startled was Vimika that it took her a moment to

respond. "What do you mean? The weather is the only one who should be apologizing."

"Putting my head on your shoulder, taking your hand... I was too... familiar, if you'll pardon the term. You were very tired, and not at your sharpest. If you feel I've taken advantage of you in some way, I-"

"Aurelai, no." *It's that stupid book!* Vimika thought. *Of course she would think something so innocent was the height of impropriety.*

Somehow, this time, such outdated notions didn't seem all that funny. "Please... don't. You've nothing to apologize for."

"That's very kind." Aurelai said, and brushed the last remaining bird seed from her hand in swift, jerky movements. "I feel like I know you better than I actually do. I've seen you through Borrowed eyes for months, watching, making sure that you were the one I could trust. And I did. Do. But you didn't even know I existed until yesterday. I was presumptuous in how you would respond."

"Aurelai... you presumed correctly. We're wizards. Contact between us is important. I don't doubt it was instinctive. I'm not offended. At all," Vimika added.

"You aren't?"

This conversation couldn't be happening. Illusion or dream, it was at least lucid, and waking up once was enough for today. "No. I wouldn't change anything about last night."

"Neither would I. Well, a little less cold, perhaps," Aurelai said.

Then who would keep me warm? would have been the suave thing to say, but Vimika's tongue was busy trying to swallow itself.

Amidst an impossible spring, they stood not an arm's length from one another, neither sure about what to do next. Then the very last remnants of the storm suddenly gusted along the wall of the house, blowing loose strands of Vimika's hair in every direction at once, exploding around her head to wrap her indecision in threads of dark brown.

Through the fog of her own hair, she saw Aurelai smiling.

"Would you like me to brush that out for you? I don't think it's used to freedom yet. You can eat as I do it. Take whatever you like, but please finish whatever you take."

Vimika's stomach gave the thunder a run for its money as the loudest, grumbliest sound of the last twelve hours.

~

At a small garden table on a spring day in winter, the sun was shining and even the trees were cooperating, whispering with only the wind. It was warm enough Vimika had forgone the robe and sat with the sleeves of her tunic rolled up.

With melon juice on her chin and Aurelai's fingers in her hair, she was coming dangerously close to being happy. Well, perhaps not *happy*, her magic was still scrambled, but something that at least hailed from the same neighborhood. And with each gentle tug, each bar of the nothing Aurelai was humming, the closer she got.

Oliver was a tight coil of sparkly fur curled up on the ground beside them. Ears the size of Vimika's hand stood up from what was otherwise one contiguous ball of fuzz, only twitching when he seemed to notice he was being addressed. He had put away his own share of melon with impressive eagerness for a being animated purely by magic without need to actually eat, but thinking about that any deeper would make Vimika's own portion quickly unappetizing.

She was quite enjoying appetizing.

"You have such beautiful hair," Vimika said between bites, "how do you manage to keep it like that all by yourself? I guess you spend every evening brushing it out."

"I never do anything to it," Aurelai said, taking up another fistful of Vimika's and running a brush through it.

"How is that possible?"

Aurelai shrugged as she began work on the set of snarls she found. "Doesn't yours take care of itself?"

"Does it look like it does?"

She had been stupid not to put it up before bed the night before, but in her defense she had been both exhausted and distracted. With how the morning was shaping up thus far however, she was no longer sure that was such a bad thing.

"Well, no, but... you flew here, right? With the wind and all..."

"No, I usually do a better job of keeping it tame, if you can believe it. I have a whole drawer full of ties, and if there's one thing three sisters with long hair learn to do, it's braid. But you, all by yourself? I guess there's something to strong mage blood after all. I wouldn't have guessed perfect hair among the benefits, though."

"Father was bald."

"I stand corrected. And a little jealous," Vimika said. "You are quite possibly older than my grandmother, but look my age. You can talk to animals and you can have hair down to your thighs that takes care of itself. Is that right?"

"I don't... talk to them. Well, I do, but not *to* them, more *at* them really, since they're not terribly good at carrying a conversation. I more... suggest where I'd like them to go, what to do. I only speak out loud to hear myself talk and confirm I still can..." Aurelai's hands dropped into her lap. "You must think me very peculiar."

Vimika shot a look of commiseration over her shoulder. "Does that have to be a bad thing? I would say you're more normal than some wizards I've met, especially given what's happened to you. I can't imagine. How did you not go insane?"

Aurelai spun the lacquered wood brush, casting little glints of sunlight into her eyes. "By working very hard at staying sane. Borrowing requires focus and discipline; if I wanted to see outside, I had no choice but to learn both. Though there were many times where I was tempted to simply lose myself in the animals. To let them carry my mind away from this place forever. In this body, it's trapped here, but in the birds, I could go anywhere. I think I thought I was a bird once."

"What made you come back?"

"Inhabiting a bird isn't true escape. A bird's mind is too simple and too small to contain ours. Only a withered, diminished piece of me would be free. What good would that do? This mind, this body are too... precious to simply throw away in despondency."

"On that we agree," Vimika said.

Another handful of Vimika's hair was lifted up and Aurelai resumed her brushing. "Thank you for understanding."

Several snarls and two knots fell to Aurelai's labor in silence. For having so little experience, she was proving adept at it without causing pain or giving up and reaching for a pair of scissors. She was patient and methodical, traits that had more than likely also served her well. Vimika was happy to let her exercise them if it meant undoing the mess she'd made of herself.

When the worst had been taken care of, Aurelai settled into a more rhythmic stroking that, had it not freed up her concentration, Vimika would have been content to sit for until the sun went down.

Unfortunately, it had.

"When you were in the Forest... what did you see?" Aurelai asked without preamble or warning of any kind.

Vimika's jaw stopped moving, and she wiped her chin with the back of her hand. "What makes you ask?"

"I've tried to not think about Father very much, but if we are to begin undoing his work, I no longer have much choice.

He let you through, and I can't figure out why. You weren't sure you had even made it through the illusions when I met you. You were covered in snow and dirt, which was real, but... did you overpower the illusions, or did they collapse? Did you see any hint of Father? Did you know it was magic right away? Didn't you feel it before you went in?"

The questions sped up the more they accumulated, piling on top of one another until Vimika felt crushed under the weight of the reminder of why she was here in the first place.

She had been so enjoying her morning, too.

"I suppose I would have to talk about it eventually."

Aurelai's hands slowed, but didn't stop. "Was it so awful?"

The melon settled into its own greenish reflection, wobbling in a puddle of juice before stilling. "I saw... myself."

"Yourself?"

Vimika nodded. "I talked to me, but it wasn't me. She was... mean. Showed me things. Used my own memories against me. My fears. Made me remember things I ran all the way to Durn to forget. Things that make me glad I live under a tavern so I can try to every night."

Following a tidal wave of questions came a tidal wave of answers. That the two were only slightly connected revealed that there was a lot more that needed saying still. It was inevitable, but even a few minutes of escape made it that much harder to get back to work. Vimika's hands were trembling with just how hard.

"I had no idea they were strong enough to access memory," Aurelai said. "They only confused me, turned me in circles. That's a sign that there's more out there than I'd known, or feared. If the illusions know what you're thinking, then they'll be able to counter whatever we try to do while inside them. But how can we act on them from the outside? Perhaps working to crack the base spells, soften the foundations, but those would be the best protected. Tapping thoughts is very advanced, maybe to the point of being unstable, we could..." she trailed away, flattening one palm against Vimika's back as if to steady herself. "No. No, Father assaulted you. That's... Vimika, I'm sorry."

"Not your fault."

Aurelai didn't remove her hand. "He was my father, and he hurt you to keep you away. He never weaponized my memories beyond making them in the first place."

Vimika looked down at her reflection looking back from the puddle of melon juice on her plate. Warped and unstable, it was even more accurate than Not-Vimika had been. "And I chose to continue on through it."

"For Oliver," Aurelai said.

"Yes. In my defense, I didn't know you were here. If I had, I..." Vimika had to stop herself. As far as she could tell, the melon wasn't fermented, but it had almost loosened her tongue all the same.

Alone for too long, Aurelai wasn't about to let anything go unsaid, or didn't know that she was supposed to. Either way, Vimika was doomed.

"If you had, you... what?"

Vimika glanced over her shoulder. "Might have come a lot sooner."

Aurelai set aside the brush and began running her fingers through the length of Vimika's hair. As they descended they grazed along her shoulders and down her back, and she leaned into the touch without even realizing she was doing it.

"If that's the case, I'm sorry it took me so long to work out a way to get you here," Aurelai said, her voice coming from a lot closer than it had been.

Vimika's arms and neck erupted in gooseflesh, but she said nothing in the fear that it would settle back down again. "You're lucky the old woman pays so well. Or, I thought she had. I turned back once, you know."

"I saw," Aurelai said.

"Sorry. If I had known..."

"Ssh." Aurelai ran her fingertips along Vimika's temples as she began gathering hair to be braided. "You didn't. That's sort of the point of the illusions, isn't it?"

Somehow that didn't make Vimika feel any better. "Still, knowing that you've been here all along, and no one had any idea... It must have been torture to be so close and so far at the same time."

"It wasn't easy, no. Especially after the mines opened. I always hoped they would come out this way to prospect at the very least, but they haven't come close yet," Aurelai said as she separated Vimika's hair into sections.

Vimika glanced down at Oliver and thought about the astronomical cost of his creation, and of what would have enabled the Tarsebaums to pay it. "There's no reason to. The mines that are already open are going to be enough to supply demand for decades, and the four houses have a total monopoly on all of it. Didn't you wonder why their house wizards are so strong for being out in the middle of nowhere?"

"No," Aurelai said.

"I guess you wouldn't have. I forget how much you don't know, you're so easy to talk to," Vimika said.

"I've been waiting a while for my chance. And... I like talking to you." Aurelai folded Vimika's hair over itself into a single, simple braid.

"Me, too," Vimika said.

Why was she being so stupid? She shouldn't be feeling anything other than suspicion and mistrust. Aurelai had been *waiting* for her, had all but summoned her.

Because no one has touched you in ages and you're starved for companionship. Of course you're going to let the most beautiful woman you've ever met braid your hair, and smile when she bats those big black eyes at you. It'll only hurt if you're dumb enough to believe that it means anything.

She needs you.

And you need her, another part of her countered traitorously. So traitorously, her heart rate sped up.

At the sensation of such familiar motions being carried out by unfamiliar hands, Vimika was forced to acknowledge that there might be some truth to it. It had been ages since she'd let someone braid her hair, and once again, it was something she hadn't even known she'd been missing. She'd been so tied up in what she was avoiding, she hadn't spared a thought for what she'd given up in order to do so.

But after Aurelai was finished and had tied off the braid, Vimika was made acutely aware of other things she'd been denying herself when Aurelai's thumbs found her shoulder blades and began to trace along the edges. It wasn't quite a massage, more an exploration, which made sense since it was unlikely Aurelai had ever worked out a way to feel her own shoulder blades, unless she had flexibility to equal her balance.

And wouldn't you just like to find out?

"Well!" Vimika squeaked, "I think I need to get out of the sun. Thank you for doing my hair."

A wooshing noise blew across her ear that might have been a laugh, or a sigh. Without being able to see Aurelai's face, Vimika couldn't tell. But when strong, cool fingers began idly stroking the back of her neck, she had a much better idea.

"You're welcome." Aurelai already had a dusky voice, but from an only an inch away, it was thick with *night*, the kind that you could put on and wear like a cloak.

"Ah, well... perhaps we should get to work?"

~

125

With breakfast cleared away and Oliver off doing whatever it was a magical creature that couldn't die did all day, the question of where to even start with a problem of the scale they were facing needed tackling. Without being able to access magic, there weren't many avenues open to Vimika that could hope to bear fruit. Luckily, her years in school gave her an idea.

"This level of magic is too complicated to memorize. Your father had to have kept books on it, right? I don't need magic to read. I hope."

"Yes, of course. Some have been ensorcelled to keep me from opening them. You're welcome to try, though. Did... you like breakfast?" Aurelai's voice was light and thin, nothing like what she'd sounded like earlier.

Vimika held back from mentioning it. "Yes, thank you. And again for taming my hair. It's been a while since I'd done much more than enough to stuff it under my hat."

"I could tell. Oh! Oh, no, that.... you're welcome! Ah, we should probably get started," Aurelai said, slow to take her eyes off Vimika before leading them back to the laboratory.

After a night's sleep, some food and not being laid out on the slab that dominated it, the lab was much less intimidating than the first time Vimika saw it. Now (mostly) free from the fear of having the tools hanging on the wall used on her, she found herself drawn to them. They were spotless, and bore almost no sign of wear.

As a wizard's research and experimentation was mostly done with words and not hammers, it wasn't surprising. Then she thought of Oliver, and just what was holding up that outer artifice, and they took on a patina that was altogether less innocuous.

"I don't use them," Aurelai said with a look of sympathy. "Come."

At the touch of a nondescript point on the wall, a hidden

door popped open, the edges jagged with teeth made of wood panels. Aurelai pulled it the rest of the way to reveal darkness beyond.

"You have a secret passage?" Vimika asked without bothering to hide her jealousy.

"Father never took any chances. I suppose I should be glad he even showed me that it existed," Aurelai said as she stared into a hole as dark as her eyes.

"Where does it go?"

"The library."

It was a short, cramped crawl, with Aurelai's magelight leading the way, to a space Vimika immediately knew was big by how much darkness it contained. The light was more than enough until it suddenly wasn't, and Aurelai had to add another to help.

The moment Vimika set eyes on the collection however, she knew she was in more trouble than she'd imagined. There were books, and then there were *books*. The kind that have a self-evident amount of import and weight that makes it impossible for them to be spoken or written about in any other way.

Then she started reading the titles.

"*Time Can't Run Out if It's Standing Still*? *Levitation is Like Flying Only Easier*? These must be *original* copies!"

There was a time when a wizard's greatest defense was a cracking sense of whimsy. It was terribly disarming and had been thought to make magic seem less scary. How they got from there to body snatching (and making) was a history unto itself, and not one that Vimika had any desire to sleep through more than once. Now, however, she wished she'd drunk more coffee in school.

"This… this is the foundation of magical theory! The copies I have at home are half this long! What's *in* here?" Vimika asked as she flipped madly through one of the *books*.

It had to be hundreds of years old, but felt like it had been bound a decade ago. Worn and well-read, it still hung quite nicely together. A wizard wasn't one to put a price on knowledge, but when it was written in the original hand of the one who'd thought it up and in such good condition, it was worth somewhere between an amount that required swearing to properly convey and one that just made you faint dead away. Or get a cramp from writing all the zeroes.

"'Before Levitating a subject, adding Lightness is advised. This will reduce strain on the caster and get them into the subject's good graces. If the subject is inanimate, the added Lightness can be displaced upon the next casting of Weight.'"

Vimika looked up, her eyes working in her head as a thousand thoughts banged against each other behind them.

"Does that make sense to you?" Aurelai asked.

"Only because I already know how to do it. Who writes like this? 'Ascent is achieved by subtracting gravity.' 'Weight is subjective. If subject is resistant to being acted upon, turn your attention to the ground and reduce its pull instead.' This is *so* much more complicated than it needs to be."

"It's a first draft," Aurelai said.

Vimika turned to her like she'd just said the sky was green. "What makes you say that?"

"Father thought he could sell it someday if he needed money."

"*He* wrote this?" Vimika riffled through the book until she found the name of the author on the very last page. The word that usually preceded Azrabaleth Kalinostrafal's name in history books was either 'wicked' or 'evil,' unless it was written by a revisionist, then it was 'misguided'. 'Genius' was only whispered about in dark rooms full of wizards and the smell of alcohol. She'd never seen 'by' before, and had no idea if the reason was prudence or whitewashing.

"Is that good?"

The world tried to spin away from Vimika then, but she grabbed it by the scruff and made it stay put. The collection, the illusions, the house, all of it suddenly came into such sharp focus she had to screw her eyes shut against the intensity of it. To accomplish all of those feats, the one responsible would have to have been a great mage, yes, but not *the* great mage. None would admit it, no matter how drunk they got, but the (loud) consensus was that Azrabaleth Kalinostrafal was an inhumane, greedy, overly-ambitious walking epithet, yet also (quietly) perhaps the greatest of them all in terms of both theory and craft.

Flipping through his original notes, Vimika could see they were the product of an obsessive, one given entirely to his work. There wasn't enough space left in the margins for anything else, and the else that was missing became more and more obvious the further she read.

"Aurelai, who was your mother?" Vimika asked.

She shouldn't have. She knew the instant she said the words, and she would have done anything to take them back.

"I never knew her," Aurelai said. "Father never spoke of her. Whenever I asked, he would leave the room. He never got angry, he would just... leave. But he was the only person here... I had to stop asking."

Vimika shook her head pathetically. Against what she was seeing, against what she'd been so stupid as to say, and most of all, the pain in Aurelai's voice. "I'm sorry. I got too excited. This is all history to me, but to you..."

"It's all right. I only knew I was supposed to have a mother because everyone in books did."

So much missing, so much unsaid, all of Vimika's education and upbringing were screaming at her to figure it out, to solve the mystery, to *know*, but Vimika the woman, who still felt things like empathy, kept her mouth shut and tried not to cry. There was so much pain in Aurelai's features.

For as odd as her body's movements were, those of her face were perfectly normal, only now there was nothing perfect or normal about them. If anyone anywhere had ever *needed* a hug, it was Aurelai then, and Vimika tossed aside the priceless tome to give one to her.

Nothing within Vimika could stop it. Aurelai was a wizard, and a woman in obvious torment at being made to remember things she would rather not, and the pang of sympathy that reverberated within Vimika when she pulled them together was deafening. Even still, she held Aurelai close, the only thing that needed doing or saying.

Or so Vimika thought.

Aurelai fought against the need to cry, her chest hitching and jerking. Her hands worked against Vimika's back as she struggled with whatever was roiling within her. Grinding her forehead into Vimika's shoulder, Aurelai shook her head in denial.

"It's all right, I'm here. You can talk to me. You're not alone anymore," Vimika said.

Pressed as tightly as they were, she *felt* the emotional dam within Aurelai burst.

"I know... and... I'm sorry. I'm sorry I tricked you into coming here. I'm sorry your magic is gone. I'm sorry I lured you into something even I don't understand. I was just so lonely... I needed to be found... to *exist*... to be more than the memory of a dead man... and I saw you. Independent, living your own life, making your own choices, answering to nobody. I wanted you to be the perfect savior so badly I didn't think about you as a person, or what this place would do to you. I'm so sorry!" She burst into tears, gripping Vimika's shoulders from the back. "I was selfish! What if we can't get out? What if I trapped you here with me forever, what if Father won't let you leave with knowledge of me? What if--"

"Aurelai, stop, please. Why are you apologizing? You've done nothing wrong! I don't blame you for trying, and I'm flattered you chose me, of all people. Because I'm none of those things," Vimika said. "I just wanted to be left alone."

Aurelai pulled back, her obsidian eyes searching. "Why? Why would you want that? You have people who care about you. You have a life! A family!"

Those smoke-black eyes needed an answer, needed to try to understand why Vimika's mind had been twisted into knots over that very question. The forest had almost gotten it out of her by force, but the pleading in Aurelai's features was infinitely more effective in drawing out that particular truth.

"Because no one can hurt me that way. They can't stare, or point, or laugh. There's no one to whisper behind my back when they think I can't hear, no one to tell me they'll be there when they won't. I can't be betrayed, or lied to," Vimika said. "*That's* what the forest showed me. The truth."

She glanced about the library, to the priceless knowledge that soared away from her, and back to the woman standing in the middle of it. "I envy you here."

"Because you don't know. You just want to think you do. Whatever happened to you… you didn't deserve, if it can make you think that this is a way to live." Aurelai threw an accusatory finger at the passage they'd come in through. "That? Out there? Is a *prison*."

In one great sucking breath, Aurelai regained her composure like it had never left. She placed her hands on Vimika's temples, holding her still and giving each of them no choice but to look the other in the eye. "And so's this. I barely know you. I've seen you from afar, and maybe the Vimika I built in my mind isn't who you really are, but I doubt it. I wouldn't have chosen you if I didn't think I could trust you. I would have never shown you the books. Never let you near *me*."

"I don't know you, either." Vimika had to tear the words out like a rotten tooth, all at once and before she could change her mind. "I just... *found* you. In this impossible place that shouldn't be. How do I know *you're* not impossible, too? You've been so generous, so kind, but... you need my help."

"Yes, of course I do... do- you think I'm being nice just so you'll help me?"

Vimika tried to shake her head against the answer, but Aurelai held her fast. "No. I don't... know. I... Aurelai, I... you don't understand. This is all too perfect. You... just waiting for me? Showing me such beautiful things, such kindness, feeding me, keeping me warm, laughing... I don't get to have those things, Aurelai. They get taken."

"Things I've never had. Things I can't have. Things I dream of, but can't hold. More illusions. But you're real! You're here. You came and you stayed. Vimika... am I wrong to want to keep you?"

"You don't know the real me. The me that drinks too much and hides under her sheets, the me that hates herself because she's let herself be hurt too many times and is too big a coward to do anything about it except run. The me that fled as far as she could from home, but found it wasn't far enough."

It was all pouring out and Vimika didn't know how to stop it. Each word felt like poison, but she didn't know to whom. She'd been keeping it bottled up so long it had begun to fester, and now she was spraying it all over someone who had done nothing but ask for help and be nice to her.

Aurelai's dark eyes held a bottomless well of pleading. "I want to know the real you! Don't you?"

"Aurelai... I don't know what I want."

"Well I *do*."

With no distance between them, Vimika was being kissed before she knew that Aurelai was moving. There was no question it was her first, but Vimika yielded to it gratefully. Tears pricked her eyes as she cradled Aurelai's face, fingers working through sleek black hair. Her lips were cool and soft, insistent and *genuine* as they chased after Vimika's. Cool skin closed on the back of her neck and she leaned into it. The softness of Aurelai's touch, her hair, her lips, her very nature, Vimika sank into them all at the same time, losing herself in a world of sable and velvet.

She allowed Aurelai's hands to roam where they would, from her neck and down, shivering when they found the small of her back. She mirrored every movement, letting Aurelai control the pace and find her own boundaries.

But there were none, and Vimika felt unsure fingers start to work at the buttons of her tunic from the bottom up. Just grazing her breasts, they soon reached her neck and the fabric parted, whispering the length of her body to the floor.

Aurelai beheld her a moment, staring with wide, jubilant eyes that wanted, *needed*, and were filled to overflowing in seconds. Vimika sucked in a gasp as Aurelai's hands found her again, closing over the bare skin of her arms, her back, fingers tracing up her spine until they closed on her face, pulling her into another kiss.

Vimika probed Aurelai's lips with her tongue. She gave in to the pressure as Vimika's fingers deftly worked the ties holding Aurelai's dress together until it, too, collapsed, sighing against her skin into a pile atop Vimika's shirt. Aurelai shuddered as Vimika's hands slid over skin smooth and unblemished, learning every curve and nuance without needing to look. Tracing down the shallow valley of her spine, they settled on Vimika's favorite curves of them all.

Aurelai tried to take a step back, her face suddenly hesitant. "I've never done this before."

"I have," Vimika breathed, and guided Aurelai gently to the soft rushes laid out across the floor.

Aurelai gasped, both of her magelights winking out as Vimika's mouth closed on the hollow of her neck and worked gently upward to find her ear. Vimika took her time sliding the length of it along her cheek until she came to the pointed tip, taking it softly between her teeth. When she touched the tip of her tongue to the tip of Aurelai's ear, there was a snapping sound of magic arcing between them, faint but unmistakable.

"I... didn't know... that could happen," Aurelai managed between breaths.

"Wizard secret. It seems you need my help in more ways than one," Vimika breathed, kissing the last word into the side of Aurelai's neck. She nuzzled against her, relishing her sudden warmth, her closeness, all doubt and hesitation banished into the darkness.

Aurelai's hair was like silk, soft and luxuriant as it slid between them in decadent sheets. Vimika's body responded, pressing closer as her lips sought out more opportunities for instruction. Aurelai writhed as she learned. Against such intense, unfamiliar stimulation, her legs worked at random without ever breaking contact, sliding up and down Vimika's.

Though Aurelai's movements were unsure, her strength was still evident as she dragged her fingers along Vimika's back, clawing at her shoulders and digging into her waist.

"More," Aurelai pleaded into Vimika's ear. "Please, show me *every*thing!"

Vimika felt along Aurelai's arms to take her hands, entwining their fingers tightly as she pressed their noses together, looking deeply into the depths of those dark, alien eyes. "Be careful what you ask for, wizard."

With speed to match her strength, Aurelai clamped her legs around Vimika's waist, pinning them together so tightly it stole the breath from her.

"Then I won't," Aurelai said, seizing Vimika's lips once

more. From between them came the hesitant probe of Aurelai's tongue, and with it magic sharp and biting, more potent than before. Vimika had been denied it so long, she pressed their bodies tighter to take in everything she could, wrapping herself in the other wizard and luxuriating in everything her body had to tell her.

Aurelai smelled of earth and clean air, of the forest and the mountains, skin cool like the early days of spring, eyes smoldering like volcanic glass not yet cooled. But even for her strength and rigid, inexperienced movements, she was soft everywhere Vimika's hands and lips fell to, responding with hitched breaths, ribboning streaks of fire down Vimika's back with every touch, every sensation she'd never felt before. Vimika grew addicted to helping Aurelai feel, to showing her everything she had been missing, and she responded with grateful and guiding hands unashamed of what they wanted.

However Aurelai moved in daylight, in darkness she was like smoke, smoothly curling around Vimika's every curve, warm and clinging, rising from the fire that burned within them both. Whispers and intimations, hands and lips, experience and utter, helpless need wound Aurelai around Vimika's patient guidance.

Writhing like a snake, Aurelai squirmed under even the barest touch, breaths coming faster and shallower, while Vimika's took their time, blooming over her breasts and down, every rise of Aurelai's belly met by awaiting lips as Vimika kissed her way over a field of rolling snow to the dark forest awaiting in the far south.

A single breath had barely caressed Aurelai's apex when she suddenly cried out, her back snapping off the floor in a great arch as her release took her without warning. Low, wordless sounds erupted from her at the peak of her pleasure until after a few sharp jerks, she collapsed, chest heaving and eyes unseeing.

"Vimika?" she eventually asked the ceiling in a breathy, far-away voice.

"Yes, Aurelai?"

"I... feel... like... I'm on fire."

"That's normal," Vimika replied with no little satisfaction.

When her breath finally evened out, Aurelai raised her head, looking down the length of her body at Vimika with lethargic, almost drunken eyes. "I didn't know it could feel like that."

"Savor it." If she could do nothing else for Aurelai, she could do this, and part of that was making sure she took her time coming back to herself. Vimika's hands were still occupied running up and down Aurelai's legs when they were lifted away and their fingers once again entwined. Vimika didn't try to pull away, perfectly content to hold hands if that's what Aurelai wanted.

"I will. But... would you mind if I did it somewhere more comfortable?"

Vimika met Aurelai's eyes over the gentle swell of her belly. "Did you have somewhere in mind?"

Aurelai nodded. "Just... let me remember how to stand up first."

8

There are few stretches like the one Vimika had upon waking up the next morning. Long, tingly, like all her joints were going to come undone, but *good*. She knew where every ounce of blood in her body was as it raced through her, curling her toes and *whoosh*ing in her ears, like it had all been replaced with liquid lightning, only less explode-y and only slightly quieter. Her arms flew out like wings, flying over sheets that were too cold and too flat.

She'd awoken alone.

Again.

It had been... too long since she'd last awoken in someone else's bed, yet nothing had changed, including the company, and she curled back in on herself. Nestled in a pile of blankets and warmer than she had been in days, she wrapped her arms about her chest and pulled her legs in so tightly she was more egg than wizard. Cocooned in warmth her bare skin was eager to pass on to a brain that wasn't inclined to enjoy it very much, she was loathe to move more than her eyes, but even when she forced them open, there wasn't much to see. Aurelai's bedroom was even sparser than her own. The empty other pillow, a bare wall beyond, and... that was it, really.

But what more could she expect? What had she really wanted after last night? Aurelai had thrown herself at her, what was she supposed to say, no? It was better this way. The glances, the touches, the tension between them had snapped spectacularly, wasn't that enough? Aurelai was satisfied, maybe they could get to work on the real problem now that the most animal parts of their brains had had their yapping mouths stuffed stupid.

And yet.

Would it have been so bad to wake up to those fathomless black eyes? To a smile? To *something* other than a blank wall?

But the empty, unadorned walls turned out to have one advantage: amplifying the sounds coming down the hall from the kitchen.

The bright clink of metal, bare footsteps, the hiss of heat being applied to whatever was making the delicious smells wafting in the open door, and above it all, singing.

Vimika's blood surged, the sound of that dusky voice raised in song filling her with memories of what it had been raised in the night before, and she curled in on herself involuntarily this time, her face suddenly as warm in open air as the rest of her was under the blankets. She stilled herself so she could listen.

Aurelai sang like her birds, albeit ones that had only ever heard *people* sing in a tavern, leaving it gloriously off-key and belted with the raw enthusiasm of someone who didn't know any better.

The same way she does certain other things, Vimika thought.

She was a grown woman a decade and several partners on from her first time, why would such a thought make her giggle the way it would have if she still used words like 'It' and 'The Act' to describe the reason her clothes were in a different room than she was?

But there was no time to lay there *thinking,* she might miss breakfast, and few thoughts got her out of bed faster than that.

She rolled to her feet only to realize she didn't have anything to put on.

The tantalizing hints of magic she'd tasted the night before had not heralded any great breakthrough in her magic shock, so she had no idea which of the drawers and cabinets were bespelled. She couldn't risk breaking an important one or worse, setting off some kind of booby trap. All she had were the sheets, so with a grunted apology, she yanked them off and wrapped them about herself. Clutching them closed over her chest, she shuffled into the hall.

So much did she enjoy being swathed in Aurelai that Vimika didn't even think about where she was going, following her nose and ears as if she were in a trance.

Arriving at the kitchen did nothing to shake her out of it.

There was Aurelai, in the pure piercing light of a winter's morning. Skin that had been milky was now radiant, as if it had been dusted in silver, the tips of her ears twin snow-capped peaks amidst rolling plains of sable, her silhouette shod in little more than a suggestion of white fabric as she moved with liquid grace in time to a song from the age of the truly great mages, one of magic and power, wisdom and history. Vimika knew the words, but had never heard the melody before. Few living had. It wasn't something that wizards passed down anymore.

But the sound of it, the sight of Aurelai moving to her own time with the freedom that came from a complete lack of self-consciousness, the joy in her voice, all while Vimika was clad in the sheets they had shared brought out her inner romantic. Who cared if it didn't mean anything, she *wanted* it. So as best she could, she mimicked Aurelai's motions as she approached from behind, swaying and moving along with her, step by step, side-to-side, until she was only an arm's length away.

With a contented sigh, she slipped her arms around Aurelai's waist and pulled her close, submerging her face in a fragrant sea of black.

When she surfaced, the first thing she became aware of was being slumped against the wall. That, and there being another Aurelai in the room. Both had identical frying pans in their hands and the same wide-eyed look of surprise on their faces.

"Vimika!" the Aurelais exclaimed, dropping their pans onto the stove and rushing forward. "Oh! Oh, I'm so sorry! I've never been snuck up on before! Oh, oh, what did I do to you?"

"I think you hit me," Vimika said, blinking as slowly and deliberately as Aurelai did while trying to remember if they'd used the pans or their fists.

Is that why Aurelai blinked that way? Why would she hit herself with a frying pan? Were all legitimate questions thought by someone who had just been knocked across the room by a blow to the head.

"Oh," Aurelai said, and began fretting with Vimika's hair, searching for a bump or bruise, but her hands were quickly stayed.

"It's all right," Vimika said as Aurelai coalesced into a single individual once more. There was a stray thought about what Vimika would have done with two, but it healed over as well, sealed within a sarcophagus made of the sense to never mention it to anyone.

She was still holding Aurelai's hands.

"Good morning."

Whatever lingering pain there might have been was instantly dispelled when Aurelai kissed her on the forehead. Vimika may have melted a bit. Or maybe it was the contented sigh that made her slump a little lower.

"Good morning. I'm sorry."

"No, I should have known better," Vimika said, somehow managing to stay in the sheets while finding her way vertical again. "What were you making?"

"Nothing very special I'm afraid, but I thought you would be hungry after..." Brilliant scarlet cascaded down Aurelai's features from the crown of her head to plunge below her neckline.

It was all Vimika could do to not go chasing after to find out where it stopped. "I am, thank you. But... aren't you cold?"

Aurelai barely glanced down at the gossamer sheath that ended well above her knees, hanging from her shoulders by straps so thin they looked like they could be snapped with a thought. "You made me feel beautiful last night. I wanted to look it when you woke up."

Within Vimika's chest there was a great big *thud*, which resulted in a little puff of disbelief rocketing out of her parted lips. "You... *are* beautiful," she said. She hoped. Words were harder now than before she'd had her head caved in. Or perhaps easier.

"Thank you. So are you," Aurelai said.

She leaned in for a proper kiss this time, which Vimika returned enthusiastically. In daylight, with the sobriety of proper sleep, it was a different, *better* kiss. It was more real. It wasn't driven by curiosity, longing or mere lust, but because it was what you did in moments like this, one that *made* it a moment like this. A kiss that was new, but wonderfully familiar, a kiss that tingled with magic...

Then Vimika started giggling and had to pull away. "You taste like basil."

Aurelai licked her lips, looking down at her fingers in that fascinating way she had, a bird peering down at a bit of seed it hadn't expected to come across. "I thought you would like it."

"I do! I just... didn't expect it. Nicking from the pan while I was still asleep?" Vimika teased.

"I had to see if it was any good. I've only ever cooked for Father. I doubt you share the same palate." Aurelai turned back to the counter, where she speared a steaming mushroom with a fork. When Vimika reached out to take it, Aurelai shook her head. "Let me."

Vimika opened her mouth gratefully, and let herself be fed the little morsel without a second thought. She couldn't remember the last time she'd had a cooked mushroom that had been made that way in anything other than oil, butter or lard, leaving it considerably more mushroom-y than she was used to. Flavorful would have been a better word, but her higher thoughts were preoccupied with the look of nervous anticipation on Aurelai's face and her continued lack of real clothing.

"Ish qua' good." Vimika said as she chewed.

A new, brighter light came to Aurelai's eyes and she came back with a chunk of tomato the size of her thumbnail. When she turned for a third time, Vimika suggested that perhaps the table would make breakfast slightly less laborious. She would still obediently open her mouth when there was food aimed at it, but there, at least, she could return the favor.

Without cheese, bread, butter or oil of any kind, it was the healthiest meal ever put away by someone who had a tavern owner as a landlord. By the time they were done, Vimika was full but not *full*, and had the kind of energy that she imagined people were supposed to have after eating, and insisted on doing the washing up.

With a kiss of thanks, Aurelai left to change, leaving Vimika with the thoughts she should have had much earlier. What was happening here? And now that she was allowed to have rational thoughts again, they handed her a note that said 'You barely know this woman, she's quite possibly older than your grandmother and has been living alone for upwards of two centuries in a prison built by her own (dead) criminal father, and you still can't access your magic. Make sure you can clear that pit before you try to jump over it. And that there aren't a bunch of snakes at the bottom.'

All good points, but Vimika had already finished the dishes and still wasn't wearing any clothes, which made them invalid.

Somehow.

Something bright caught her peripheral vision and she looked over to see Oliver staring up at her.

"Good morning. I... uh, don't know what she usually gives you. And I... already did the washing up. Do you even need to eat?"

As he was an animal, Oliver said nothing, but there was something to his eyes that made it feel like an insult to reduce him that way. For a split second, she had genuinely expected an answer.

"You really are a little miracle, aren't you?"

Vimika sucked in a deep breath at that thought, only realizing after she'd done so that she'd held the sheets to her nose while she'd done it.

"So's this," she said with a smile.

Oliver padded over to sniff at the unfamiliar fabric. Cocking his head in either approval or confirmation, he trotted away the way he'd come.

Unsure of what to make of the encounter, Vimika returned to the bedroom to find Aurelai just doing the ties up the side of a different dress than the one Vimika had had the privilege of removing. A deep green trimmed in black lace, it was in perfect repair, the same as the towels and blankets had been, and for the first time, Vimika found herself glad that her magic was on the fritz. The amount necessary to maintain the preservation spells on the textiles alone must be near blinding, to say nothing of something like the stasis slab.

"How do I look?" Aurelai asked as she did a little twirl, the hem of her dress fanning out to reveal that she was doing so on the very tips of her toes.

"Wonderful," Vimika said a hair too absent-mindedly.

Aurelai settled flat on her feet, her dress swishing about before settling as straight as her hair. "What is it?"

Vimika looked up and around, running her fingers down the door frame as if she expected something to happen.

"I just saw Oliver. But I can't *See* him. I can't sense *any* of the magic that's saturating this place. If what you've said is true, it's been... marinating... for centuries. It must have a life of its own by now, but I can't feel it. Just like I couldn't feel that other me in the forest. I know it's the magic shock, it *has* to be. The alternative is... Aurelai, is any of this real?"

"Real enough," Aurelai said brightly.

"Don't. Please. After the Forest, after last night... I don't want this to be a dream or an illusion. Besides, you owe me for hurling me into the wall."

Aurelai met some success in stifling her grin. "You're right. Vimika, to the best of my knowledge, everything you've seen and experienced since waking in the lab is real. Yes, Father's magic is... intense, but I've never known it to do anything unless I leave the clearing. It's like a- a moat. Do castles still have those?"

"The tackier ones do," Vimika said.

"A moat. Or a wall, since it's powered by hundred-foot trees."

"A prison with golden bars is still a prison."

"Yes. But at least I've finally been allowed one visitor," Aurelai said.

"As much good as I've been thus far."

"I've quite enjoyed our time together." Aurelai's eyebrows bowed upward, her brow furrowed in sudden thought.

"Haven't you? I... I'm sorry. If you want to sleep in the den, I can unlock some more blankets. You probably need more rest, I've made you exert yourself too much. I will go fetch some of the most promising books for you so you have something to read. There are candles if magelight is too difficult, I just have to remember where I put them."

Aurelai made to leave, but Vimika snatched her by the wrist and spun her back, pinning her to the wall with a look. "Don't apologize to me anymore. If I think you've done something wrong, you won't have to guess, all right? I regret nothing of what has happened since I arrived here. Do you?"

"No. No, I've enjoyed every moment," Aurelai replied.

"Good." Vimika let go of the bed sheet and snaked a hand around the back of Aurelai's neck.

"Oh! It's not even dark!" Aurelai exclaimed with a trill of nervous laughter, nonetheless plunging her fingers into Vimika's hair as lips closed on her shoulder.

Silken hair gliding along her chest and over her ears, Vimika didn't break the chain of kisses she laid down Aurelai's arm. Magic tingled. "All the easier for you to see what you've been missing."

It was for the best that Aurelai was barefoot, as she quickly found herself standing in a pool of emerald.

~

"I think I may need to borrow something to wear," Vimika said as she shrugged into her tunic and trousers again. Creeping into the library completely naked to fetch them had been far more intriguing a prospect than it was an exercise. Windowless as both it and the laboratory were, there was something about doing so in broad daylight surrounded by magic she couldn't sense that made it feel as though windows weren't entirely necessary to be seen by someone, or

145

some*thing.*

But the someone who definitely *had* seen her was nothing but appreciative. Aurelai's eyes were wide and completely unselfconscious about staring as Vimika thought better of doing up the tie that would close her collar, revealing a subtle shadow in the deep 'V' of a neckline that hadn't been there before.

Aurelai had slithered back into her emerald dress while Vimika was gone, looking good enough to attend the coronation of the next king in the time it took for Vimika to walk across the house and back. As she had no plans to ever take part in anything so formal, she told herself it wasn't jealousy she felt at the sight.

"You can try on anything you wish," Aurelai said, crossing to the nearest closet. Pressing her palm to the wooden door, she whispered a few non-words and it consented to open. Inside were several substantial chests stacked on top of one another. Aurelai hauled out the top one with an ease that meant in addition to the null time, it had also been cast with Lightness, otherwise it would have been impossible for Aurelai to move by herself.

That Vimika was having to deduce such things and not See them soured her mood for the brief moment it took for Aurelai to throw open the lid and reveal what was inside.

Color. Vibrant, shimmering colors from rich amethyst to brilliant amber. Sapphire, jade, pearl, the trunk might as well have been a treasure chest. Aurelai took out the topmost garment, a dress as nice as the one she was already wearing, only an amethyst so vibrant and deep it shamed any gemstone that could be dug out of the Dragonbacks.

Aurelai held it to the light, turned it this way and that. "I... er... rather like this one. Do you mind if I...?"

"Go right on ahead. It's yours, after all. Besides, I can't see needing anything like that around the house. Or ever, really, "

Vimika said in spite of the fact it was the only kind of thing she'd ever seen Aurelai wear.

"Thank you!"

But further pillaging, all the way to the bare boards of the bottom of the chest, revealed that formal was all there was. So did the next one. The lack of any real options beyond ostentatious gowns laid to rest any lingering doubts about just how long they had been sealed up. Women hadn't worn anything else back when they'd been shut, even wizards. Before the robes, before the hats, this is what the titular *Polite Magical Society* had actually looked like, and Vimika couldn't decide how she felt about it. The garments were all gorgeous, more costume than clothing, but having no choice in needing to put them on to go outside struck a raw nerve. The only thing that had changed in 200 years was the quality of their uniforms.

"What did you wear before I got here?" Vimika asked as she ran decadently soft sleeves of amber fabric between her fingers. Say what she would about how it may appear in modern times, it was *nice*.

"I never had guests or anyone to impress, so I mostly wore sleeping clothes. Usually until they fell apart. They were quite comfortable," Aurelai said.

The *embroidery* sparkled! "So you dressed up this way for me?"

"It only seemed polite when hosting a guest, especially when I had something to ask of her. Besides, I rather like the way I look like this," Aurelai said, sweeping a hand over her dress, hair falling forward in curtains.

"Me too," Vimika said.

A grin of genuine appreciation touched Aurelai's eyes. "Thank you. Now, you've been clutching that one like a blanket, would you like to try it on?"

Vimika held the dress up to the light, trying to picture

what she would end up looking like in something so ridiculous and old-fashioned.

Aurelai. You'll look like Aurelai, idiot.

Though chastising, the thought was both helpful and accurate. "I suppose I do. Is there a dressing screen I can use?"

Aurelai's head quirked to one side. "I've seen you naked already."

"That- that's not the point!" Vimika brandished the dress, with its dangling strings and myriad folds and layers. "Most magic is less complicated than this thing!"

And I don't want to look like a fool in front of you, any more than I already do, she didn't say and tried to will Aurelai into understanding without having to.

But Aurelai's long isolation won out. "And?"

"And!" Vimika took a breath. "And, I feel stupid not knowing how to put it on."

But there was no judgment in Aurelai's look, only compassion. "So I'll help you. Most of these were never designed to be donned alone. Why do you think I left them packed away? Come."

Aurelai touched a seam between two of the wood panels that made up the wall and pushed. The panel spun around, revealing a full-length (if narrow) mirror.

Vimika approached it tentatively, peering at it from the side to avoid her own reflection. "I've never seen a mirror this good before. There's no warping or fogging..."

Then she touched it. "It's glass!"

Every mirror Vimika had ever seen was highly polished metal. Magically, as was found in those owned by the wealthy, but mostly by regular old time and effort. Why hadn't Kalinostrafal tried to get rich selling *these* instead?

Aurelai demurred. "Do you like it? It used to be a table. But with no guests to entertain, I... repurposed it."

"*You* made this?" Vimika said, which was impressive, since

she'd done it with her jaw on the floor.

"I had a lot of time on my hands."

Vimika ran her finger along the beveled edge. It was perfectly smooth. "No, I mean... how?"

"Silvering is just another type of metalsmithing, is it not? Surely you've done magical metalwork before. It's so thin, it didn't take very much. Less than a single earring's worth, in fact," Aurelai said with only the faintest trace of pride.

She could have shouted it and not been out of line. "I've never heard of anyone turning a spell on its head like that. I've re-shaped silver, but you... transformed it," Vimika said, turning the mirror to run her fingers along the back. Just as Aurelai said, there was barely anything there, the precious metal reduced to something more like a film than a sheet.

"Well, it pleases me that you're impressed," Aurelai said. "Now kindly remove your clothes."

By the time Vimika was dressed again, she didn't recognize the person looking back at her. Aurelai stood behind with a look of complete satisfaction on her face.

Vimika wanted it to be from the quality of the mirror, but looking down at her sleeves put paid to that lie as fast as it took her to blink. She'd chosen the amber dress accented in gold, and it had indeed taken both of them to wriggle her into it. The fabric shone as it gripped her arms and swished around her legs with whispered rustling. The neckline was modest, but left little doubt as to the shape of her waist.

Aurelai, in her dresses, looked stunning. Radiant. A wizard from another age, when they were proud and respected.

Vimika looked like an impostor playing dress up. Aurelai's alterations had been as masterful as they were swift, and though the dress fit perfectly, it didn't *fit*. The tightness made Vimika hunch, and her hair was nowhere near as elegant as Aurelai's, bound in braids more suitable for flying or just staying out of the way than attending Court.

Her ears drooped at the sight. The Vimika in the mirror wasn't a wizard, and in her state of magic shock, she didn't *feel* like one any more than she looked. At least the hat had let her pretend.

Aurelai was still smiling, and set a hand on Vimika's shoulder. "You look very nice."

"Do you think so? I feel like a pillock."

Aurelai shook her head. "You don't look like a fish at all. I think you're lovely."

Vimika was too flattered to correct her. "If you say so."

"I do. And I mean it," Aurelai said. "But if you don't like it, I can try to find some more sleeping clothes, at least. There should be more buried somewhere..."

"You think I'm lovely?" Vimika suddenly asked their reflection. It had taken a moment for it to sink in that Aurelai hadn't included 'looked' in her compliment. There was flattered, then there was 'lightheaded with ears on fire,' and Vimika's were distinctly pink, right out to the tips.

The stars in Aurelai's midnight eyes came out. "Apologies, I must have misspoken. You *are* lovely."

Vimika swallowed. "No one's ever said that to me before."

Aurelai took Vimika's hand in her own and brought it to her lips. "Then there are more fools in the outside world than you've led me to believe."

Heart racing away from her in a gallop, Vimika felt as though she'd just taken on a lot more than a new wardrobe, but there wasn't a mirror fine enough to tell her how well it was going to fit.

~

Days and nights began to blend together after that, as did Vimika and Aurelai, now that they were sharing clothes as well as sheets. Aurelai proved time and again to be the master of the former, while Vimika was happy to continue playing instructor in the latter. But the talent they shared was magic. Through their close contact, Vimika's had shown tantalizing hints of life, but until it was resurrected fully, their only outlet for hoping to crack their predicament was the library.

Sitting at a desk in a dress wasn't all that unlike doing it in robes, and Vimika had grown accustomed to it with surprising ease. She had never had the occasion or imagination to do so, but the fabrics were so soft, they felt like nothing Vimika had ever worn, which went a long way to helping the transition. This was further aided by Vimika being not at all displeased with the fact it was impossible to put on most of her new garments without Aurelai's help. That they were so easy to get *off* was, Vimika would admit, suspicious, but she was grateful for Aurelai's help with that, too.

What Vimika had needed her help more for, however, was sorting through the library's deceptively vast collection. Between the dimness and how cramped it was, it was hard to get a sense of the scale. But when Aurelai had started pulling down both books and *book*s to reveal that they had been stuffed onto the shelves in *layers*, Vimika began to wonder how well her fancy dresses could stand up to sweat and the true wizard lifestyle: hunched over for hours at a time, reading or experimenting, day after day.

After having trawled through countless such layers without much of a catch to show for it, Aurelai produced from under a dust-riddled blanket that had very much not been the beneficiary of any preservation magic, the 'forbidden' *book*s. With a description like that, Vimika had expected them to look different. Having been bespelled by one of the most powerful mages to ever live, she'd expected chains of gold, or for them to be encased in arcane frost, hidden in a pocket dimension or at least full of teeth.

Instead, they were blank.

That was it. From the outside, they were like any other *book* in the library, like any library anywhere: pebbly covers, gilt lettering, the musty odor of reams of dead trees having been pressed against each other for ages. The only difference was that when they were opened, there was nothing to see. Not a single figure, illumination, diagram, inscription, big block letters saying something like 'PROPERTY OF HIGH COUNT MUCKETY-MUCK, IF FOUND, RETURN IMMEDIATELY ON PAIN OF YOUR FAMILY BEING DROWNED IN SACKS LIKE UNWANTED KITTENS'.

Books were expensive, and owned by a lot of awful people. These *book*s were both and neither.

Anyone who would imprison their own daughter was objectively terrible, but this anyone was dead. The magic was priceless, but the *book*s themselves outwardly worthless. Vimika strongly suspected, however, that any attempt to destroy them would be met with resistance of some sort, probably of the spectacular and painful variety. A literal dead man's switch.

At least she knew Kalinostrafal wouldn't return as a ghost. Leaving your own child imprisoned for two centuries warranted a place in an especially deep hell, which Vimika suddenly needed to believe in more than she already did in order to continue to live as anything other than a complete nihilist.

She would admit, however, that simply leaving the pages blank was quite clever. A trap or a lock invited poking around, trying to undo it, sever it, break it. To *remove* something, in a sense. To be staring down at literally nothing meant she had to figure out how to *add* something. Anything.

Or…

"Shit," Vimika said suddenly. And more effectively, since it came out of someone wearing a dress worth more than the

Double C.

Of course.

"I have to *find* it." Like a recalcitrant cat, or the impossible mechamagical miracle asleep in the corner, she had to figure out where it had run off to and track it down. It had to be here, or why else would the *books* exist at all? So she knew where to look, she just didn't know how.

"Can you do that without reliable magic?" Aurelai asked from her perch atop a chair they had dragged in from the dining room.

Vimika flicked the corner of one page under her thumbnail. "I doubt it. There's nothing here for my non-magical senses to even start with. Though it would be clever to hide it that way, wizards have all the same senses as everyone else. You couldn't make it physical. The spells would be useless to a non-wizard anyway, except as ransom or blackmail."

Which, without her magic, was exactly what they were.

She flipped the *book* closed and inspected the back cover embossed with the device of a man long dead, yet all too present. Though Azrabaleth Kalinostrafal was legendary, it was not for being stupid. He, more than anyone, would know the value of what he'd created, and wouldn't leave them lying about for anyone to find and use against his daughter.

Or by her.

Vimika looked over the heap of leather and parchment to the woman sitting on the other side.

Whatever Aurelai's father had been, she was not. She was a *victim*, arguably the worst. Leaving your daughter all alone, trapped in a prison of your own making? How could he be *worse* than what history said he was? But Aurelai wasn't history, she was flesh and blood, and very much alive. She'd worked so hard just to keep her head above water, she deserved better than to drown now.

The book was blank. Useless. Just like Vimika had been up

to this point.

How long have I been here? she asked herself. Long enough to lose track already, but what had she accomplished in that time? All she'd done was taken, what had she given back? She'd given Aurelai pleasure, yes, but had she made so much as a dent in her happiness? Vimika had raided Aurelai's closets, her garden and her body, but for what?

Whatever hints Vimika's magic had shown passively, it remained beyond her ability to actively access, and now she couldn't even read a bloody *book*. And that was just the *start* of what was going to be necessary to keep her promise.

She was clad in a dress of sapphire blue from another age, her hair done up to match, but she was no princess. Pointed ears, slitted eyes, but without magic, she was no wizard. It all suddenly seemed so petty. Pointless.

"Vimika?"

Blinking away the burning in the corner of her vision, Vimika came back to herself to find Aurelai gazing across at her with eyes full of concern. At the sight, something insidious and all-too familiar seized Vimika's heart in talons tipped with acid-soaked razor blades: fear. This lonely wizard had put her hopes in Vimika, and she'd failed to deliver. What made it more acute was that the source behind the concern in Aurelai's eyes was affection, and the talons squeezed all the harder.

She called you lovely...

Vimika flipped the *book* shut and stood. "I need to go for a walk. All my thoughts are crashing together and making too many sparks, and I'm afraid they'll catch fire. Could use some cold air on my face."

"Of course. Would you like me to come with you?"

"No, no. Stay warm. I'll just be a minute."

Outside, the stars were waiting. In a clearing in the middle of a forest at the edge of the world, they were as bright as

Vimika had never seen them. The white light somehow made the winter air seem colder and crisper, snowflakes that would never fall.

Vimika had always loved the stars. Bright with possibility, they could be anything. Holes in the sky, portals through which the gods checked on their people as they slept, the filter through which dreams could enter the world. Tonight, however, she could only see the space in between. The void in which the answers to all her problems lay. Unknowable, impenetrable and far away.

Black. Black as Aurelai's eyes, with the same shining light. Black as her hair, a river in which to drown her senses. Vimika could lose herself in either of them if she wasn't careful.

You're doing it again, she thought. *A pretty face and a kind gesture from someone who wants something from you, and you want so badly for it to mean more than that. When have you ever been right? As if this entire situation is anything other than insane to begin with. Even if she's never seen it, she's read books. She knows how to use her wiles to get what she wants, and it's not hard from you. She wasn't lying about her lack of experience, but that only makes it even more convincing, doesn't it? More sympathetic. Makes you weaker.*

It always does. All a girl has to do is touch you and you fall at her feet to promise her anything so she'll to do it again.

Vimika was a wizard. A curiosity. A mark on some rich woman's bedpost. A means to an end.

They only see the hat and the robe. Once they get them off, what's left?

Well, they were off now, only to reveal there was nothing underneath.

Time and time again, she'd been courted by the well-to-do of Maris. Wined, dined, sexed to within an inch of her sanity, but she hadn't known how to play the game. She had never and still didn't want to learn, and so she'd been torn apart, crushed into a slurry of shame and self-hatred and dumped into the gutter.

And now it was happening again, except she didn't even have her magic to justify being here in the first place.

Aurelai was the daughter of perhaps the most powerful mage to ever live, the upper echelon of what they had been at their peak of influence and power as a people. Though in the present Aurelai may have been poor in gold, her blood was liquid platinum. And now she had a problem she needed Vimika to help solve. Lured here, then dined and sexed, all that was missing was the wine before she was thrown away.

Sooner than later, if her magic didn't return.Would it be worse this time if she had no magic to offer? It was the only thing sparing her. Until Aurelai knew for a fact that Vimika couldn't help her, the great mage's daughter had to keep up the ruse.

And Vimika, sad, lonely Vimika, would let her.

Aurelai was unspeakably beautiful, with the same slant to her talents as Vimika. That, she couldn't fake. But her kindness? Her gentility, her strength, her vulnerability?

Vimika didn't doubt that Aurelai's need for help was all-too real, which meant the opposite had to be true for her overtures.

But so what if they are? What do you want from her? What are you expecting? You had sex a few times, so what? You've done that with a lot of women without having a crisis over it. Isn't that enough? Consider yourself lucky you got that much out of all this.

As much as Vimika told herself Not-Vimika was out there in the forest somewhere, she didn't need to be seen to be felt. Not-Vimika only existed out there because she already did somewhere much closer, whispering instead of shouting. And Vimika would believe her.

So she would do as she'd promised, and help Aurelai

escape, then wash her hands of all of it. Start over again, put extra locks on her heart. Run.

She called you lovely...

Clouds of breath puffed from Vimika's mouth, joining the steam that rose from the trails down her cheeks. Up they climbed into the night, to fog over the stars. At least, she thought, they helped just as much to cover the blackness in between.

Once. Just once, couldn't I be part of something beautiful that was real?

The chains she'd been keeping her heart shackled down with were heavy, and she longed to strike them off. But they had been forged at great cost, and the price to be paid for removing them prematurely would be even higher.

And yet...

In the silence of a night stilled by artificial spring, the approach of footsteps from behind were impossible to hide, even if they were barely a whisper above the one being shared amongst the trees.

"I know you said you wanted to be alone, but... I was worried," Aurelai said.

Vimika dabbed at her eyes with the corner of a sleeve. "You didn't have to come all the way out here."

"I know. I wanted to. Do you want to talk about it?"

"About what?" Vimika sniffled.

"That."

"No, it's all right. You have more than enough problems without adding mine."

"If that's how I can help, then that's what I'll do," Aurelai said.

Vimika regarded her with naked disbelief. "How are you so nice? I cannot fathom how you've lived your life and came out a good person. You should be completely mad, or speak your own private language or something. But you're a better person than many I've had the misfortune of knowing."

Better than me.

"I worked hard at it," Aurelai said.

"At being nice?"

"Yes. The animals don't respond very well to those who are unkind to them. They taught me empathy, but I taught myself discipline. To only worry about what I could control, to act when I could, instead of spewing my frustration and anger aimlessly at the trees. I think they like me better now too," Aurelai said, nodding at the jagged border gathering up the stars as the world turned.

Vimika shook her head. "You are truly remarkable, you know that? Where did you get the strength? The hope? I've had nothing but freedom my entire life, and all I seem to do is find ways to throw it away."

"I've only been disappointed by one person in my life so far. Perhaps it takes its toll."

"It does that, yes." Vimika looked back at the house. "I almost wish we could stay here."

"No you don't."

Aurelai took Vimika's hand, considered it much the same way she had the first time. Only now her touch was familiar and gentle, while the magic, again, was the torment of magic so close and yet so far. Like finding a skin of ice on the surface of a lake she'd been swimming in when she desperately needed air. Her fingers pulsed, twitching slightly with every beat of her heart, while Aurelai's were still.

"Can I ask what happened to make you this way? The Vimika whose hair I braided, who I fed mushrooms to, help to dress every day... is not the Vimika standing here now. Where did she go?"

The sigh that issued from Vimika's lips wasn't strong or swift. The thin wisp of white breath that leaked from her was more akin to dust rising from something within her that had just collapsed.

"I'm afraid," she said when it had cleared. "That I won't be able to keep my promise. Or that I will. I don't know which one will hurt more."

The subtle twitches in Vimika's fingers became violent throbs that pressed their fingers tighter with every beat.

But Aurelai's eyes were only for Vimika. "I have no desire to hurt you. I wouldn't dream of it. Why... why would you fear that if you wished we could stay here?"

"If we're here, then it's because my magic hasn't returned. What am I without it? It's all anyone needs from me. I'd be useless to everyone, especially you. And if we escape... then I'll have fulfilled my purpose. You'll have the whole world before you, and you deserve better than to spend a second of it cooped up under a tavern in the middle of nowhere."

"And if I choose to? Do *I* not get to decide that, Vimika? You said you would show me the world yourself. Are you taking it back?"

"No! It's just- that's how it goes with me. I learned the hard way the pain of indulging in optimism."

Aurelai took Vimika's other hand but kept her in place with more than physical strength. Something in Aurelai had shifted, demanding Vimika meet her eyes. She didn't want to, she wanted to look away, to run, but the sound of that twilight voice arrested her every impulse, giving her no choice but to listen.

"And what if that was the lesson I'd taken from my captivity, hm? Just given up, let Father win without a fight? Without *trying*? At least if I'd done so, the only person I would have hurt is myself. That you care so little for *my* feelings about any of this hurts, Vimika. I feel guilty about bringing you here, please don't make me outright regret it. You made a promise, and I trusted you. I'm still struggling to accept that I may have been trapped here for centuries, but

159

never once in that time did I ever indulge in this sort of maudlin self-pity. I *worked*. I *tried*, and I was rewarded." Aurelai squeezed Vimika's hand. "I've only known the you unable to access her magic, and I'm still here beside you, am I not? It was the magicless Vimika I fed, bathed, braid the hair of every night, take by the hand and lead into my bedroom... and you fear I won't want you without magic?"

"What if it's not temporary? What if I'm like this forever? I'd just be a burden to you."

"How can you say that? How can you dare presume how I would feel about you if that were the case?" There wasn't a wisp of anger in Aurelai's voice; the only thing clouding it was confusion.

"Because it's always been true! Wizards and magic are useful, not necessary. I'm nothing beyond my usefulness."

Aurelai dropped Vimika's hands to cradle her face. She searched the facets of Vimika's eyes, through the doorway to her heart and the seat of magic that they'd always been taught the slits represented. "Who did this to you? How can you say such hurtful things about yourself?"

Vimika tried to look away, but Aurelai held her fast. Firmly but gently, she forced Vimika to meet her eyes again, to bring through those doorways the noxious, rotting thing within her.

To bring out Not-Vimika.

"People I'd worked very hard to forget. But they... your father-- it's what the forest showed me. Brought me right back there, as if it was happening again. I could feel everything, smell it. He pulled it out of my memory, forced me to experience it again, and it's all I can think about when we're not together."

"*Who?*" Aurelai didn't bother to blunt the edge in her voice.

Arrested by twin pools of obsidian, Vimika had no choice but to dive in. "Rich women who just wanted a pet wizard, I won't dignify them with names. Humans of influence who wanted to show me off, to have magic done for them. Their friends had wizards working for them, so they needed to have one, too. But so did their enemies. Sometimes I felt like a tool, other times like... a puppy. Coddled, presented, doted on, made to fetch and do tricks when company came over. But puppies become dogs. Or they're no longer fashionable, or sometimes a cuter puppy comes along, or I would refuse to bite strangers.

"Every time I was scooped up, I thought it was different. I thought *this* time, my master cares about me. They all cared enough to pretend, I suppose, but only to keep me in their sway. And I fell for it. But it's one thing to be discarded or ignored. The last time, the time that made me run... she *humiliated* me. Every awful thing I'd ever felt about myself, she threw in my face. All my insecurities, my doubts, my stupid inability to learn that they didn't care about anything other than the hat and robes. She talked to others I'd been in... service... of, compared notes. I thought they'd loved me, but they worked together to show me just how little they had ever cared. So I would *know* who held the real power in Atvalia.

"So I ran. As far as I could and still be in the Empire, I ran. Ran and hid. I came in search of Oliver so I could afford to run even further. Hide even deeper, so I could forget I was a wizard. But now I can't even do that anymore. More so even than I was to those who'd betrayed me, I'm *useless*, and you deserve a lot better. When we're done... *if* I can keep my promise, I want you to go. Go see the world, live the life you deserve. I'll live the one I deserve."

Aurelai's black eyes narrowed to horizontal slits. "What are you talking about?"

"I'll stay here."

"Absolutely out of the question! You will do no such thing!"

Vimika's hands closed over Aurelai's, the trickle of magic now painful. "This place... a house in the middle of nowhere, completely isolated, cut off from the world... it's what I wanted before I came here. Can't you see why I would want to stay?"

"No! Your friends and family are out there. I don't know your family, but I've heard the way Seris and Delica talk to you. They want to help you, but you won't let them. Why? Do you enjoy wallowing so much?"

Vimika's eyes fell in shame.

"I won't let you, you know. They can't force you to stop hurting yourself, but I can. You will not squander your potential or your *life* in my house, Vimikathritas Malakandronon. You will rise above your pain, the same as I did. You will not give up or surrender to your past, you will work for your future, a *real* future. Do you understand? Against my will I have lived what you wish to volunteer for, and I won't let you subject yourself to it. Whether your magic returns or not, I want you with me."

Still cradling Vimika's face, Aurelai pulled her into a kiss infused with raw, naked truth. A lifetime of silence had made Aurelai's need to voice her feelings deafening, and she all but shouted them in her steadfast refusal to let Vimika pull away. She would not be allowed to retreat nor deny, she would be made to feel the truth of them as deeply as Aurelai did so she would *know*.

And she did. As fundamentally as she had ever known anything, the truth of Aurelai's feelings flooded into Vimika, saturating her being and leaving her no choice but to breathe them in and make them a part of herself. Overcome by warmth and relief, her legs went weak under the weight of it and she fell to her knees. Aurelai followed without letting go.

When Vimika managed to return the kiss, it was wet with the taste of salt. Through her tears, Aurelai held her, baptized herself in them, swallowed the hurt that poured into her, taking Vimika's burden within herself. She drank deeply of the tidal wave Vimika could do nothing to stop, even as another crashed into her coming the other way.

Vimika took Aurelai's loneliness, her betrayal. The elation of being found, of being touched, of being *seen*. The wonder that accompanied every new sensation and the buoyant, overwhelming relief of her hopes made real.

Twin rivers flowed in opposite directions but formed a single sea, and they swam in it together. The waters were warm, lit only by the stars, but all too soon it was time to come up for breath.

When they parted, Vimika looked into Aurelai's eyes, far enough to see the brightness of her potential. *Their* potential. Together.

"I know... I know that there is nothing I can say to prove I am not like the ones who hurt you. To be lied to, betrayed... I can only show you that I would never inflict that which I, too, have felt so acutely. But for that I need time. Can you give me that much, Vimika?"

Under the stars, shadowed by magelight, there was a spark within Vimika that had nothing to do with either. A flickering welled up from beneath the tears, fighting through a forest of pain, small yet, but growing by the moment. By the heartbeat.

"Yes."

Aurelai's eyes were almost impossibly expressive and utterly beautiful as they searched Vimika's own. They were open, just as much as her feelings, and all of Vimika's doubts and fears seemed small and unworthy in the face of it. Tears still streaked down her face, but she found herself smiling. Here, in this incredible place where time didn't matter, was an impossible alien girl, and deep within Vimika impossible alien feelings were rising in response.

The chains strained to hold them back.

"Yes," Vimika said again. She needed to. To make it true, to confirm it. It didn't matter why, she just needed to hear herself say, "Yes!"

"Thank you." Aurelai kissed her again.

The bindings that had been withering Vimika's heart shattered, and she gave herself over completely, allowing feelings to geyser up from deeper places within her than lust or loneliness, to arc across the bridge of magic that suddenly soared between them, sharper and more glorious than ever. Unshackled from fear, it roared in her ears, burned through her veins, guiding her hands as they threaded through Aurelai's hair, pulled her closer. Closer until there was nothing at all between them. No hesitation or misunderstanding, no tentativeness, no questions.

No doubt.

Vimika started as Aurelai grasped a handful of hair and tipped her head back. The pressure of her lips built until Vimika had no choice but to lean over backwards. Strong hands held her as they guided her downward until she was forced to sit. Still cradling her head with one hand, Aurelai slid the other up Vimika's bare leg, bringing the hem of her dress with it. Cool night air flooded in and her breath hitched, grip tightening. Only when Vimika was completely exposed did Aurelai relent and finally break the kiss.

A thin gossamer strand hung suspended between them, and they both snatched at it at the same moment, pressing their lips together again until they quickly parted in stifled laughter.

Aurelai smiled down on Vimika as she supported her with one arm, another display of her beguiling hidden strength. Vimika surrendered without question as it lay her flat on her back, filling her eyes with the night sky, with midnight sable, with shining obsidian.

Cool skin lovingly displaced cool air, and Vimika sucked in

a sharp breath. Aurelai's fingers were slow and unsure at first, but followed Vimika's every reaction, every twitch and movement until they were deftly matching her needs without a single word being spoken.

Black eyes looked down on bronze with unfettered exhilaration as Vimika writhed, neither willing to break eye contact even as Vimika clawed furrows into the dirt. Her back arched, already steaming with dew and sweat as she drove herself against Aurelai's ministrations.

Aurelai met her happily. Vimika's breaths grew shorter and closer together, her eyes increasingly hard to focus. Sweat beaded her forehead, wordless noises of encouragement streamed from her mouth and Aurelai took them, learned from them. Soon Vimika's every fiber was afire, muscles and tendons tensing against the need for release that Aurelai kept just beyond reach, slowing when Vimika's eyes were begging for speed, soft when she desperately craved hard.

Aurelai watched Vimika's face contort in exquisite agony as her legs kicked out, shoulders thudding into the ground. On the edge of mercy, her vision narrowed to nothing, lungs filling with the scent of grass and dew.

"Aurelai!" Vimika cried at the final surrender, and all that was black exploded with light.

Blinding and beautiful, the world was set ablaze with color as Vimika clutched helplessly at Aurelai, grasping for anything to anchor herself to as she was taken by something far more intense than just pleasure. The night sky was rendered shocking blue, every star as bright as the sun. Every tree, every flower, every blade of grass erupted in bright green, while Aurelai, her beautiful Aurelai, shone a pure white so bright she was illuminated from within. She was glory incarnate, too intense to look upon, but even when Vimika shut her eyes, she remained a shining beacon.

Vimika slowly spiraled back into herself from her dizzying

peak as the tension holding her taut began to wane, only for her breath to be snatched again when the first cool drop of realization spattered across her parched tongue.

The *alumita. Mana. Animata.*

Magic.

A second cry erupted from her as she threw her arms around Aurelai. Panting into her shoulder, Aurelai blazed white with magic, brighter than any wizard Vimika had ever met, and it took a moment to remember how to compensate, longer for her body to respond, occupied as it was.

It wasn't until Vimika managed several deep, steadying breaths that she could filter out the *animata* of the daughter of the most powerful wizard in history. That she was strong wasn't a surprise, but seeing for the first time just *how* strong left Vimika hanging limp from her shoulders.

All around her the world was naught but magic, the most brilliant concentration she had ever seen. It was beautiful and horrifying, and made it impossible to let Aurelai go. Weak as a kitten, Vimika needed Aurelai's strength just to draw enough breath to get her senses back into working order.

Tears of untrammeled joy and relief soaked into Aurelai's shoulder as Vimika looked out on this new world in wonder. Her head was buzzing with a symphony of positivity, but the single dissonant note of why she was surrounded by so much magic kept her clinging on for a little while longer.

They sat leaning against one another in silence until Vimika found the energy to lift her head, gazing into dark eyes that were now lit from within as they always should have been.

Parting strands of Vimika's sweat-soaked hair, Aurelai smiled a hesitant little smile. "Did I do it right?"

The kiss that followed was raw magic, a torrent that gushed between them with a force that only made them want more. Blending and binding them, tasting the way jumping into a hot spring after rolling in snow felt, intense to the point of approaching dangerous, but Vimika didn't want to stop.

Starved for so long, she gorged on Aurelai's magic, so strong she could taste it. Sharp and metallic, she drank until she was dizzy.

Aurelai jerked away, putting two fingers to her tongue as if she expected to find blood. "No?"

"Yes!" Vimika exclaimed. She snatched up Aurelai's still-wet fingers and pressed them against her own temple. "Here. It's back! My magic is back, Aurelai!"

A quick Look confirmed it, and Aurelai was left speechless, eyes searching.

"I can See you now," Vimika said, even if it hurt to do so directly. She'd gotten used to Aurelai as she was physically, but now with her magic's return, it was a bit of an ask to start Seeing her as the magnificently gifted wizard that she truly was. What would she be when she was finally free of this place?

Aurelai ran the backs of her fingers from Vimika's temple down the side of her face. She nuzzled them, intoxicated by the magic coursing within and between them. Even two fingers worth of contact sent Vimika's heart racing. How could she ever have thought about giving Aurelai up before knowing what she truly was? For all the worries about what Vimika had felt like, she had completely neglected the fact she was just as ignorant of how Aurelai should have truly felt. It was though Vimika had only known her shadow until now. Her ghost.

But she was very real, and very much alive. Vimika's skin tingled as Aurelai took her hand.

"How do I Look?"

"More beautiful than I had imagined... oh, and yes, you did *very* well." Vimika placed a chaste little kiss on Aurelai's forehead.

To Vimika's delight, Aurelai blushed.

"After all that?"

"It tickled!"

Just as Vimika had thought she'd regained control of her body, she lost it again, falling against Aurelai as they laughed together in pure, unbridled joy.

9

Outside, it was the height of winter. Inside, an entirely new spring had come, layered on top of the one Aurelai had created so long ago. But this one too was her doing, and even more than the one that kept her from freezing to death, Vimika was thankful.

Though blanketed in more snow than ever, the speartip pines that ringed their little world burned *mana* green for the first time since she'd stumbled through them, and she would steal unfiltered Looks at Aurelai to bask in the bright white of her *animata* for no other reason than she could. Then she would do it again for a lot of other reasons.

The magic that buzzed between them when they touched was heady and more intense than Vimika had ever experienced. The long drought had been followed by torrential spring floods, and vibrant green shoots were sprouting from places within her that she had long thought fallow. Aurelai *was* an excellent gardner after all, and tended these seedlings with utmost care and attention.

Likewise Vimika, as shepherd and guide for all things new, led Aurelai down paths she had never thought open to her, the friend and companion she had so long hoped for.

And more.

Something had happened the night Vimika's magic returned, but she still wasn't entirely sure what it was. Her heart felt like it was doing half as much work as it used to, and every time they touched, no matter how innocently (or not), it felt *right*. Whether it was the solidifying of the full magical connection or something even more profound, they would let time determine.

But that time could not be spent idle, as loathe as they were to untangle themselves from one another. When the high of being together morphed into a plateau, they strode across it hand-in-hand to find that it ended in the same place the old one had: the forest. Within it, their relationship could grow deeper, but no wider, forcing them back to the chill reality that lay beyond the warmth of their double spring.

Blissful though their isolation had become, it was still isolation.

Vimika, with the full return of her magic, was a *wizard* once more, and after another night spent in Aurelai's arms, she emerged from the house with a burning need to earn those precious moments, to pay back the weeks she'd borrowed and fulfill the trust that had been placed in her. They'd barely known each other when Vimika had made her promise, but now, if they were to be more than just friends, she needed to prove herself even more.

The sun was shining, and she'd just hacked apart a priceless gown to make the world's most expensive headband, leaving her feeling particularly aggressive in her drive to solve problems.

Vimika began her assessment by walking around the perimeter of the clearing over and over, passively absorbing everything she could magically to get a true sense of the place for the first time since arriving. The constantly shifting yet repeating perspective helped her get a sense of the scale of what she was standing in the center of.

Fortunately, it was just big enough to engage her need to figure it out, rather than to take a rock to her head in order to regain the blissful ignorance she'd been living in.

On an academic level, one that had spent several years at a school specifically designed to drill all aspects of magic into her so deeply she still had dreams about it, she'd known roughly what would be necessary to knock the magic out of her head after thwarting Aurelai for two centuries, but she was entirely unprepared to See it.

There *was* nothing that could have prepared her, as magic like this simply didn't exist anymore.

It wasn't *a* spell. It was dozens, interweaving and overlapping, a latticework of spiderwebs that were not only intricate, but dense as well. Having essentially soaked into the ground over the course of 200 years, they were deeply rooted into the forest and as much a part of it as the trees. Taking a shovel to the place would be the closest anyone could get to being able to scoop up magic itself. It was very clever, and allowed the illusions to to feed off the *mana* of the trees themselves almost indefinitely. The tree line was a hard border between the gentler climate spells and the twisted horror of the illusions, leaving no question as to who had made which. For all the trouble the latter had given Vimika on the way in, Seeing it now made her realize how lucky she'd been to only have temporarily lost her magical senses.

"I don't understand how I made it through there without losing my mind entirely," she said, pacing just beyond the reach of the ring of shadows the forest cast across the grass. It would be awhile before she trusted those again. "These spells have been feeding off of one another and interacting without maintenance for 200 years. They should have collapsed ages ago, but they've only reinforced each other. Where do you even start pulling something like this apart without activating it? It's like trying to take the shoes off a horse while it's kicking you in the face."

Aurelai kept even more distance from the shadows of the trees, and one eye constantly on the boughs above them, even as Oliver trailed behind, showing interest in, well, anything for the first time since Vimika's arrival.

But Vimika's concentration was for the forest. The more angles she Looked at it from, the longer she spent doing it, the deeper and more detailed the mental map she could make. It wasn't a uniform concentration, more like bubbles that grew out from each tree and weakened with distance, with unstable eddies and whorls appearing around trees that were old or dying.

Only when her 'map' was built up could she make out faint traces of white that had nothing to do with snow.

"There are threads of *animata* in there!" Vimika suddenly exclaimed with a stabbing finger. "That's... I'm really tired of saying impossible."

It meant that what she'd seen in Not-Vimika hadn't been an illusion. Ghostly white threads wound through the green of the *mana*, faint but unmistakable. And yes, impossible. Supposedly. Plant life didn't have *animata*, and could't use it, what the hells was it doing weaving through a forest of speartip pines?

"That's where I started, but I couldn't even begin to try to separate them out," Aurelai said.

"What do you think it is?" Vimika had a guess, but it was too nice a day to give voice to that kind of horror.

Aurelai had no such compunctions, and even seemed to take some satisfaction in saying, "It's Father. Not all of him, but it's him."

"The Last Breath?"

"I think so," Aurelai said. "The rest was waiting for it, like a catalyst, or a key."

Vimika continued to walk and Look, trying to find the

patterns that must exist amidst the complexity. It had been designed, and every design had to start somewhere, even if it was buried under 200 years of overgrowth. "Or a driver. He built the carriage and harnessed the horses, they just needed to be told where to go."

"Yes. Do you think there could be that much of him left?" Aurelai asked one tree in particular. "I want to know I'm not crazy for believing it."

Much like the spells themselves, it was going to be hard to undo the other damage he'd wrought before casting them. "Remember how I said I saw myself in there? I had a conversation with... her. It could just be a manifestation of my inner voice, like talking to a memory or a projection of my own inner monologue, but the more I've thought about it, the less I believe it. She felt... intelligent. The last thing she said to me was 'you aren't worthy of her.' I thought it was about what she'd just shown me, but... what if it was something else?"

"Like what?"

"You. What if it was your father trying to scare me off?"

"Then he could have shown you a slobbering fell beast, or a wall of fire, or a crazy person with a crossbow, not shouted something cryptic at you as you ran right towards me," Aurelai said with a dismissive wave.

"Or maybe he's had a change of heart. Could be why he let me through," Vimika ventured.

The resulting laughter was like shards of broken glass hurtling towards her face: sparkling and sharp, preceding a messy impact. "The only way my father could have a change of heart is if you ripped out the one he had first. Death was an *opportunity* for him, not an obstacle. Isn't that why everybody wanted his head? He was an obstinate, ruthless, dispassionate *villain*, and 200 years isn't nearly enough time to begin to change that. He probably *likes* being dead."

Hearing Aurelai spitting such invective sounded perverse. Vimika wasn't above a good verbal shellacking, but for Aurelai's hard-won self-discipline to slip for even a moment revealed not how deeply rooted her feelings were but also how far they could still reach. More than her blindingly intense *animata*, there was still far more to her than Vimika had been able to see until now.

"I'm sorry," Vimika said. She wanted to kiss Aurelai, but the pain in those dark eyes was too near the surface. The torment, the long years of isolation and what could only be called betrayal by the one person she had ever, *could* ever, trust, it wasn't a pain that could be kissed away, only lived.

The heat in Aurelai's face melted away until it was cool and serene once again. "It's not your fault. You only know him through books and legends. He's more like a character in a story than a real person to you, I imagine."

"I suppose so. What was he actually like?"

Aurelai gathered Oliver into her arms, cradling him with one hand and scratching behind his enormous ears with the other. For an immortal wild animal with bones made of gold, he seemed pleased with this turn of domestication.

"Our relationship was… complicated. I loved him. Or tried to. I believed him when he said we had to stay, that there were too many who wanted to hurt me out there. He was right about that much. Though his mind was starting to go when he died, his last words were 'I love you.' I cried for days afterwards... I didn't even leave the house for... I don't know how long. I must have spent months in suspension to avoid thinking about it. It was only when I had the energy to start using magic again that I noticed everything was off."

Aurelai glanced into the trees, but didn't seem to see them. "The forest felt strange and off-color to what it had before. Thinking it was a blight of some kind, I had a Look. In moments, I went from feeling completely bereft to absolutely livid. If he had *asked*! Told me! Consulted me in any way, I might have agreed to some sort of protection, to living behind magical walls, but he didn't. My entire life, he'd never given me a choice in anything, and he kept right on doing it! Even in death he denied me, as part of me still believed that it was too dangerous to try to leave. I lived with that fear for years. It's why I... settled. Why I set up the climate spells and started farming.

"Eventually, whether it was loneliness or insanity, I decided that whatever was out there was better than in here, but every time I tried to leave, the forest would turn me around. No matter how hard I tried to walk straight, or for how long, I would end up back here again. Days and nights I would be gone, following false stars, but always the same outcome."

She shook her head at the memory and Oliver burrowed himself more tightly into her arms. The smile Aurelai had for him was beatific, at complete odds with her story.

She continued, "Anger became despair when I couldn't untangle the magic. It fought me like it knew me. Adapted to everything I tried before I'd tried it. That's when I knew what that *animata* was out there. He actively thwarted me, Vimika. My own dead father. His last words were the only ones I'd ever wanted to hear from him, and they were a lie."

Vimika looked into the trees with a renewed, uglier type of disgust. "He never appeared to you out there?"

"No. I never saw any other evidence of consciousness beyond it fighting back when I tried to undo it."

"Huh. What about him?" Vimika asked, joining Aurelai in giving Oliver a right proper doting. "It doesn't seem to have affected him at all, even though he's pretty much made of magic. I'd've thought a field that intense would do something to him. Scare him, at least."

A long tongue curled out of a longer yawn, as if Oliver found the idea rather droll. Viewed with Sight, he was bright white, concentrated *animata* with none of the impurities that were found in normal animals and people. They had things like minerals and iron in their blood, muscle, sinew, things that were suffused with *animata*, but acted more like a sponge for it. Mechamagical creations weren't strictly speaking alive, according to the propaganda of the last few centuries, but Vimika could See the truth now. Oliver was a living, thinking being, and utterly beautiful. He should have died of old age while Aurelai's father was still alive, but his eyes were sharp, nose wet, no sign of any injury or infection having ever plagued him. He was, for all intents and purposes, perfect.

That's traitor talk, Vimika reminded herself. Perhaps she'd had her hat off for too long and forgotten just what tragedy the creation and trafficking of these creatures had wrought on her people.

But is that their *fault?*

"He doesn't fear much anymore, it would seem," Aurelai said. "I think he knows what he is. When I touch his mind, he doesn't feel like other animals. He's more... complicated. Even the thought of Borrowing him is repugnant, it would be like trying to Borrow you."

Vimika stroked Oliver under the chin and he looked up at her with soulful brown eyes. "He's certainly had a long time to think about things."

"Maybe he's been here before. Father made him, after all, perhaps he welcomed Oliver home."

"You'd never seen him before?" Vimika asked in surprise.

Aurelai shook her head. "He must have been made before... before. For one of Tarsebaum's ancestors?"

"Likely. I have no idea how you would acquire a mechamagical animal after the Purges. The penalties for harboring one are extreme. For us, at least. Maybe it's easier for a wealthy non-wizard to find a few loopholes in the back of their vault. They would be quite a prize for someone who has everything."

As always, Vimika thought. Us and Them, with different rules for each. Since the return of her magic, she'd been lulled into forgetting what actually lay in wait for them when they made good their escape. It was going to be less sightseeing and adventure than running and hiding.

In secret. Even if they managed to spirit Oliver away (there was no chance of returning him to Tarsebaum now), powerful people had a vested interest in keeping the fact he had ever existed hidden. The obvious choice was to flee Atvalia completely, but they were wizards, and wizards who *did* manage to get themselves away to safety would only guarantee the consequences fell squarely on their families. It was one reason the government turned a blind eye to big wizard families. They were collateral.

Something bumped against Vimika's side, and she looked down to see her hands shaking.

"Don't think about it, Vimika. Anger doesn't suit you."

"Nor you."

"Mm. Perhaps I was a bit optimistic. That you would walk in here and already know the answers, or immediately see something I couldn't and we'd be gone in an hour," Aurelai said with an eye on Oliver. 'We' had come to mean 'three' without need for discussion.

"To be fair, this is the first time I've been able to put any real thought into this. You're going to have to give me some time too, Sweet Beak."

Aurelai looked up, eyes sparkling. "Why did you call me that?"

"You said you liked it. I was paying attention, you know," Vimika said.

A small, slightly embarrassed smile spread across Aurelai's lips. "Is that so? What color were the birds, then?"

"Not to them."

Aurelai wetted her lips. "I think I like this charming Vimika. Some kind of spell, is it?"

Vimika took Aurelai's free hand and brought it to her lips. "Magic, yes. But not cast by me."

"Oh, you... you!" Aurelai's cheeks washed over scarlet. "You'll get what's coming to you, just you wait."

"I'd better. But not now. This," Vimika tossed a hand at the forest, "is too much to bite off at once. I can See it now, and that's enough to start. I hope. We should go back to the library. Maybe I can find some chink in this thing there."

"I've been through every book in there a hundred times, I told you," Aurelai said.

"Even the blank ones?"

"Why would I look through those? Father died before writing in them."

Vimika shrugged. "Maybe so. Or maybe that's where you missed something. I may not be as powerful as you old wizards, but we've made up for it with a fair bit of cunning along with having a vested interest in hiding magic from people."

"Fair enough," Aurelai said, setting Oliver down.

As they fell into step beside each other, Vimika reached out for Aurelai's hand, but found only a swift column of moving air where it should have been.

"*Old* wizards, you said?"

"A*ha*... ha..." Vimika wasn't the strongest swimmer, and all the rocks she tried scrabbling over to rescue herself were slippery. And cold. Then the current got faster and was that a shark? "As in... legendary. More of a... style... than age. A... way of thinking."

There was a unique, altogether new type of pressure that came with eyes that didn't blink terribly often. Or at all, as was the case at the moment.

A slender eyebrow arched over one of them.

With sharks nibbling at her toes and a horizon quickly vanishing in a decidedly waterfall-y way ahead, Vimika lunged for a low-hanging vine. "Sweet Beak?"

With a wry smile, Aurelai surrendered her hand.

The library could wait.

~

Their first attempt at a bath together went as well as could be expected in a tub built for one, resulting in the mutual conclusion that it wasn't nearly what stories made it out to be. Their next attempt would have to wait until they came to a river or a lake.

"Or a bathhouse," Vimika said as she shrugged into a robe that was decidedly not for modern wizards. Or to be worn outside. Or be seen by anyone, really. Prim and proper the old ways may have been, when it came to dressing down, they dressed *down*. But up or down, Vimika was coming to enjoy being dressed by someone else, especially when that someone smiled every time. Though Vimika still wasn't fond of the mirror, she was beginning to delight in being seen.

"A whathouse? Why would you need such a thing?" Aurelai asked, hair dripping in thick black ropes as she led them outside into the dying light of the setting sun.

"They're really nice! You build them on top of natural springs so you don't need any complicated pumps or to expend a bunch of magic to make the water hot."

Vimika hadn't been very often and only with her family, a rare treat for one made up of seven wizards.

"You go... somewhere else, to take a bath? Somewhere public?" Aurelai's face said everything about how she felt about the idea: pinched and uncomfortable.

"Trust me, after the hike it takes to reach most of them, you're glad for a long soak in mineral water that leaves you pink when you get out."

Aurelai's dressing gown was thicker but slightly worn from having seen actual use in the last two centuries. Modest compared to the one Vimika wore, it was designed to be seen by servants in. Aurelai tugged her belt tighter. "With other people."

"They give you a towel. At any rate, they're expensive and hard to get to. Hold still."

Vimika muttered a few non-words and ran her hands down the long cascade of Aurelai's hair. By the time they reached the end, there wasn't a single drop of water left, leaving it to hang once more as a single silky curtain.

"Thank you," Aurelai said, gathering a handful and looping it around her waist like she was checking her tail for twigs or insects. Satisfied, she set about returning the favor for Vimika.

"No, wait!" But Vimika's, so used to being bound, was overzealous in enjoying its freedom and exploded outward as Aurelai's hands flew down Vimika's back in a single, swift arc. In the the time it took to blink, her ears vanished without a trace.

"You see why I'm so jealous of yours?" Vimika asked as she felt out the size of the dark brown cloud now enveloping her head.

Though Aurelai had gotten better at policing her features, a crime spree was now running rampant across her face. "Oh! Oh... dear. How did *that* happen?"

"You dried it too quickly." Something tugged at the corner of Vimika's lips. "I suspect on purpose."

"*Do* you now? How unfortunate. I guess that means you'll have to jump back in the bath?" Aurelai said, the gleam in her eye taking on a somewhat lecherous hue.

"No. I look ridiculous, and your punishment is being the one who has to see it," Vimika said with a satisfied smile and an indignant crossing of the arms. "So there."

The law returned to Aurelai's face. The sentence was to flip her smile upside down and for her eyebrows to fight to the death.   "What? No... that's not what was supposed to happen!"

"Sorry, I don't make the rules."

"What rules? Where? Where are these rules written? Tell me, Vimika," Aurelai demanded with endearing sincerity.

"Oh, you don't know? That's too bad. Because they say that now I can torture you as much as I want. That's what happens to naughty wizards who abuse their power. Sorry."

"They do not," Aurelai said. Her eyes flicked off to one side.

"They do. Page seven, paragraph four, subsection b: 'A female wizard's hair is a gigantic pain in the arse and isn't to be trifled with without said wizard's permission. Infractions shall be emended at the plaintiff's discretion.'"

"You're making that up."

"'However, exceptions can be made, and the record of the offender expunged if she gives Vimika a kiss and says she's sorry.' See? All there. Straightforward as can be."

Aurelai crossed her arms. "What if she's not sorry?"

"Then I'm going to go play with Oliver. *He* likes me. I think. Oliver!"

Magelight swelled from Vimika's fingertips, but not one of ethereal fire, but liquid. When it reached just the right size, she let it drip onto the grass, where it bounced, a glowing yellow blob.

Oliver came trotting up, espying the globule immediately.

Before he could decide what to do with this turn of events, Vimika's foot shot out and sent it skittering across the grass. "Go get it!"

White lightning raced out to follow, catching up to it in a flash. When Oliver leapt atop his prize, it shattered into four smaller copies, squirting out in as many directions. He stood puzzled for only a moment before deciding which of his prey to go after, which he did with gusto.

"He will literally never get tired, you know," Aurelai said. What was now eight lights danced in her eyes as they flicked to Vimika's hair. She bit back a smile.

"That thought occurred to me round about when my foot connected. Thankfully I have you here to spell me, don't I?" Vimika teased.

"I don't know any stamina spells. I could have a look, but-"

"What? No. Spell... as in 'take over' for me. Not... magic spell."

As Aurelai watched Oliver bat two magelights into one another, sending them careening off in opposite directions, she looped an arm through Vimika's. "You know, there are times I wonder how we can communicate at all. Language has changed more than I would have thought in 200 years. I have books older than that, but I can read them without issue."

Vimika patted the back of Aurelai's hand, letting their magic swirl and combine before speaking. "People talk differently than they write. I imagine Delica was even harder to understand through a cat's ears."

"It was... difficult, I admit," Aurelai said.

"There's no shame in that, you know. I live below her, but it took me a good few weeks to figure out what she was saying. Every time I walked into the Double C, I would just smile and nod. She was always so nice! I thought she fancied me for a little while. That's how I met Seris. She, ah, rescued me from myself. Had quite the egg on my face." Vimika saw the question forming. "Means I was embarrassed. No, I don't know why."

"Oh," Aurelai said with a little pout.

One Vimika had to keep from trying to chew off.

Now that she was whole again, not only did the world

seem brighter magically, it did in many other ways as well, and the brightest beacon of them all was Aurelai. With the blinders that had been Vimika's anxieties about her usefulness removed, she could see Aurelai how she deserved to be seen.

Oliver came trotting back, and Aurelai formed her own magelight globule, tossing it away for him to go harrying after.

Playing fetch with, well, not a dog exactly, but a short fuzzy companion with a black nose and big ears, was one of life's simple joys, one Aurelai hadn't discovered until her third century. But in so doing, she was *alive* as never before. There was a light within her that had nothing to do with *animata* and everything to do with her happiness.

Vimika made her happy.

When had that happened?

The return of Vimika's magic had solidified something nebulous between them, allowing them to get on with... whatever it was they had been doing over the last... however long it had been.

Living, she realized.

That was what they were doing. It didn't matter how long they'd been doing it. Poring over books, helping each other prepare meals, tending the garden, playing with Oliver. Talking, holding hands, spending their days *and* nights together... a lot more was happening than Vimika had been able to see, or had wanted to.

Vimika watched Aurelai be completely normal in wonder. Not only had she not destroyed herself in madness or grief in her time alone, she'd grown from the experience. She was a better person for it! That kind of ability to overcome adversity made her even more formidable than Vimika had thought her to be, and that much harder to not be taken by.

Aurelai was beautiful, kind, intelligent, and stronger than

virtually anyone Vimika had ever met— there was nothing she could want in someone more.

Vimika didn't believe in love at first sight, that was just lust that had been gussied up so you could tell your grandchildren about it, and so it had proven. But now, after weeks together, they were well beyond firsts and into regular life. Alarms rang in Vimika's mind at the thought, even as a thousand holes opened in her heart, waiting to be filled by the woman before her. Holes that had been opened before, every time more painfully for having to rip apart the scars that had formed the last time they'd closed.

They had met as prisoners of separate jailers, and had promised to help free one another. For Vimika to escape the one she'd built for herself, she had to trust Aurelai. To the surprise of the self-assessment brought on by something that walked and talked an awful lot like contentment, Vimika did.

Yes, Aurelai was odd, but who wasn't, really? There were gaps in her knowledge, but Vimika was coming to quite enjoy being a teacher, no matter the subject. The intermingling of their magic was potent to near inebriating (after long enough contact, she would say that it *was*), and they had settled into effortless rapport with so little effort Vimika hadn't even noticed it happening.

"Vimika," Aurelai called.

A response took several blinks to formulate. "Yes?"

"Is there something wrong with me?"

More blinks. "What? No... of course not. Why?"

"It's just that you've been staring at me for a while now."

"I... do you mind?"

Aurelai flushed. "I can't say that I do. Though Oliver might have some feelings on the matter."

At Vimika's feet sat a gilded fennec, eyes wide with anticipation.

"I think yours taste better," Aurelai said.

Vimika let another magelight globule distend from her fingers, but this one she didn't let fall, swinging it to and fro on a glowing thread of raw magic. Oliver leapt at it, swiping and biting, but he was limited by physics, while his object of desire was controlled by willpower alone.

"He's never going to leave us alone after this," Vimika said through a broad grin.

Aurelai knelt down, swatting at Oliver's tail in idle affection. "He's been good about it so far. He deserves to have his fun, too."

Vimika took her eyes off Oliver for a moment, and the globule exploded, pinging off in seven directions. He bounded off after one, bowling over Aurelai and sending her tumbling onto her back.

"Are you all right?" Vimika asked as she extended a hand.

"Perfectly," Aurelai managed through her laughter. She took Vimika's hand. "Come down here and join me, would you?"

Vimika settled onto the grass, chill against her back through the thin fabric. They stared up at the sky together, the high clouds afire with scarlet and orange, watching in silence as they were slowly extinguished by the eternity beyond.

"Does the sky look different outside?" Aurelai asked.

Vimika weaved their fingers together.

"No. Everything is where is should be."

Then the wind began to pick up, and the voice of the forest swelled alongside it, whispering and conspiring with the newborn twilight.

Everything except them.

The first stars began to appear. The Wolf's Eye. The Dagger of Kolom. The Wanderer.

There was still much work left to be done before Aurelai could see the rest.

10

In all her time at school, Vimika had only ever been punished for falling asleep at her books. Now, for the first time, after weeks of effort, she had been rewarded.

They had spoken to her.

There was magic in them all right, hidden in plain sight, because who would think to listen to a book? That was only supposed to be for *old* objects that absorbed magic naturally over time spans far longer than the life of the caster. To do it on purpose was as clever as Azrabaleth Kalinostrafal's reputation made him out to be.

Too clever.

"Boiled piss!"

The sound of footsteps swishing on the bare walls preceded Aurelai coming speeding down the passage.

Vimika couldn't bear to turn around. She knew the look on her own face, she didn't want Aurelai to see it. Or worse, share it.

"You've been at this for hours. Come to bed," Aurelai said as she approached. Vimika leaned into Aurelai's arms as they snaked over her shoulders. Now that they were used to such contact, the need for it was nearly akin to pain after any time apart, but the garden had needed tending, the books listening.

At least one of them had been productive.

"I can't now. I have to start all over," Vimika said.

The pause that followed was so pregnant it had an entire litter when it was over. It was birthed from Vimika's mouth in a long sigh. "These blank books have the basis for the illusions in them."

"But that's wonderful!" Aurelai exclaimed.

"It would be if I'd gotten here... I don't know, a century ago, perhaps?" Vimika's finger thudded down on the open page so hard it left a dent. "This is how it started. It's all here. But that shit out there is nothing like this. It wasn't just you. The magic itself *evolved*.   There's all kinds of diagrams and hypotheses in here, I can see how he started, the underlying structure. But he kept working on it *after he died*!" Vimika swiped the book off the desk and it crashed to the ground with a satisfyingly awkward sound.

"You're swearing too much, dear heart. You're tired."

They had been so close. So *close*, and he had thwarted them *again*. Vimika settled her hand over Aurelai's, giving it a gentle squeeze completely at odds with how she felt. "If I may speak frankly with you?"

"You don't need to ask me that."

"I know, but I felt like I needed to preface it: your father was a right bastard," Vimika said.

Soft laughter blossomed in her ear. "I've called him much worse."

"Seemed only polite to ask."

Surrounded by books that could very well add up to being one of the greatest libraries of magic in Atvalia, Vimika had no idea what to do next. The answer should have been here, and the fact that that was *partly* true made it all the more frustrating. It's as though he was teasing them. The magic needed to be written down, it was too complicated to keep in your head, even for him, and he'd known someone would come looking (or listening) eventually.

He'd known all along, and going by the look and feel of it, he'd *planned* to keep working after he was gone. Wizards believed in an afterlife, but to just go ahead and forge your own was completely pants-on-head, upside-down insane, and Azrabaleth Kalinostrafal had pulled it off. He'd died and gone to prison, and made himself the warden.

Vimika craned to look at its only prisoner. For now. "I'm sorry."

"Don't be." Aurelai kissed her gently on the cheek. "It's just one more way that won't work. That leaves fewer to try."

There was looking on the bright side, then there was blinding yourself so you couldn't see reality.

Yet Aurelai was still here, still trying. "You're going to have to teach me how you do that."

"Live without a choice and practice. There. Now, you've gotten your swears out, what are we going to do next? I've already tried everything I can think of. Earn your room and board, wizard." Aurelai's hands retreated to clamp down on Vimika's shoulders.

"What are you- Oh!" Vimika piped as Aurelai began to rub with rough, insistent movements. Vimika held her tongue. She was going to need rough and insistent to get the blood flowing through her brain again, even if she did bruise afterward. She winced and hissed as Aurelai mauled her in ways Vimika's hands would have immediately cramped up attempting, but melted in gratitude all the same.

The good news was that it worked, her mind was working again.

The bad news was the conclusion it drew.

"If we can't untangle it, we may have to destroy it. What about the *alumita*?" she asked.

"I'm going to stop if you're just going to joke," Aurelai

replied.

"I'm not. It's there, isn't it?" Vimika pointed up.

"Yes, and I was never desperate enough to try it. I thought about it, but I knew there would always be another way if I was patient enough. I wasn't about to kill myself out of spite. He would have won," Aurelai said.

"He's your father! Whatever else he may be, I don't think he would have wanted that. Besides, it doesn't *have* to be a death sentence."

"Has there been some breakthrough in *alumita* harnessing in the last 200 years? Is that why our people were decimated and live like second-class citizens? Because if you've managed to figure out how to safely wield the fundamental creation energies of the universe, I can't imagine you would let that stand for very long before you started vaporizing cities."

As Aurelai spoke, Vimika found herself being ground into her chair, squashed until her face almost reached the desk. She squirted out sideways, twisting from Aurelai's grip to stare at her with a grimace she didn't try to suppress.

"That hurts!"

Aurelai stood with her hands on the back of the chair staring down at them. "I'm sorry."

Vimika rolled her shoulders this way and that, and the pain began to ebb. "I didn't think it would be such a sensitive topic."

"I was tempted, you know." Aurelai's gaze was hollow and distant. "To just... end it to spite him. Undo *everything* at once so we could scream at each other about it for the rest of time as wraiths. But I knew I could bear this... purgatory longer if I worked at it. And I have. You are my best hope, Vimika. Anyone else would see me imprisoned or dead. I am to them as Oliver was to you. A means to an end. Together I... *we* have a chance. I've never wanted to live more than since I met you,

I can't risk the *alumita*."

"I could. The magic field is dense enough, maybe it could even out the flow of discharge, lessen the chaos-"

"No, Vimika! That's not why I brought you here, and I won't ask that kind of risk for my sake. No. There's *always* another way."

"Finding it will take time."

There was no mirth in Aurelai's smile. "We have a lot of that here, it would seem. And if there is one thing I have gotten very good at, it's waiting. When you first came here, I had hoped we could be gone quickly. But now... I don't mind a little more time together before I have to share you with the world."

Heat crawled up the back of Vimika's neck and found her ears. "That's very sweet. I want that too, but the world out there isn't going to stop for us. It's almost spring, and it's hard to be presumed snowed in somewhere when there's no snow. If I'm not back by the time it's gone, people will start asking questions, if they haven't already. By now, Malivia probably thinks I ran off with the money. If she's mad enough, maybe even sent her house wizard after me to get it back. And since we don't know why I made it through the illusions, we can't say that they won't be able to do it, too. If what you say is true, 'the world' may already be on its way. We have to do this ourselves, and quickly."

"I will have to trust you on outside matters," Aurelai said, eyes downcast. She stared down at her hands still in the claw-like shape they'd gripped Vimika's shoulders in.

"What is it?"

"I didn't anticipate any of this. I don't... *know* anything. I never even considered that she would follow you, or even that she would pay you, let alone what I assume is a large amount of money?"

Vimika nodded.

"I didn't even know that." Aurelai sank into the chair. "I didn't think beyond my own desire to escape."

Unable to stand the distance between them anymore, Vimika returned to Aurelai and knelt beside her. "It's understandable, though."

"A lifetime of waiting and it could all come unraveled because I couldn't anymore," Aurelai said in a voice quivering against her self-discipline.

Vimika placed a finger under Aurelai's chin, gently raising her eyes. "That's the nature of risk."

"Yes. But now everything feels more... real," Aurelai said. "I lived in my own head for so long, it became difficult to see possibilities beyond the ones I wanted. Things had gone wrong for me so often, I thought I only needed an outside perspective to fix everything. I didn't care about consequences anymore. Maybe I should have."

Vimika shook her head. "Aurelai, this isn't over. Not even close."

"I want to believe that. But I have no conception of time. At least, not the way you do. 'Soon' doesn't mean anything to me. By sunset? By the time true spring comes? Can I afford to while away any more time in your arms?" Aurelai reached for Vimika's hand, and she gave it without question.

Magic tingled, their connection strong and steady. Or ironclad, given that Vimika tasted metal. Humans may have used the word 'chemistry' to describe the nature of their relationships, but for wizards it was more alchemy.

Vimika curled her fingers through Aurelai's, locking them together. Tendrils of raw magic flowed through their joined palms, and they sighed simultaneously at the rush of the connection. "When I was lost in doubt, you rescued me. Now it's my turn. We want the same things, and face the same obstacles. But we *will* get over them. It's going to be even harder than we already thought, and painful, but neither of us is alone. One of us has already freed the other from her prison, that only leaves one to go, right?"

Black eyes took on an extra layer of shine in the flickering magelight. "It does."

"I will get you out of here, I promise. I promised when I arrived and I am promising again. No matter what happens or how, you will be free, Aurelai. I swear on my life."

The magic streaming between them took on a new intensity, but it was nothing like pain. In concentrated, pulsing waves, Vimika *felt* Aurelai respond even before she moved.

When she did, it was with the same grace she showed when she danced and made love as she flowed out of the chair to kneel eye level with Vimika. "I accept. But I am no passive princess waiting in a tower. My prince has come, and I will help her however I can."

"You know the *Jewel in the Tower*?"

"There's more than just magic books in here. Literature, poetry, fairy tales. You'd be surprised what I know."

"Then you should know that princes don't get kissed until afterward. I haven't done anything yet," Vimika said.

"Yet."

When their lips met, every hair on Vimika's body shot up at once, along with her heart rate. Veins swelled with Aurelai's passion and magic, and Vimika's mind began to race as though they were thinking as one, a thousand thoughts and images swirling around that were part memory, part imagination.

No passive princess...

Vimika jerked away with a wet smack to see Aurelai's eyes as wide open as her own.

"You found me through Borrowed eyes! How did you do that? How did you thread a magical field of that intensity in a way stable enough to maintain connection to the animals?"

Vimika asked breathlessly, as though the words would evaporate if she didn't spit them out first.

"Carefully..." Aurelai looked about, needing to gather thoughts that were whizzing around as fast as Vimika's. "It... it took awhile before I worked out I could use them as a kind of anchor. Father's spells don't work on animals, so they could pass through it, bringing me with them. I learned to thread the field without interacting with it directly, so it didn't activate. I always did it from the house to keep my body safe, and so I would know where I left it."

Vimika nodded. She could almost see it as Aurelai said it. "And Oliver? You Called him, didn't you?"

"Yes, but I didn't know it would work. I had no idea it was Father who had made him until he got here."

"But it *did* work. How did you get the Call out?"

Thoughts, images, ideas, all catapulting about Vimika's mind, so close to coming together...

"Through Borrowing. I sort of... projected it outward from one of my Familiars."

They slowed down to make sure they caught that last part.

"You sent a Call *through another* animal?"

"Is that bad?"

"It's impossible! Wait, did it explode?"

"Of course not!"

"Then it's impossible! Or should be. How did you to do that?" Vimika asked with the nervous energy that came with knowing she was on the verge of something.

"I just... did it. I was desperate."

"But if you can get a Call out, and just need an anchor to lock onto..."

Everything snapped into place at once, and Vimika smacked her forehead hard enough to hurt her ears more than her hand. "Mother's tits, of course! We don't have to undo any of this! I flew in, we can just fly out! We can relay

194

the Summon through a hawk or something! It's sitting out in the snow, waiting for me! So stupid! Piss and hellfire, I could kiss you!"

"Heaven forfend."

Vimika bolted forward, knocking Aurelai onto her back to dole out her just reward.

When they separated, Aurelai was grinning like Vimika had sucked the sense out of her head.

Maybe she had, she was feeling pretty clever at the moment.

"Let's go upstairs and try!" Vimika bounded towards the door, yanking Aurelai by the hand. But if there was another thing Aurelai had had ample practice at, it was staying in one place, and Vimika jerked to a halt at the end of Aurelai's fingers.

"It's dark by now and you're exhausted. It can wait another night," Aurelai said.

Vimika's grip tightened, even as her eyes softened. "But what about time? You said we can't while. This is whiling."

"Yes, but the spells adapt, remember," Aurelai said. "If we're going to do it right the first time, we should have an actual strategy. Contingencies. 'A hawk or something' isn't going to get us very far if we only get once chance."

Vimika chewed her lower lip. "Conceded. It's your decision."

"Thank you." Aurelai let herself be helped to her feet. "Let's talk about this over dinner, shall we?"

"Yes. But." An impish grin pulled at Vimika's lip. "If we're sparing ourselves, when we go to bed, it's to *sleep*."

"I- wh... well, I didn't..." Aurelai's cheeks reddened to the point they looked like they were trying to boil themselves off of her face.

"You did. And so do I."

Aurelai bit her lower lip in such a way Vimika felt *things* happen within her, and her ruse collapsed.

"Now?" Aurelai asked.

"If this is our last night here, well, I'm sure there's somewhere I haven't had you yet."

"The kitchen and the laboratory," Aurelai said a hair too quickly.

"Kitchen it is, then. Hmm..." Vimika gave Aurelai a mock assessment up and down. "As an aperitif? I bet you pair well with melon juice."

"Vimika!" Aurelai's eyes widened with scandal only to immediately hood with intrigue. "Too runny. I do have some preserves I was saving, however."

~

With a (mostly) full night's sleep and a hearty breakfast in her, Vimika craned her neck to the sky and gave it a good Look. Just as she'd hoped, the magic field above them wasn't nearly as strong as it was straight outward. It was there, no doubt, but it almost felt like an afterthought compared to the rest. If there was any *animata* present Vimika couldn't See it, and that gave them a chance to outwit it.

At least, that was the plan.

"How come you never tried to fly out yourself?" she asked.

"I could never get the enchantments to stick. My toes barely got off the ground before I ended up on my face."

"Hmm. Now that I think about it, I bet those flying instructions in your books are crap on purpose. If the forest had to work going both ways as well as tap into memory and whatnot, he could save energy by making the sky more like a net." Vimika said, working it out as she took in what she Saw. "Without an instructor to tell you what you were doing wrong, you would have never made it out."

"But you can?" Aurelai asked, turning her face to the sky.

The forest at least looked like a wall full of shadows, but above them was nothing but daylight. Now that they were this close to freedom, Vimika didn't know which was more intimidating.

"Flying's come a long way in the last few centuries, hopefully it's something he can't have anticipated. But before we try, there's something we didn't talk about last night: you need to decide what to do with everything here. Your father's books are priceless, the magic used in this place could take years to unrav-"

"Burn it."

Two syllables of solid ice thudded into the ground and dared anyone who'd heard to touch them.

Vimika had no choice. "Are you sure? Think about it for more than a second."

"I've been thinking about it for two hundred years. All of it. To the ground. If my father is as terrible to people out there as you say he is, why should any of his work survive? They would wonder where it came from. No, it will only follow me for the rest of my life. I don't even know how I can explain *my* existence to other wizards, let alone that kind of work suddenly appearing centuries after Father's death."

"You won't have to explain where you came from to any wizards," Vimika said softly.

"Of course I will. They can See me."

Vimika gathered Aurelai's hands along with her attention. "Then we'll find a way to leave Atvalia. Go somewhere it doesn't matter. Or where we can be alone if it does."

"But you have a life to go back to. People who will miss you. Your family will be in danger!"

"I promised you I would show you the world, Aurelai. I intend to keep that promise. We'll find a way," Vimika said. She had no idea how, but there were a thousand steps to take before she had to figure it out.

Aurelai's features were still a moment before she spoke. "Do you mean that? Truly?"

Vimika met her eyes. Magic arced between them, but not near quickly enough to catch the feelings that raced out ahead of it.

"Yes," she said, resonant with the most confidence she'd ever heard come from her own mouth.

Aurelai must have heard it, too. "Where will we go?"

"I don't know. All that matters is that we do. Together. And if you feel strongly enough about destroying the house, I won't stop you. It's yours to do with as you please. All I want is what's best for you, and for you to be happy. But... once you do, you can't undo it."

"I made my choice a long time ago. The only reason I never did was because it was my only shelter."

"Do you want to bring *any*thing? For a museum, at least?" Vimika asked with a raised eyebrow.

"No. Anything I take could tie me to Father and his poison. I want a clean break. When this is over, I want it to well and truly *end*. I'll only take what I can wear, and only until I can find something else. You have extra clothes, don't you?"

Vimika glanced down. "I may have something lying around. Nothing compared to what you're used to, though."

"That will be the least I have to adjust to," Aurelai said. "I could do worse than looking and smelling like you."

"I told you I live under a tavern, right?"

"You could live next to a tannery for all I care."

"Thankfully, things aren't that bad." Vimika tugged her hat down more snugly and made doubly sure her robe was cinched closed. Wearing her old clothes would keep her hair out of her face and eliminate at least one question when they were back in the real world. There would be more than enough of those waiting as it was.

Then came what they had been waiting for.

Overhead, silhouetted against the clear blue sky was a black shape wheeling on currents of air.

A reaper hawk.

"All right, well, let's see if this works. It's to the north... somewhere. I cast Weight on it, so it should be easy to find. If we're lucky, it'll be the only mark in the snow for miles."

"What did you enchant, anyway? It's not a broom, is it?" Aurelai asked as she sat down in the grass.

"You'll see," Vimika said as she gathered Aurelai into her arms to stabilize her body while her mind was elsewhere. Internalizing such a thing was also on the list of topics they should have talked about last night, but then Aurelai had brought out *peach* preserves, and, well... they hadn't.

"I don't actually know what my body does while I'm Borrowing, so if I elbow you because I'm trying to flap wings I don't have, I'd like to apologize now."

Vimika firmed up her grip, and swallowed back the peaches that wanted to make a second pass at her tongue. "Good to know."

"Wish me luck."

With a kiss on the temple, Vimika did just that. "Let's get out of here."

The world lurched as Aurelai's magic surged, launching her consciousness northward.

Closing her eyes, Vimika reached out with her own, extending her awareness to tap into the thread of Aurelai that was already snaking its way through the illusion matrix with astonishing speed born from years of practice.

Aurelai weaved through the trees like a greased serpent. The spells were stronger closer to their energy source, so she was essentially threading her way through a series of circles, staying as far away from the centers as possible. It was an astonishing feat of magic all by itself, feeling more like flying than flying did. There was no weight shifting or changes in inertia, just raw momentum propelling her forward in one continuous motion.

Before Vimika knew it Aurelai's probe rocketed out the other side, free and clear of the tree line and into the head of the reaper hawk, whose thoughts registered surprise a moment before they were shoved to the back of its mind.

Wind. Wings. Vision sharper than Vimika had imagined possible seemed to take in the whole world as it stretched unfathomably far in every direction.

It had been gliding east, but was persuaded to wheel around west again, towards a nondescript mound in the snow. Normally, that would never draw the keen eyes of a hawk, since normally, the hawk was in control of them and would rather search for tasty things that go *squeak* when their lungs are perforated by four-inch talons.

Luckily it was enough, and through the combination of Aurelai and the hawk, Vimika could sense her own pool of magic just ahead. With breathless excitement (and apology to the hawk), she speared the waiting door with her consciousness and hauled with everything she had.

The Weight spell shattered and the door exploded from the snow, leaping straight into the air. Chunks of white streamed away and thumped into the unmarred field, leaving a trail of bumpy craters as it flew up and over the trees and the magic they harbored.

Without being atop it, Vimika didn't feel like a bird, or anything else that was free of the bonds of gravity. More like she was flying half of a two-handed kite, with Aurelai holding the other string and an enormous, rather confused raptor in between.

When the door was directly overhead, Aurelai retreated back to the hawk, leaving Vimika in sole control as their way out plunged downward.

To cut straight through what felt like molasses made of bad

intentions was exhilarating, but revealing of just how little had been standing between Aurelai and freedom. The magic field overhead barely went past the tops of the trees, meaning she'd been less than a hundred feet from the outside world her entire life.

"Here it comes," Vimika announced as Aurelai shifted with her return to her body.

The door arrowed straight towards them so fast it clipped the top of a tree, snow bursting into fog and curling into the vortex the door's flight left behind. It stopped without slowing down, coming to rest waist-high above the ground with the same stability it would have if Vimika had set it on a table.

"It's a door!" Aurelai exclaimed as she paced around it, looking for the joke. When one failed to appear, she looked at Vimika with beseeching eyes. "You enchanted a *door*? Why?"

Gathering her robes about her, Vimika hopped up into her normal traveling position. For something that had been purely utilitarian for so long, it felt like she'd mounted a throne she'd thought lost to a usurper after a long civil war. Or maybe that was just a wizard's acute sense of history and the fragility of taking things for granted.

"Why not?" Vimika asked, hooking one ankle behind the other and kicking the air. Her door was the closest thing she had to a security blanket anymore, even if that thought hadn't occurred to her until the moment someone questioned it.

"This is only half of it!"

Vimika glanced backwards. "And? It was free and no one would ever think to steal it," she said a hair defensively. She extended her hand. "Come on."

"What about the house?"

"Let's make sure we can get out of here before we torch our only shelter if this all goes pear-shaped," Vimika said as she tucked her robes securely under her legs.

"What's a pear?"

"A kind of fruit. Like an apple, but with hips. Sort of. I'm not crazy, don't look at me like that."

"And an apple with hips… means a plan goes bad?"

"It… yes. Idioms have gotten weird since your books were written," Vimika said, helping Aurelai up. "Bind or sit on your dress, unless you want to wear it on your face."

The moment Aurelai settled her weight onto the door, it tipped sideways, and Vimika dumped a panicked surge of magic to right it, flinging Aurelai into her hard enough to nearly knock Vimika off.

"What happened?" Aurelai asked, clutching her chest in surprise.

"I must've forgot to compensate for the weight shift. I've never had a passenger before," Vimika said. But it should have been automatic. The intrinsic balance was one of the reasons it took so long to enchant objects for flight use. Then again, between the restrained chaos of Azrabaleth's magic and Vimika's having been scrambled for who-knows how long, she was lucky to have not catapulted them both into the trees.

Hovering steadily now, however, Vimika goosed the door upwards a few inches, eliciting a squeak of surprise from Aurelai, who threw her arm through Vimika's, pulling them tightly together.

"It's all right, I know what I'm doing," Vimika said. She wanted to sound reassuring, but now that Aurelai's life was in her hands, she suddenly doubted every second it had taken to make her door flyable. When she'd made it, it was only for herself, someone she didn't care for very much at the time. Now?

They were still close enough to the ground Aurelai could simply slide off onto her feet, yet she peered down as though she would have a long while to contemplate what would happen before she landed. "Don't let me fall."

"I won't. Are you afraid of heights?"

"I don't know." Aurelai's neck bulged as she swallowed what looked like an invisible tangerine.

"Then keep hold of me and close your eyes. We're going to have to do this fast, so your stomach is going to feel like its trying to find your feet. That's normal."

"I would disagree."

Vimika threaded her finger's through Aurelai's, gripping them tightly. "It's all right. I won't let anything happen to you. Are you ready?"

Aurelai screwed her eyes shut, her knuckles going as white as the mountaintops awaiting them beyond the trees. "Yes."

"All right." Vimika gathered her magics about her for a single, hard push that would rocket them straight up, and hopefully through the magic field before it knew they were there. She would worry about sideways after that.

With a single, sharp release and a barked mental command, Vimika's stomach indeed sought her feet, her hat pressing harder onto her head as they shot up, the ground racing away at terrific speed. Her entire body trilled with elation as the wind whipped at her hair, the cold bite on her cheeks as they reached the height of the trees in a heartbeat.

Then it all went wrong.

The door suddenly pitched over to the right, and Aurelai screamed as she was jolted and began sliding away. Her hand snapped out to snatch Vimika's arm just in time to keep from spilling off.

"Aurelai!" Vimika cried, recklessly pouring magic into the door to right it, but she could tell instantly that it wasn't the door.

The higher they got, the more Aurelai seemed to weigh. The magical net holding her in was not only working, it was getting stronger!

Pain lanced Vimika's arm, and there was the tearing of fabric, even as she tried to keep the door between them and the ground. But no matter how much magic she used, Vimika couldn't get the door to budge. She simply couldn't generate enough power to tear Aurelai through the net.

"Vimika!" Aurelai cried as she threw another hand over Vimika's arm, her legs now dangling straight underneath her as she kicked at thin air as though trying to fend off what had grasped her. Raw, unshaped magic erupted from her in a torrent, so fast Vimika barely had time to channel it into the door. But even as it began vibrating from the amount of magic she was pouring into it, Aurelai was being held down.

Blinded by tears, Vimika couldn't see the terror she knew was twisting Aurelai's features as badly as it was her own. "I won't let go of you!"

The pain in her arm was excruciating, clamped in the vice of Aurleai's hands while being torn away from her body at the same time. But if Azrabaleth wanted his daughter that badly, he would have to take Vimika's arm, too.

A brave thought, but the scream tore from her throat all the same. A scream of not only pain, but frustration. She could feel the emptiness of the sky only yards away, but no matter how much willpower she exerted or how much of their combined magic spilled out of them, there was no progress to be had.

"Stop, Vimika! We'll find another way!" Aurelai shouted.

"No! We're too close!"

"If you don't, we'll crash!"

"*He can't have you!*" Vimika roared, and threw everything she had into a final push, magic erupting from her like a dying star.

In an instant, the weight was gone, and so was the pain.

~

The world Vimika awoke to was strewn with stars. But not those of night, or the ephemeral ones of snow, but ones that only she could see, swirling and dancing with every movement of her eyes. Everything beyond them refused to focus, in a dreamlike haze of pain and discombobulation.

The only thing she knew for certain was that she had found the ground.

Everything hurt and she tasted blood. Her probing tongue discovered a loosened tooth, and she went completely still so that it would heal straight.

"Aurelai?" she croaked once she was satisfied it had. "Aurelai!"

"I'm here," was the response from not terribly far away. It wasn't a voice elated to find that it was still alive enough to speak. Instead it was heavy with dejection. Of resignation.

No, Vimika thought. A clear, piercing thought that cut through the haze and dispelled the stars enough for her to orient herself. With a grunt of effort, she rolled onto her side to face Aurelai's direction.

She was there, but not as much as should have been. Only her nose and a spiky cloud of hair were visible above the ground.

Vimika blinked several times, but it still failed to make sense until she pushed herself up high enough to see that Aurelai had landed so hard she'd made a crater. Dark, damp dirt sprayed out all around her like a brown spiderweb.

"Aurelai?" Vimika's nails gouged strips out of the earth as she began to drag herself closer. If Aurelai had landed that hard… "Are you all right!?"

"No. I'll live."

In that crater there should have been a broken body, limbs askew and awash with blood. But Aurelai's limbs were as they should be, not a finger out of joint, and there wasn't a drop of blood to be seen.

Only the glint of gold.

11

Aurelai's beautiful black eyes were staring straight up, the light shining in them dimmed by the fact that the right one was now ringed in sparkling metal. A gash had opened up from temple to jaw on that side, revealing that those perfectly-sculpted cheekbones had, in fact, been sculpted. The skin on her right arm had split open as though it had burst from the inside, leaving a ragged tear behind. But beneath it was no muscle, no fat, sinew nor tendon, only bones of bright, shining gold.

Panic, terror, and dumb, animal incomprehension seized Vimika like a bear, choking the breath from her and pressing her into the dirt so hard she couldn't take another.

"Wh... what?" was all she could get out. She knew what she was seeing, there was nothing else it could be, and her gorge rose in response.

"Vimika..." Aurelai said, her voice as equally close to tears as her face.

Her beautiful, flawless, *false* face.

"You... no. No, this is an illusion! It has to be!" Vimika said, her head whirling to every part of the forest. "You said they didn't come in here! You can't... be!"

Vimika spilled onto her backside in scrambling denial,

pushing away from the crater with her heels. She plowed a track of retreat towards the trees, preferring whatever may lay be lying in wait within them to whatever was laying before her. At least if she made it, she might be allowed to see something else.

Or maybe she already had. "I never woke up, this is still the forest!" she said, shaking her head so violently stars exploded across her vision again. Breath was coming so fast it hurt, but she still felt like she was going to pass out. The world was swimming as it faded in and out, and she had to swallow her gorge back down every few breaths to keep from being sick. "You're impossible."

A hand emerged to grip the rim of the crater.

"No! Stay down there!" Vimika shouted.

A dark cloud, a pair of empty voids, polished, gleaming gold. "Please. It hurts..."

There was pain in that voice, so much so that an answering one tore across Vimika's heart. That voice should never feel pain, she thought. Something within her screamed a primal rejection of anything that could make it come to be so.

Her Aurelai was in pain, but the thing clambering out of the ground was... what?

"Vimika... please."

A hand reached out, and Vimika's began to shake at the urge to take it. She *had* to, it was Aurelai's. She'd held it, kissed it, let it explore her most intimate places, but the skin hanging from it wasn't skin. The bones beneath weren't bones.

"You're not real," Vimika said. She didn't know herself how she'd meant it. Illusion, dream, artificial creature *pretending* to be alive... they were all true. And not.

"Vimika..."

The eyes. Those beautiful, infinitely deep wells were unchanged. They looked at Vimika the way they always had, the soul behind them just the same as the one that Vimika had fallen for so thoroughly.

That she'd *trusted*.

"*Why didn't you tell me?*" The words tore from Vimika as though she'd reached down her throat and spelled them out with her own guts. Her chest was heaving, but there wasn't enough air in the world to calm her.

Aurelai's eyes swelled with tears, and she winced in obvious pain every time one dripped into her wound. She looked down at her hand, considering it. "I thought you knew."

A low, mournful laugh bubbled up from within Vimika. Slow and mirthless, the laugh of the dying and the damned. It burst from her all at once, the absurdity, the sheer *impossibility* of what was happening geysering from her so hard she convulsed with the strain, doubling her forward. Closer to Aurelai.

"How could I *possibly* have known that?! There *aren't any* mechamagical people!"

It's why wizards had been purged and not exterminated. Why the practice and anyone capable of it wiped out.

But it had happened anyway.

To Aurelai. Why *Aurelai*?

Twin streaks of liquid anguish burned down Vimika's cheeks, making Aurelai waver and dissolve before snapping back into harsh, unforgiving reality.

Aurelai sat back on her heels, perfectly balanced. "I weigh over 400 pounds. I move like one of your clocks. I only breathe when I remember to, I'm cold to the touch. My *animata* is as pure and bright at Oliver's, I'm *two centuries* older than you, but look younger. The most powerful mage in history set in motion his second-greatest masterwork with his Last Breath to keep me hidden. How did you *not*?"

"I... I didn't... think about any of it... This place is so

strange, so saturated in weird, powerful magic, it could explain anything!"

The pain on Aurelai's face was excruciating to witness, made all the worse by the fact that only a tiny fraction of it was from having her skin peeled to the bone. "You mean you denied it."

White-hot fire tore open Vimika's heart, the pure, piercing lance of bare, polished truth. The tears returned with savage intensity, falling like scalding rain.

The evidence had been there all along, but she'd been too short-sighted to put it together. Everything she'd experienced since waking up on the slab had felt impossible, why not one more?

As though she had seen every thought in Vimika's head, Aurelai answered in an achingly soft voice. "Maybe I ignored what I didn't want to see, too. I thought you'd accepted what I was. It made me so happy I forgot to question it."

Vimika couldn't bear to look at her, but couldn't bring herself to look away. "You… you should have told me as soon as I arrived."

Aurelai shot to her feet with blinding speed to look down on Vimika with eyes of utter heartbreak, hiding the light and leaving only the darkness.

"*Why*? Would you have even talked to me then? Helped me? Made love to me? *Treated me like a person*? Or would you have *run*? Abandoned me here, just like the only other person who's ever pretended to care about me?"

Tears streamed freely from Aurelai's eyes, full of betrayal and confusion but not surprise, and that was what hurt most of all.

"Look at me, Vimika. *Look at me!*" Propelled by the flexing of golden ribs, her command rang from every tree trunk and off the flat sides of the house, amplifying it ten times over. With a single sharp yank, Aurelai tore a chunk of dangling 'skin' from her forearm, revealing even more gold. Her bones were brilliant and untarnished, works of art in and of themselves, and through Sight, solid shafts of blinding white. "Here, the truth you wanted so badly: I'm a mechamagical monster. An abomination, unworthy of anything but contempt and fear. Is this what you wanted? Is this how I should have greeted you that day instead?"

"You lied to me!" Vimika cried.

"I showed you who I was! *Me*, Vimika, not my bones! Everything I've ever said to you, every kindness I've shown you, every word, every touch, every glance, every moment we've had together is the *real* truth! This," Aurelai shook her exposed arm, the ragged edges of her 'skin' fluttering like cloth, "isn't me. I didn't choose this. This is *my father's* truth, and so is this awful place! What's in here is who I am, and who I have been to you since the moment you arrived." Aurelai thumped her chest, and some kind of fluid splattered over her dress in a great red slash from shoulder to waist. Red, but the wrong red. It was the color of blood, but too thin, like wine.

Her veins were full of wine, and you were stupid enough to drink yourself insensible from them.

Aurelai was right. The signs were all there. Even when Vimika's magic had returned, she didn't want to see it, and in response her eyes stung to the point she could barely keep them open. Her heart was pounding against her ribs so hard it felt like someone was trying to tear it out.

Or two someones. Aurelai with her lies, and Vimika with her own. For daring to hope that this time was different. Her time with Aurelai had been like building a castle made of crystal, brick by brick, every drop of mortar her own blood and tears. The gravity of her past had been pulling at it, trying to tear it down around her, but she had propped it up with belief. With hope.

211

And now Aurelai had shattered it with a single blow, rendering it dust too dangerous to breathe.

With your help.

"I was genuine to you, Vimika. I've never had a chance to lie to anyone, how good do you think I would be at it? But I should have known. I should have been smarter than to believe you were who I'd hoped you were. Who you pretended to be."

Vimika stared at the... woman across from her, fingers flexing without thought or intent as a knife drove itself into her heart with agonizing slowness, killing her in degrees. With every beat it sank deeper, every breath twisting it a little more until in one anguished cry, it ruptured her completely. Wordless tortured agony echoed through the clearing, a whisper compared to what Aurelai's had done.

"I should have never brought you here. Never allowed myself to hope." Aurelai looked down, dark eyes bright with tears. "It hurts so much more than I thought it would."

Vimika looked up, clutching her chest. On that much they could agree. "The traps, the illusions... I understand why now. He had to do it."

Brightness returned to Aurelai's eyes: the searing, chaotic fury of lightning.

"He wouldn't have had to if he hadn't *MADE ME!*" She slashed her wounded arm down, slinging 'blood' in a great arc between them. "Do you think I asked for this? Do you think I *want* to be an immortal monster, living forever with the borrowed soul of someone else? I don't even know what to call that woman! My mother? My sister? What are your hurts to mine? You know *nothing* of betrayal. When your own father rejects you because you didn't come to life with the memories of the dead daughter he was trying to duplicate, but to then have to look out through her eyes, speak with her voice, wear her face and plead with him to accept you as someone else, only for him to say *no,* right up until he forgets what he'd done..."

Rigid self-discipline descended with a shuddering breath. "But I helped you. I listened, I dried your tears... and it doesn't matter. You've already made up your mind."

Vimika stared out into space. Into nothing. Into the lightless void that yawned out in front of her, all the darker for having been such a bright future only moments earlier. "I can't stay here."

Struggling to her feet, she looked about for her door to see it mercifully still intact. She stumbled towards where it had embedded itself like a snapped saw blade, feet swishing through grass that she could no longer trust as actually existing.

"You're going to leave me? Like he did?"

"Do you know how dangerous it would be if you got out?" Vimika tossed over her shoulder as the door slowly rose into the air. She couldn't look back or she'd stop moving. If she stopped moving, she'd start thinking, and then she would have to consider that Aurelai might be right.

"Dangerous to whom?"

"Everyone. You most of all. Staying here means you're safe," Vimika said, each word dripping from her lips like the vile poison they were. That they were the truth made her swallow every drop.

When Aurelai next spoke, it reached Vimika's heart and worked into the wound, so painful as to be blinding: "That's *exactly* what he said."

Vimika settled her weight onto the door, and the two of them stared at one another long enough for a lifetime of words to pass between them in silence. A thousand insults, a thousand pleas, a thousand confessions and ten million apologies.

The door began to move.

"I thought you were different," they said together.

But even as Vimika rose into the sky, she paid no attention to the fact she met no resistance; it was entirely for Aurelai as she shrank away. The house, the garden, none of it mattered save the look on her face, the one that Vimika could see perfectly even as all the other details became lost by distance: betrayal.

Vimika couldn't bring herself to make the turn. Unable to look away, it was only the clouds that broke their gaze, and soon enough Vimika was all alone with no refuge from her thoughts but the wide-open sky.

~

There was nowhere for Vimika to go.

Above the wind, above the clouds, the sun beat down on her unimpeded as she let the air sink its teeth into her nose and cheeks, the cold gnawing at her fingertips, her ears. Only the brim of her hat spared her eyes as they stared straight down onto a world that held nothing for her anymore.

She was well and truly alone.

The rim of the world stretched out before her, the sky darker above than ahead, while behind her the Dragonbacks rose up from the clouds like the jaws of a slavering animal, sundering them without pity in the hopes of inviting her over to throw herself upon them.

Snow, cloud, sky, sun. The world was unbearably bright.

The only shadow lay beneath her hat, the darkest place in her existence.

How could this have happened?

She could still feel Aurelai's fingers atop her own, smell her hair, taste her lips, the brew of their combined magic to which they had each become so addicted. The warmth of her skin, the unfathomable depths within dark and open eyes. The

214

sound of her voice, spoken and in song, about beautiful things and their even more beautiful future.

A future Vimika had long been convinced would be spent as alone as she was now, joyless and without intrigue or challenge. Simple and pathetic. How easy it had been to lull herself into believing it could be any other way. That destiny had anything in store for Vimika but heartache.

Tears fell into empty space, torn into mist by the scything wind.

Aurelai.

Impossible for one reason, and now another entirely.

It made complete sense for Aurelai to be mechamagical. Every point she'd made was blindingly obvious now, but one could only be blinded if they could see in the first place. Couldn't she understand how dangerous it was to be anywhere else? The reaction that would be sure to happen if it were ever revealed that there was a mechamagical *person* in the world?

No one would care that it had been done centuries ago by a dead man, and that the secrets had died with him. One look at those golden bones and they would be lucky if they only cut their heads off. Then it would be on to Vimika's family and every other wizard in Atvalia. It would be the end of them for good this time.

How could she have kept that secret? How could she have... tricked me into letting her go? Vimika thought. Or was it Not-Vimika? Was there really any difference?

Yes, what a monster, wanting to be treated like a person, another part of her responded. *A victim didn't want to call attention to what she's innocent of?*

Because she wanted to be accepted for who she was, and not what? To want to not be judged for things she couldn't help?

You're the worst kind of hypocrite, Vimikathritas. For shame.

Vimika stared down at her hands as they trembled and shook, no longer confident it was only from the temperature.

Aurelai was mechamagical, yes. But she didn't choose to be, did she? Aurelai hadn't always been Aurelai. She'd been *made*. But the only way to do that was to rip the soul out of someone else and move it.

But who had she been before?

Vimika had to fight the sudden urge to vomit.

Two victims. Both innocent.

And who knew Aurelai's father better than she had? Knew what she was better than she did? She *knew* the risks to herself. She could have lured anyone in to help her. Summoned any and every mechamagical animal within Calling distance, leading trails as bright as comets straight to her if she only wanted out. If the local house wizards were already being blackmailed by their presence, what difference would it make to them to follow if their masters thought the reward was big enough?

She asked you *because they would have killed her, and she knew it.*

The status quo required stability. A little blackmail afforded the four families in Durn security, put them equal with the others up north that had wizards, and kept the miners in line without needing an army. Knowledge of a mechamagical person would have upended the order of everything overnight if the wider world found out. Uprisings from the commoners and the execution of every wizard in Atvalia, the four families destroyed for being the ones responsible.

It was a struggle for the tears to fall now, creeping down Vimika's cheeks in halting, jerking clumps of ice.

She listened to every wizard in Durn, and believed you were different. She needed you to be.

And you, wizard, wanted so badly to be hurt again, you found your reason regardless of what it did to her. Of what had been done *to her. Why would she lie to you? You truly were her only hope.*

And now, hundreds of years after the worst betrayal it's possible to endure, Aurelai had suffered another. Perhaps for a third time.

Vimika doubled over so strongly she very nearly pitched off of her door. She screamed into the clouds, needing to expel enough of her shame so that she wouldn't let herself.

Go to her. Talk, at least. She's done nothing more than you would have.

Than she'd already done.

With sickening speed, Vimika arrowed straight down, bursting through the clouds to find nothing but sharp Speartips pointing straight back up at her. She shot out over the treetops so close they whipped at the hem of her robe, snapping and tearing in a bid to yank her from the sky.

But as she scanned about for the clearing, she couldn't find it. There was no break in the trees whatsoever, only dense forest all the way to the mountains.

How could that be? She'd gone straight up and then straight down again! She boosted her altitude until her hat was cutting a trail in the belly of the clouds, but even that wasn't enough.

Aurelai was gone.

12

Vimika circled around where she thought the clearing had been several times, in wider and wider spirals until she was gliding over the edge of the forest. She made out the disturbance in the snow the door had made when it took off, the only blemish on the vast expanse of white, while the trees were darker than she remembered, already having shed a great deal of their winter burden.

The magic, however, remained. It was all about her, but not the thick, choking fog that it had been the first time, more like the smoke trailing away from a recently-snuffed candle. Still irritating and visible, but easy enough to wave away. Below her however, it was far more tangible, a boiling vat she was very conscious of not wanting to fall into again.

Kalinostrafal, bastard that he was, had been smart to never teach Aurelai how to fly. It had made an entire dimension to his cage a trifle, and removed the possibility of anyone overhead being snared and crashing into it on accident. Visually, however, it was just as effective as if Vimika had been inside it. Though she'd been here before, nothing was familiar beside the sticky sense of dread that permeated the whole area.

Except the border of shadow, she realized.

Viewed from above, it was really an arc. Unwilling to trust her Sight when it came to anything Kalinostrafal had a hand in while airborne, she could just make out the circle it described with the naked eye. With a little yip of triumph, she shot up again to hover directly over where the center should be. But with no sign of anything other than more trees, she cursed. Peeking out through one eye, she risked a quick look with unfiltered Sight.

Sure enough, a blazing white star of *animata* pulsed directly below her, orbited by a dimmer planet.

The allure of being so close, combined with the driving need for recompense drew Vimika down.

"Aurelai!" she shouted. "Can you hear me? Aurelai, I'm sorry! I-"

The star moved, but no sound came up to meet her.

"I'm coming! Just... hold on!"

So close to the trees now she could have reached down and touched them, Vimika skimmed the Forest in frantic search of some crack, some fracture or break in the magical field she could pry open, or if she was feeling more reckless, try to dive through. But it had sealed itself perfectly. Only Aurelai and Oliver gave away anything was abnormal, and that, Vimika suspected, was only because she already knew they were there. There had been no sign of anything save Oliver's trail the first time, and now they were as obvious as the mountains.

What wasn't was how she was going to reach them. She could risk a blind plunge, but the illusions could easily trick her into thinking the ground was farther away than it was, or overwhelm her magic again mid-air, which would end poorly.

But she had to get back. She couldn't leave Aurelai...

Ever.

The thought came so suddenly and so clearly it occupied

the entirety of Vimika's mind. It wasn't about the place, or what she was, or anything resembling an objective argument about what *might* happen, and she wanted to cry out at her own stupidity for how she'd reacted.

She wanted to be with *Aurelai*, the Aurelai she knew, the Aurelai that was, regardless of what she was made of our how. Aurelai the woman was all Vimika had ever known, and all she ever wanted to know. The Aurelai she had vowed to show the world, to see it with, to *share* it with.

And what was stopping Vimika?

Her own stupidity, and Aurelai's dead father.

The first she could do something about. The latter, however…

A second thunderbolt struck Vimika square in the brain. With Aurelai the sum total of her thoughts, they were flowing as freely and clearly as they had when they'd connected in the library, and were coming so quickly she could barely work out how to apply them before another one came along to shove it out of the way.

Vimika had talked to herself.

In the forest below, there was that ephemeral strand of *animata*. From above, it was even more obvious, weaving the patchwork of spells together in a web-like pattern, appropriate for ensnaring anyone who wandered into it. The one that could have turned her around, scared her even worse than it already had or just never let her out at all, letting her die of exposure or starvation. But it hadn't.

"You are unworthy," Vimika whispered.

With sudden decisiveness, Vimika wheeled the door around. "Aurelai! I'm coming for you! I'll be back soon!" she shouted, and shot away north until she found where her door had spent the winter.

She set down on the snow and stared into the trees.

This time, what lay beyond was more than money, more

than intrigue. It was the other half of her heart, and nothing would keep her from making it whole again.

Selfish witch.

It wasn't about Vimika's heart. It was about Aurelai's. *She* was the one in true pain, through no fault of her own. *She* was the one robbed of choice her entire life. *She* was the one who needed to be made solid after living an entire lifetime as a shadow. *She* was the one who deserved to be loved for who she was, and not what.

She was the one.

Vimika turned north.

Out there, just over the horizon, *they* were waiting. Tarsebaum, her wizard, the other house wizards of Durn, and beyond them the whole of Atvalia. They would find her. Sooner than later, they would come, and they would take her. Tear her apart to see how she worked, experimenting, testing, *then* howling about what an abomination she was and killing her. Aurelai had to get away. Now.

After so long in an artificial spring, the bite of winter's breath on Vimika's face was sharper than ever, whipping at her robes, tugging at her hat. It stung her eyes, made them tear up, but for all that she could see more clearly than ever. Without direction for so long beyond *away*, she could now look towards.

Towards the south, to See the Shadowbridge Forest awash in the green of *mana*, with that eerie single thread of white *animata* weaving through it. Above was blue. Bluer than the most perfect sky, more intense than any feeling could ever be. The high magic, left over from the birth of the universe.

The *alumita* called to her. The eternal temptation of every wizard, and the last, to all who answered. It was said to be the power of the gods themselves, not meant for mortal wizards.

But Aurelai wasn't mortal. She would outlive Vimika, and

deserved to do so free and unharmed. The moment Vimika had agreed to find Oliver, she'd all but signed her own death warrant anyway. Or at least condemned what years remained her to a kind of indentured servitude, which was the same thing.

Craning her face to the cloudless sky, she Saw her chance to set it all right at once. Her friends and family would be safe, Malivia and her greed thwarted, and above all, Aurelai would be free.

When Vimika's work was done, there wouldn't be enough evidence left to find her with.

~

Calling on the *alumita* wasn't that different than calling on *mana*, it was the discharging of it that exploded you. A wizard's body made a decent enough receptacle for magic with enough training, but a terrible conduit for it to actually move *through*. There was a reason forest fires started with lightning, and it wasn't because the tree that was struck kept all the energy neatly contained.

Standing in the snowfield apart from the forest, Vimika felt very much like a lightning rod, only one that was chanting the words that would guarantee a strike. All around her the air itself was conveying twisted shapes and unnameable colors as the light passing through it *bent.*

Ironically, power of the type Vimika was calling on didn't leave much of a wake. There was no howling wind, no flurries of snow kicked up, no scattering of birds or baying of dogs, because everything was changing together, all at once. From an external viewpoint, *alumita* barely interacted with the physical world at all. From Vimika's, it was twisting its very fabric.

As the energies built she saw thunder and tasted lightning,

while all she could smell was the color blue. Her long wizard ears heard nothing, as the air could no longer move fast enough to convey sound.

It would have been fascinating if it weren't so incredibly painful.

She grit her teeth to near bursting, tears and drool running freely down her face. She'd long ago lost any sense of her body, every ounce of her having been replaced with arcane fire. But she couldn't scream or budge while she was siphoning, that would risk early and catastrophic discharge. The latter was always going to be true no matter what she did, but the former would make the entire enterprise pointless.

She had no idea how much she would need to destroy the illusion field, so she took as much as she could handle and still maintain the ability to think. It wasn't like she was going to get another chance. Besides, the universe would never run out of *alumita*, making it impossible to waste.

Whatever the final amount, it had to be enough.

Every inch of her burned with the strain, but still she called it down, and she began to feel the first inkling of what it was like to be a god. She could do *anything* with this kind of power. Unmake the illusions? She could unmake the *world*!

As the power grew, the more light bent around her, and blackness closed in.

Surrounded by it, sheathed in it, it whispered against her.

Like Aurelai's hair.

Her bottomless eyes.

With a single barked command, the flow of *alumita* ceased, and light returned. The world straightened itself again, only now it *tasted* blue.

But she couldn't dwell on it. Without knowing what kind of range she was going to get, she had to reach the heart of the forest to shatter the illusions from the inside without

224

getting too close to Aurelai when she did.

Each step was agony as her body tried to reshape the near-divine power within her to match the movement of her very mortal arms and legs, but it was sheer bloody determination that led her to charge over the shadow line without slowing down, kicking up clumps of snow behind her as she stalked it like a predator. When the silence descended, she didn't flinch. She pressed a hand to her neck, encouraged by her heartbeat and the raw energy coursing through her. They were signs of life, the reassurance that she could still make things right. Aurelai would be free of this place whether the ghost who called it home allowed it or not.

"Show yourself!" Vimika shouted, the words surging under her fingers as strongly as they had sounded in her mind. "If you're going to try to stop me, do it or get out of my way!"

Without waiting for a response, she forged ahead. She knew where the house was without question, guided by the blazing star of Aurelai straight ahead. There was no magic of any kind that could steal that light away now. Vimika locked on to it, held it in her mind's eye, her Sight, her soul, holding it tightly and threading it through the piece of Aurelai lodged in her own heart.

No matter how this ended, she would *not* lose it again.

As though approaching from a distance, the sound of her own footsteps began to grow gradually louder, the hushed whisper of the wind through the trees closer to that of the rush of water. The call of birds returned, the crush of fallen needles beneath her feet, the crisp, clean light reflecting off the snow in the boughs, a blanket adding an extra kind of white to crystals of ice that had yet to melt.

When the silence lifted completely, a shadow fell across her path.

"I was right about you. The moment you had the means, you fled," Not-Vimika said.

"And returned." Vimika's voice had been squeezed into a frog-like croak from being strangled by the fundamental energies that had birthed the universe. Managing to speak at all was a good effort, she thought.

"Indeed. Why?"

Even without the *alumita* to help pierce it, the artifice skinning Not-Vimika was as thin as paper now, the face it wore just a veneer over something altogether not Vimika. Beneath was the entire thread of *animata*. Concentrated into a space the size and shape of a young female wizard, it Looked more like molded fog than anything solid, but a glance around confirmed that's all there was.

"Show me your face, Azrabaleth. Your real face. I want to know what kind of man does this to his own daughter. Daughters, I should say."

"My real face is rotted to dust by now. Far more efficient to pluck one from your memory. *Why* have you returned, Malakandronon?"

"For Aurelai. To make sure that she knows there was one person in the world who cared about what she wanted. And to say I'm sorry, which is more than you've ever done for her," Vimika said. She could barely stand to look at herself through the pain, but whatever *he* was now, she was going to look him in the eye.

"I couldn't lose her. Not again," Azrabaleth-as-Vimika said.

Vimika huffed both in discomfort and disappointment at such a weak defense. "Why? Why did you do this to her? She didn't do anything to deserve what she's been through!"

"As I said, I couldn't lose her again."

"Stop talking around it! She's your *daughter*!" It was getting harder to form words. Vimika's tongue felt like it had been coated in grease made of acid.

"Yes," Azrabaleth-as-Vimika said. "And no. I was a grieving old man who couldn't bear to look upon that face and see anyone but who I'd lost. Aurelai exists because I couldn't accept that loss. First her mother, then our daughter... I couldn't. Wouldn't."

Vimika had to tamp down the urge to be sick. "What happened to your first daughter?"

"Her name was Greldefara. We sought refuge here from our persecution, but she soon took ill. I was no apothecary, and breaking the defenses to seek out a healer would have killed us both. This place is rich in metals, so when the time came, I did what I could with what I had. But when the girl on the slab opened her eyes, it was not Greldefara looking out from them."

"That's not her fault!" The need to discharge the *alumita* was making every word explosive, she had to shout everything now just to vent what pressure she could.

Azrabaleth-as-Vimika shook her head. "No. Nothing personal to my Grelde survived the process. I didn't see Aurelai as my daughter, only as a creation. One so dangerous she needed to be locked away forever. Only in death did I realize what I had truly done, but then it was too late."

"So let her go!"

And talk faster!

"Where? Into a world that would see her destroyed? Pulled apart and inspected like a broken timepiece?"

"Because of you! You're the whole reason any of this happened in the first place!"

"Do you think those first contracts just appeared from nowhere, Vimikathritas? That I expended all that time and energy on a whim? I did what I did because there was a demand for it. I did it in concert with the people who later turned on us. It was the mages who had no scruples, and no business attempting the process that doomed us, not my perfecting of it. I gave people what they wanted! I made confessions of undying love genuinely possible.... something I promised to my wife the day I married her. But she was taken from me. I kept it for Grelde."

Fire and pain lanced Vimika's insides, which meant they were either liquifying or she was going to start shitting lightning. "Where was Aurelai's promise of undying love?!"

"I've confessed my mistake already, Vimikathritas. What of yours? I was right to call you unworthy, and you dare speak to me of promises made to my daughter? You broke her heart as thoroughly as I did, so tell me why I should let you near her again."

"Because I'm still alive to make up for it!" Vimika bore down on the foreign magic churning within her, forcing it to let her speak long enough that he would know why his (after)life's work was about to be undone. "I was a afraid. And a fool. I'm neither of those things anymore, and you are not going to stop me from seeing her again. I will keep my promise, and she will know she is loved the way she *deserves* to be loved."

"And if I continue to believe you unworthy, then what?"

A small comfort fluttered through Vimika's torment. He couldn't sense the *alumita*. He was no longer a real wizard. Fragments of images danced on the corners of her vision, but the illusions had no hope against the power ravaging her body. Standing before her was a ghost, and those were easy enough to walk through when you didn't believe in them anymore.

The *animata* was all here, tied directly into the patchwork of the entire field. It was all connected, centered not an arm's reach away.

It all seemed so simple now.

"Then I will *prove* myself worthy."

Vimika reached a glowing blue hand to her *animata* facsimile, placing it over her heart.

Azrabaleth-as-Vimika cocked its head as realization

dawned. "You'll die."

"Probably. But Aurelai will live."

The power of heaven exploded the world a blinding blue.

13

There are multiple destinations wizards believe lie beyond death, most of them a hell of some type. Unlike the conception of many human belief systems, the hells weren't necessarily for punishment, merely a place where the soul could be... laundered. Life lessons collated and pondered, rewards and punishments doled out depending on how one lived their life, all manner of things to make it ready to return to the world of the living in another form. This, wizards believed, was the source of good and evil. Good people had learned, bad people hadn't.

Then there was the one Heaven, a place of true enlightenment accessed after millennia of incremental improvements have made the soul ready for even attempting conversation with the gods, sometimes even to become gods themselves.

Or, it was possible to remain in the world as a benign spirit, communing with people who would never be believed, assisting in ways that they would never completely understand. Intuition, conscience, premonition.

Wizards who died violent deaths by their own hand became wraiths, magically-charged entities always on the edge of tangibility. A torment that would never end until they were exorcised or the world ended, as punishment for the abuse of their gifts.

Vimika had never felt particularly enlightened, so she was fully prepared to be scooped up, fed into some kind of interminable queue and made to fill out paperwork of some kind. She hadn't been terribly responsible with her body after all, which probably meant she would have to sign for it. Then she remembered why she was having these thoughts, and suddenly having a familiar sky above her made a lot more sense. She looked down at her hand to see something black and smoke-like wafting around it.

"Oh," she said.

Maybe being a wraith wouldn't be so bad. She could float around, pass through walls, and... what? Keep an eye on the world, but have no power to interact with it? Condemned to *remember* what it was like to eat, drink and make love... forever?

The corners of her eyes began to burn.

No. First, no matter what her form, she had to check on Aurelai. If it hadn't worked, and Vimika had damned herself for eternity...

The black threads on her hand slipped away.

"Vimika!"

That wasn't a demon's voice, or another ghost's.

"You're awake!"

"No, I'm dead. I think you have me confused with someone else."

The daylight vanished, replaced by a smiling face framed in midnight, twin pools of stars gazing down on her with beatific concern. "You're quite alive, Vimika."

Impossibly soft fingers settled against her face. Warmth radiated from them, along with the unmistakable current of magic.

"You came back for me."

"Aurelai? You can see me?"

"Of course I can! How else could I have dragged you here?"

'Here' was Aurelai's lawn again, only now everything around it was smoldering and emitting some flavor of smoke. Sometimes wood, sometimes metal, sometimes blue.

"I didn't explode?"

Aurelai laughed her throaty, luscious laugh. Vimika bolted up to cut it short. It was a deep, languid kiss, but not terribly long, as Vimika went quickly dizzy and had to lay back down again.

"Don't overtax yourself. No, you didn't explode, but you came awfully close."

Vimika snatched up Aurelai's hand and held it to her cheek. "I'm sorry. I'm so sorry! You were hurt and I left you. All my fears took over, I was scared and upset..." The words tumbled out of Vimika faster than she could think them. Overwhelmed with relief, she had to get them out before something else came along to take away her chance.

But Aurelai set a finger gently over Vimika's trembling lips. "Ssh, my prince. This isn't the place."

A gust of wind brought more smoke, making Vimika not only cough, but aware of the fact the only thing she was wearing was a blanket.

"Where are my clothes?" she asked, staring down at her bare toes in disbelief.

"Those *did* explode, so you might be breathing your hat. We should probably go inside." Aurelai said, and gathered Vimika into her arms using a strength she didn't bother to hide.

Vimika was deposited on the cushions in front of the hearth feeling like she'd aged a thousand years. Everything hurt, even her hair somehow. Pain, at least, confirmed she was alive.

"How...?"

Aurelai sat down, foisting a cup of tea with one hand and stroking Vimika's arm with the other. "I felt it. Father's *animata* was the heart of the whole latticework. By starting there, you gave the *alumita* direction to discharge into. If you'd done it from anywhere else, you would have been killed. That was smart of you."

"I just wanted to make sure I got him. Did I?"

"Yes. It cascaded through everything that was connected, and went around the house. I'm safe. Oliver is safe," Aurelai said.

Vimika blew out a long breath and took a sip of tea.

Aurelai narrowed her eyes in both concern and no little suspicion. "You expected to die, didn't you?"

"Yes," Vimika said to her reflection.

"For me?"

"He was going to keep you in here forever. After my stupid mistake, he was never going to let anyone else in."

Aurelai traced a finger up Vimika's bare arm as she considered this. "You talked to him?"

"What there was of him. He tried explaining. He told me about Greldefara. She died naturally, you know. You didn't take anything from her."

Aurelai nodded, but said nothing, her eyes far away.

It was too much. Vimika set the tea aside and threw herself at Aurelai without care for how much it hurt. The dam on her earlier apologies cracked wide open, and the words came pouring over Aurelai's shoulder in a torrent of sobs and half-formed syllables. "I'm sorry. When I saw what you were, I reacted like a frightened animal, not a wizard, and certainly not someone who cares about you. I was everything I shouldn't have been when you needed me and worse, everything I hate and decry in others. I was no better. I can't begin to wash away the shame of what I did, or that I can ever make it right, but know I will try. I was *stupid*, and couldn't stop myself from making the biggest mistake of my life."

To her relief, Aurelai returned the embrace, but only briefly. "You hurt me, Vimika... in places I didn't know I could hurt."

Vimika didn't deserve to ask forgiveness. "Aurelai, I'm so sorry. Please-"

"But," Aurelai ran her hands through Vimika's hair as she thought, nails grazing against the skin. "Neither of us were at our best in that moment. I accept your apology."

Vimika buried her face deeper into Aurelai's shoulder and clutched her back, pulling them so tightly together Vimika could hardly breathe. "Thank you."

"And what's more... I'm sorry, too. I should never have left something so important up to misinterpretation. I should have told you, no matter the cost to me. And... I said awful things to you, too. Things I can never take back."

"No," Vimika said, shaking her head to clear her eyes of hair and tears both. "You've nothing to apologize for. You were right about most of it. You deserve nothing of what's happened to you, least of all the hurt *I* caused."

She ran her fingers over the right side of Aurelai's face, to the shimmer just below the surface. The wound had already healed considerably, but there would likely be scars. Mechamagical or not, Aurelai was still a wizard, and not even they healed from wounds so egregious without a cost.

"Does it still hurt?"

Aurelai found Vimika's fingers, guided them. "A little, but it's much better than before."

"When I left you. I'm so-"

Aurelai cut her off with a finger to the lips. "Enough. We're both sorry."

Vimika kissed the back of Aurelai's right hand, her wrist, up her arm. Her skin was warm, and Vimika nuzzled against it, holding Aurelai's eyes as she did, shining bronze searching obsidian black.

Aurelai watched her in fascination. "These hands have wielded the *alumita*, yet they're still here to hold mine. Hm... what made you do something so reckless?"

"I wanted to keep my promise."

"I would have taken a broken promise over losing you."

"Breaking a promise *is* losing me."

Aurelai fingered loops of Vimika's hair, flicking charred bits off the ends. "Is there something past romantic? My books aren't clear."

"Only the truth."

"What truth?"

She held Aurelai's hand out, considering the shining skin where her lips had pressed against it, and curled their fingers together. The connection took them, stronger than ever, magic and emotion rising to meet the words rushing to leap from Vimika's tongue.

After all, there was magic, and then there was *magic*.

"I love you. And I will never leave you again."

"Nor I you. *And* I you! What? No! I love you, too!" Aurelai spilled forward, knocking Vimika onto her back, shattering the pall that had held them.

Tussling and giggling, they rolled over the pillows, snatching more kisses and wiping tears. Bit by bit, Aurelai lost her clothing until they were each swathed only in the moment.

Vimika's aches and pains faded into a haze of pleasure as they made love in the warmth of not only the sun, but the relief and elation that came with the confession of the feelings that matched their magic.

What arced between them now was sweet and life-affirming, nothing like the torture of the *alumita*. It filled Vimika's veins and her lungs, flooded her every sense as her tight gasps peppered Aurelai's succulent moans, their bodies bearing out the truth of their words as they rose in climax together, each crying the other's name.

When they came drifting back down again, Vimika laid her head on Aurelai's chest.

"It's... not fair... you don't have to breathe..."

"Mmm... you'll see its advantages when I don't come up for air next time." Aurelai laid a tender kiss on the top of Vimika's head so at odds with her intimation it made them both smile. "You've been through a lot today, I didn't want to push you."

The silence of someone absorbing a promise she was very much considering calling in immediately passed, but Aurelai made to get up before Vimika could decide.

"I want to stay like this too, dear heart, but the forest exploded. We have to get moving before someone comes to find out why."

Reluctant in the face of good sense, Vimika lifted her head, now without pain or dizziness. And looking forward to laying it upon her beloved's chest once more, another reminder from the forest that would never hurt her again.

"What will we do now? Spring has come. Real spring," she said as Aurelai stepped into her dress with graceful, assured movements. Whether it was the emotions, their shared magic or just having observed Vimika for awhile, Aurelai's odd tics had disappeared, and there was no small part of Vimika that was sad about it. She alone had been privy to that Aurelai, and would cherish those memories forever.

"You almost died. Go home and see your family," Aurelai said.

The euphoria of their lovemaking suddenly faded, the sun dimmed. For the first time since awakening, Vimika took her eyes off Aurelai to look out the window at the smoke rising from the ashes of her prison.

It was only their first barrier to freedom, and Vimika's near death the lowest price.

"I can't do that," she said slowly, the truth of it dawning on her as she did. She pointed outside. "You were right. People *will* come looking. People who know I'm gone and why. One Look will tell any wizard what happened, and being able to connect me to you and Oliver would doom my family. So would trying to leave Atvalia... if I was... alive. For their sake, and that of Delica and Seris for that matter, I *did* die out there."

It was a strangely comforting thought. There was a finality to it that was freeing, even if she knew that the true cost would come later.

"Vimika.. I'm-"

"No. I asked you to stop apologizing." Vimika went to Aurelai and brushed the hair from her face. "I didn't have to follow Oliver out here. That was my own greed and short-sightedness, not you."

"But it's your *family*. Your friends, your *life*! I can't ask you to-"

"You didn't. I'm telling you."

Aurelai shook her head, leaning into Vimika's touch. "I never intended for you to have to give up everything for me."

"I know. Which is why I'm doing it. You called me to your service, and in it I will remain, Princess Sweet Beak."

Cheeks reddened beneath black eyes gone aglitter. "Then, if you insist, I heartily accept. Prince Silver Tongue."

Vimika was able to reconfirm her wizard healing was working when the smile that broke out on her face didn't hurt. "Oh, I don't know about *that*. Do I talk so well?"

"Talk?"

Laughing softly and not entirely with humor, Vimika rolled her forehead against Aurelai's. "I hope they write something nice about me in my obituary."

"I'm sure they will. And when it happens... I know

someone who has a lot of practice being a ghost."

"Then we both get to start over. Together."

Vimika looked into Aurelai's eyes. Black and bottomless, Vimika willingly hurled herself into them. Rushing up to meet her came a relentless tide of pure joy that washed them both clean. When their lips parted, they were afloat and adrift, carried by the current rushing between them in a direction that neither of them had ever charted before.

As if the emotions of the moment weren't enough to unbalance her, something heavy tried to knock Vimika's legs out from under her. She looked to see Oliver looking back with wide, knowing eyes. "Would you like to come, too?"

His tail had barely completed two swishes before Aurelai gathered him into her arms, holding him between them like the spoiled child he was. "As if I would think of leaving my little brother behind."

At any other point in Vimika's life, it might have qualified as the most ridiculous thing she'd ever heard. Now, however, it was the most appropriate.

In all the world, Aurelai was unique, but that would never again mean the same thing as alone.

Epilogue

The world was filled with noise unlike anything Vimika had ever heard. The rush of wind through the tall grass that wafted back and forth in the alien air was a gentle whisper compared to the full-throated roar coming from just ahead. Something black and wet squished between her toes as she worked them into it more deeply, as elated as she was slightly alarmed by the feeling. Humidity as she'd never experienced blanketed her, pregnant with rain that had yet only threatened to fall.

Straight ahead, the perfectly flat horizon was a deep steel gray shading to blue.

Beside her, Aurelai stared out with eyes widened to take in every detail, filling them to bursting since she couldn't be bothered to blink.

"This is the ocean?" she asked.

Vimika stood with her arms outstretched, dressed as they both were in simple tunics and trousers. All the unnecessary weight of their lives and heritage had been scythed away, leaving behind wizards of their own definition to look out over the breaking waves.

There was color in Vimika's cheeks permanently now, the tips of her ears darkened from near-constant sun, which had had the opposite effect on her hair, lightening it and shooting it through with golden streaks. Shorter now for traveling, she felt Aurelai reach up to finger the ends affectionately, prodding Vimika out of her reverie.

Taking the hand from her hair, she kissed each and every finger on it without even glancing at the scars. She saved her gaze for Aurelai's, matching it with a growing smile. The elements had been no match for her mechamagical body, and despite the sun, she was still sheathed in fresh cream, her midnight hair hanging down to her thighs without a strand out of place. The blades of her ears were still as pale as snow, as were her cheeks, the right one creased by a faint line just below her eye.

Vimika hadn't had a drop of alcohol since leaving Durn, yet she still spent every day intoxicated.

"It's wonderful, isn't it?"

Three weeks they had traveled already, enough to leave Atvalia completely, and into the Kingdom of Il-Tahana. It had been a lot of flying, but also the first taste of true freedom for both of them as they played hide and seek amongst the clouds, both from each other and those on the ground. A thousand miles from anywhere Vimika had ever called home, she had yet to feel a single impulse to return.

Being dead was glorious.

"Does it go on forever?" Aurelai asked.

"No, not forever."

"What's on the other side?"

"No one really knows. Could be anything."

Aurelai took her hand and squeezed. "Dragons?"

Vimika squeezed back. "I certainly hope so."

In the far, far distance, somewhere just over the rim of the world, she thought she could make out something in the air. Maybe it was a cloud, a play of the light. A mirage.

Or maybe it wasn't.

"Shall we?" she asked.

Nodding, Aurelai summoned her transportation.

Sliding to a stop behind them was the top half of an old door, and a a blackened, charred wooden beam. To the back of the latter was strapped two lightweight packs, while from Vimika's doorknob hung her well-traveled satchel. Looking out from it was Oliver, eyes wide with boundless curiosity, tongue lolled out in satisfaction at what they saw.

Vimika met Aurelai for a final kiss before mounting up.

"Let's go see what there is to see."

Thank You

Thank you for reading the paperback version of *Midnight Magic*! Hopefully it was exactly the story you needed for the world we find ourselves in as of this writing, or at the very least, made you feel something positive for a few hours.

I don't know that I can express in words how much I needed to write this book. If you're reading this in the future, then know that I wrote it during the height of the Coronavirus pandemic that engulfed the world in the spring of 2020. Immediately before that, my family was devastated by tragedy, and the funny little love story between Vimika and Aurelai that you've just read was my way of coping with so much awfulness befalling me all at once. I needed to write something positive, funny and beautiful, but not vapid or weightless. As such, no matter how many books I write or characters I create, Vimika and Aurelai will always have a special place in my heart. They are both very different from who I initially conceived (Vimika so much so I had to change her name!), but their journey of love and escape never did. Aurelai's little island out of time was mine too, and I looked forward to visiting it every single day.

I hope you did, as well.

Thank you from the bottom of my heart for giving it a chance.

On a final note, reviews mean a lot to writers, especially indie ones. They're tangible evidence that you enjoy our work, and not only tell other readers what you thought, but us as well. Writing novels is a lonely experience, and to know that you like what we do goes a *long* way to inspiring us to do even more (and usually faster). Doesn't have to be much, just a few words. To know that my little magic kissing book put a smile on your face would mean the world to me.

If you'd like to painlessly find out when my next book comes out, please use the 'Follow Author' button on this book's Amazon page and you'll be notified automatically when it does! Otherwise, give me a follow on Twitter @cdarrowwrites for announcements and whatnot. My email address is cdarrowwrites@gmail.com if you'd like to contact me more personally.

Thank you again for taking this journey with Vimika and Aurelai, I sincerely hope you enjoyed your time with them. And me.

-Cameron Darrow, September 2020

Acknowledgements

I want to say thank you to all my friends and family who supported me through the writing of this book. They know how much this one means to me and why, and without them it wouldn't exist. So many have and continue to support me on this mad quest, I only hope the end results live up to all you have done for me. Brooke, without you this book would be a lot worse (and quite a bit shorter); you've helped make all of my books better.

ALSO BY CAMERON DARROW

Printed in Great Britain
by Amazon